DEVELOPING MURDER

A LISA MARCH MYSTERY

BY HARVEY S. CARAS

Developing Murder

A Lisa March Mystery

Copyright © 2021 by Harvey S. Caras

ISBN 978-0-578-87231-5

First Printing, March 2021

Cover design by Carasmatic Design

Published by YM Press

Printed in the United States of America

*To Joanne, my real life JoJo, who inspires me every day with
her energy, love, style, and passion for everything she does.
To Jonathan, Rachel, and Mickey,
who have made me the proudest dad on the planet.
To Sarah, Dan, and Leah,
whose love for my children makes my heart sing.
To Zahava, Shalom, Chaya, Vivian, Yossi, Adam,
Kobi, Rivka, Amy, Mendel, Chana, Sarale,
and all of the little Caras's to come.
To Lisa November and all of the friends who have been kind
enough to join me on this novel writing journey.*

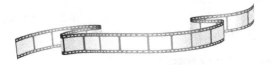

CHAPTER 1

"*Three, two, one......*"

"*Good afternoon, everyone. This is Chris White with TV 12 news at noon. I'm here with my partner, Lynn Farrell.*"

"*Well, Chris, some exciting developments in Port St. Lucie today. The ground breaking ceremony for a brand new community that promises to be something we've never seen before.*"

"*That's right, Lynn, and for that story let's go to our correspondent, Dory Cameron, live on the scene in Port St. Lucie.*"

"*Hello, Lynn and Chris, and hello everyone. I'm here in Port St. Lucie for the ceremonial ground breaking of a hot new development by Porter Homes, a project that has a lot of people talking.*"

"*I'm joined here by the Vice President of Marketing for Porter Homes, Tim Cleveland. Hi Tim!*"

"*Hi Dory. Yes we're all very excited about this new concept in adult living, and we know from the number of people waiting to purchase homes here*" that we're breaking ground today on a truly ground breaking concept in senior living."

"Tim, what makes this new development different from the many other senior communities that seemed to have sprung up throughout Port St. Lucie?"

"Well, Dory, as you can see by the sign here, our new community is called Serenity."

"Yes, I noticed that, Tim, so why Serenity?"

"Up until now, Dory, all of the fifty-five plus communities have catered to adults who want to be active. They feature swimming, jogging, tennis, Pickleball, fitness centers, and bike trails."

"Those seem to be very popular."

"They are, Dory, and Porter Homes has developed several communities like that throughout Florida."

"But Serenity is different?"

"What makes Serenity so unique is that this community is for seniors who want to relax, and the whole community is being built with that in mind."

"So, no physical activities?"

"Of course, we'll have plenty of activities for those who want them, but on a smaller scale. Our focus will be on providing a calming atmosphere for seniors who just want to get away from the hustle and bustle of the world."

"How so, Tim?"

"For example, Dory, our entire community will be built using Feng Shui as our guiding principle. We have a full time Feng Shui consultant who will oversee the construction of all of our facilities and homes."

"That sounds very interesting."

"We're also planning a beautiful butterfly sanctuary and a series of orchid gardens, each built and maintained by a full-time staff of experts."

"Okay, and what activities will there be for residents?"

"Our pools, for example, will feature lazy rivers, where our residents can lie back in an inner tube and be gently moved along the river while calming music plays."

"That's really relaxing, Tim, so what else?

"Our homes will be totally maintenance free, Dory. We plan to have a full time staff of maintenance specialists available to handle anything our residents need."

"That sounds great! I know my husband would appreciate that at our house! So what other special activities can we look forward to at Serenity?"

"Yoga will be taught every day in our special yoga studio, Dory, and we'll have meditation, massages, acupuncture, chiropractic, and reiki for those who want them. We'll also have a fully staffed urgent care facility on site that will be available for our residents twenty-four, seven."

"That's important."

"But I think the most important feature of our community will be twenty-four hour concierge service for our residents."

"Concierge? What does that entail, Tim?"

"It means that the residents of Serenity can do as much or as little as they want to do in their daily lives. Anything they don't want to do for themselves we'll do for them."

"For example?"

"For example, our concierge staff will make reservations for restaurants, doctors appointments, and other activities, just like a five start hotel would do. They'll even shop for the residents, online or in stores. There's nothing that a Serenity resident could ask for that won't be done for them. Our goal is to make life as easy and peaceful as we can."

"Sounds very interesting, Tim. Have people started buying homes in Serenity yet?"

"Dory, the response has been overwhelming. People keep asking when we're gonna start selling homes in Serenity."

"So, what answer are they getting to that question?"

"Well, our models are under construction now, and, as you can see behind us, the equipment is just getting started on our entrance. I'm very excited about this entrance because I can assure you that this entrance will be like nothing Port St. Lucie has ever seen before. We hope to have our models completed by the end of January and then we'll begin selling homes."

"Let's take a look at what's happening behind us, Tim. I see that a man is walking towards us. What is that he's carrying?"

"Folks, you won't believe this. But it looks like the construction crew here at Serenity has unearthed a skull! Back to you in the studio."

"Does it look like a human skull, Dory?"

"It looks like it to me, Lynn. Oh yes, that is definitely the skull of a person!"

"Well, Chris, apparently that place wasn't serenity for at least one poor soul!"

"You know, Lynn, here at TV 12 we've always wanted to be featured on the national news. I think we will tonight!"

"You're right about that, Chris. Let's go to a commercial while we figure out exactly what's going on at Serenity in Port St. Lucie."

CHAPTER 2

NOVEMBER 14, 2018, 1:00 PM

POLICE HEADQUARTERS

PORT ST. LUCIE, FLORIDA

"March, Worthington, my office," came the booming voice of Captain Bob Davis.

Davis was a grizzled thirty year veteran of the force and everyone knew that when he called you by your last name it meant you were either in trouble or you were needed for something important.

Within seconds Detectives Lisa March and JoJo Worthington were in the captain's office.

"What's up, boss?" Lisa said.

"I got a strange one for you guys," Davis replied, "they just found a human skull at a construction site off Becker Road.

"Just the skull?" JoJo asked, "Where's the rest of the skeleton?"

"I imagine it's not too far away from where they found the skull," Lisa replied. "Are they looking for it, boss?"

"Not yet, Lisa." Davis responded, "that's why I need you guys over there."

"You want us to shut them down?"

"Do whatever you have to do to get them to cooperate, okay?" Captain Davis said, "we need to find the rest of the skeleton and I don't have the budget to pay for a crew to look for it."

"I got ya', boss, we'll take care of it." Lisa said.

As JoJo exited the office to pick up her bag, Lisa stayed behind to speak with the captain.

"Why'd you do it, boss?" Lisa asked quietly.

"Do what?" Captain Davis responded.

"Why did you take Danny Torres away from me and pair me up with Worthington?"

"Well," the captain replied, "after Lonny Carter died, Beth Danelo needed a new partner. I thought Torres would work well with her, so I paired them up."

"But Danny and I made a great team!" Lisa pleaded, "you know that, boss!"

"No denying that, Lisa, you guys cracked the Pickleball case. You're two of my best so I decided to split you up and make two strong teams."

"Okay," Lisa responded, "I get that, but why me and the hat lady?"

"The hat lady?"

"Come on, Captain," Lisa said, "she wears a different hat every day. You never noticed?"

"Of course I noticed," Captain Davis replied, "but I don't give a rat's ass what she wears, I think you guys will be great together, even if you don't think so!"

"But boss, it's just..."

"Just what, March, just what?"

"It's like we clash, Captain. We're like oil and water, that's all."

"Well then get over it, you hear me? You're both professionals and I expect you to act like it, got it?"

"Got it, Captain," Lisa said stoically.

Lisa March and JoJo Worthington were as different as night day. Both forty-three and both long term veterans of the department, that's where the similarities ended. Lisa had dark curly hair, was a conservative wife and mother who dressed in dark slacks and gray tops, fitting of a serious detective, she thought.

JoJo, on the other hand, was a blond who, to Lisa, never seemed serious about her career. She loved to wear bright, outrageous, and totally inappropriate clothes that were bought for her by her wealthy husband. Lisa couldn't remember ever seeing JoJo in the same outfit twice.

These differences carried over to their styles as detectives, too. Lisa cherished her reputation as a tough, hard nosed cop who wasn't afraid to mix it up with anyone. At five feet tall and barely one hundred pounds she was by far the star of the department.

JoJo Worthington, Lisa thought, was her polar opposite. She loved being the center of attention, often bringing homemade cookies and other treats for everyone in the precinct. It seemed to Lisa that JoJo was more interested in the attention she got for her hour glass figure, her inappropriate clothes, and her collection of hats than what she got from solving crimes.

The bottom line was that Lisa missed the team she had built with Dan Torres and was not looking forward to working with a flake like JoJo Worthington.

In spite of her feelings, however, Lisa knew that she needed to find a way to work successfully with JoJo, or they both would suffer the wrath of Captain Davis.

As they walked toward their car, Lisa looked at JoJo and said, "you know we're going to a construction site, don't you?"

"Of course I do, Lisa, why?" JoJo replied.

Lisa looked at JoJo's pink dress, pink hat, pink purse, and pink open-toed shoes. "You wanna change first?"

"Sorry, partner," JoJo replied, "this is all I got, but don't worry, I'll make it work."

"Uh huh," Lisa replied, "I'm sure you will."

Within ten minutes Lisa and JoJo were at the Serenity construction site. As they walked closer Lisa noticed that all of the men had stopped working and were sitting on top of their heavy equipment. A few catcalls greeted them.

A team of uniformed officers was keeping the TV crew and gawkers at bay.

JoJo and Lisa pushed their way through the crowd. Within seconds they were met by two men, one of whom was carrying a large plastic bag.

"Gentlemen," Lisa began, flashing her badge, "my name is detective Lisa March and this is detective Joanne Worthington."

The younger of the two men spoke first.

"My name is Tim Cleveland. I'm the vice president of marketing for Porter Homes, and this is our construction superintendent, Tony Bianco."

"Gentlemen, I understand you had a big surprise today," JoJo said.

"We sure did," Bianco replied, holding up the plastic bag and handing it to Lisa.

"Is this the skull?" Lisa said as she peeked inside the bag.

"One of our front end loaders came up with it right over there'" Bianco said, pointing to an area just behind them.

"Any other parts of the skeleton turn up yet?" JoJo asked.

"No," Bianco replied, "we stopped digging until you guys could get here. We didn't want to mess things up for you."

"I appreciate that, Mr. Bianco," Lisa replied, "once you dug up that skull this whole area became a crime scene."

"Crime scene?" Tim Cleveland asked, "what does that mean for us?"

"I'm afraid It means that we have to shut this project down until we find the rest of that skeleton," JoJo replied.

"But, how long will that take?' Cleveland asked.

"That's up to you guys," Lisa replied.

"How is that up to us?" Bianco asked.

"If we have to bring in a new construction crew to dig things up in here it could take a month before we get them in place," JoJo said.

"We can't wait that long!" Cleveland yelled. "We've got a deadline to meet."

"Well then," Lisa replied, "we can make things go a lot faster if we can use your crew and equipment to do the digging."

"Okay," Bianco said, "my team is here. Just tell us what you want us to do."

"I was hoping you would say that," Lisa responded, "we'll have a team of officers out here at 8 a.m. sharp tomorrow morning to supervise the search. They'll probably bring a cadaver dog."

"My team will be here, too," Bianco said.

"If the skull was found here then the rest of the body shouldn't be too far away," JoJo said.

"I'm not so sure," Cleveland relied, "this site was dug up about ten years ago by another developer, but they went bankrupt and never finished the job."

"So the rest of the skeleton could be anywhere," Lisa said.

"Wherever it is, we'll find it," Cleveland replied.

As Lisa and JoJo stepped into their car, Lisa once again looked at the skull inside the bag. "Poor bastard," she said quietly.

"Think we can figure out who it is?" JoJo asked.

"We've got the best coroner and forensics team in the state," Lisa replied, "if they can't do it, nobody can."

"Hey Lisa," JoJo said, "that was a great job we did getting them to do the digging for us, wasn't it?"

"Captain Davis should be happy about that!" Lisa replied.

"I think we're gonna make a great team, partner!" JoJo said with a grin.

The jury's still out on that one, Lisa thought.

CHAPTER 3

NOVEMBER 14, 2018, 7:00 PM
THE HOME OF LISA AND RICK MARCH

"Get the camera ready, Rick," Lisa said, "they're walking up to the door now."

"Shhh," Lisa's sister, Carol whispered, "don't spoil the surprise."

The front door opened and Lisa's parents, Gloria and Ernie Goodman, came walking in.

"Surprise!" came the roar from the assembled group of twelve guests.

"Happy birthday, Daddy!" Lisa said, as she hugged her father.

"Oh, what a surprise!" Ernie said, "I never expected this. Hello everybody, thanks for coming!"

"Happy birthday, Ernie," Rick said with a smile.

Lisa hugged her mother.

"I told him about the surprise, Lisa."

"Why'd you do that, Mom?"

"Look, honey, your father's eighty years old. I didn't want him to have a heart attack when he walked in here."

Typical Mom, Lisa thought, always needs to do things her way.

"Hey, Dad," Lisa said, "Rick, Lexie, and I bought you a birthday present."

"You didn't need to do that, Lisa!"

"I know, Dad, you're always doing things for us but you never want us to dote on you. Well, guess what? Today's your day!"

Ernie Goodman was a small man, standing no more than five foot four. A retired police captain in Broward County, Ernie was still as sharp as ever.

For their whole lives he had always been the rock of Gibraltar to Lisa and her sister, Carol. While Mom was often moody and sullen, Dad was upbeat and happy. I don't know how he stayed so happy living with Mom, Lisa often said.

Ernie opened the present. "A Pickleball paddle!" he said with a grin, "and you got exactly the brand I wanted. Thanks!"

"Now that I'm taking lessons, Daddy, you and I are gonna play together."

The party consisted of four pizzas that Rick had ordered, punch that Lisa made, and a chocolate ice cream birthday cake that Carol had brought. All of their guests were gone by 9:00.

"I hope they had a good time, Mom," Lisa said, "cause they left awfully early."

"No, honey'" her mother replied, "that's what time all of our parties end!"

After saying goodbye to the last guest, Ernie turned his attention to his daughter.

"Hey, honey," Ernie said softly, "I heard you're working on a skull that got dug up in a construction site."

"Yeah, Dad, I am."

"Did you figure out who it is yet?"

"Not yet, Dad, " Lisa replied, "the only thing we know for sure is that it's a man, and he's been dead between twenty and thirty years."

"Any word from the coroner about trauma to the skull?" Ernie asked, "do they know how it was separated from the rest of the body?"

"Good question, Dad," Lisa replied, "I thought maybe we had a deranged killer who beheaded the victim, but the coroner assured me that the head was broken off by the construction equipment"

"Could they figure out from the skull how the victim died?"

"Apparently the vic was shot through the mouth."

"Ouch! That'll do it! So the teeth are gone?"

"I'm afraid so. Nothing to match dental records with."

"How about results from the DNA?"

"You're so funny, Dad," Lisa laughed, "you retired before they even had DNA!"

"Almost, it was just getting started when I left the force. But I know that DNA solves every crime now, dear," Ernie said, "we both know that!"

"Yes, Dad, I suppose that's true," Lisa replied, "and we did get DNA from the skull, but so far no matches in the CODUS system."

"So you don't know who he is, or was?"

"No, not yet. All we know is how long he'd been dead," Lisa said, "Oh, and that he was between thirty-five and forty-five when he died."

"Any more body parts show up at the crime scene?"

"Yesterday they found a left leg that matches the skull, so they say now the guy was about six feet tall to six foot two."

"So, what do you do next?"

"Well, we've spent the last three days searching through every missing persons case between 1985 and two thousand to see if we can find a thirty-five to forty-five year old man."

"Any luck?"

"Nothing so far."

"Geez, honey, have you thought about Jimmy Foster?"

"Who?"

"Jimmy Foster," Ernie replied, "I guess you don't remember him, but your mother and I will never forget him."

"Is he the guy that stole your money?"

"That's him," Ernie said, "it was 1995, you were in college and Carol had just married Martin, so your mother and I decided to downsize and move up here to the new Jimmy Foster adult community in Port St. Lucie."

"I remember now. I was at FSU, but I remember how you guys got screwed."

"Us, and about five hundred other couples, honey. We lost thirty grand!"

"Jimmy Foster disappeared with all of the deposits and he never built the houses, right?"

"That's what we all thought, Lisa," Ernie replied, "but maybe he didn't disappear, maybe he's been dead all these years. Maybe that's his body. It's worth looking into, don't you think?"

"It's definitely worth looking into, Dad. Thanks!"

"We'll see you back here for Thanksgiving next week," Rick said.

"You want me to make the food?" Gloria asked.

"No, Mom," Lisa replied with a grin, "Rick, Lexie, and I have everything under control."

"Uh huh!" her mother grunted.

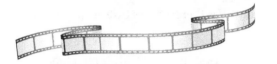

CHAPTER 4

As Lisa entered the office she couldn't help but notice that JoJo was already hard at work. She was sitting at her desk searching through a pile of folders. Today's outfit, yellow.

"What's up, Jo?" Lisa asked, "how long have you been here?"

"I've been here since six this morning," JoJo replied, "I like working when it's quiet."

"Any luck yet?"

"Nope. I've gone through eighty-four missing persons cases, but nothing about a man who fits our victim."

"Did you happen to come across a file for a guy named James Foster?" Lisa asked.

"Not on the list, Lisa, why do you ask?"

"Something my dad said the other night. There was a guy named Jimmy Foster who disappeared in '95 and stole millions."

"He's not here, Lisa," JoJo replied, "I guess nobody filed a missing persons report on him."

"Yeah, probably not," Lisa said, "but there must have been a case against him for fraud or something."

"Okay, if it's in our files, I'll find it."

Lisa grabbed her cell phone and dialed up her father.

"Dad," she said. "Was there a fraud case against Jimmy Foster when he disappeared?"

"Of course!" Ernie Goodman replied, "I remember talking to a detective from your office back then, let me see if I can remember, I think his name was Appleton, or Arrington, Mike or Marty, something like that."

"Thanks Dad, you've been a big help!"

"I've got a personal interest in this case, honey."

Lisa ended the call and walked to Captain Davis' office. She knocked quietly on the glass and waited for the captain to wave her in.

"What's up, March?" Davis asked, "any more bones show up today?"

"Not yet, boss," Lisa replied, "but I do have a question for you."

"Fire away!"

"Back in 1995, did this office have a detective named Appleton or Arrington?"

"Matt Arroyo?" the captain replied, "he was a crazy son of a bitch, retired about twenty years ago, before I became a detective."

"Do you remember him working on a case involving a guy named Jimmy Foster?"

"Of course I remember Jimmy Foster," the captain replied, "he's the builder guy that ran off with millions of dollars that he collected from the buyers. It was big news, but I was a uniformed officer back then and we didn't get involved in the detectives' cases unless they needed us.

"Any idea where Matt Arroyo is today?"

"Last I heard he was living in a high rise condo on Hutchinson Island, why?"

"I'm gonna go talk to him."

"Do you think the skull might belong to this Jimmy Foster guy?" Captain Davis asked.

"I don't know, boss," Lisa replied, "that's what I'm trying to find out."

As Lisa walked out of the captain's office, JoJo handed her a slip of paper.

"What's this?" Lisa asked.

"It's Matt Arroyo's address," JoJo replied, "you know how thin the walls are in the boss's office!"

"Good work, JoJo," Lisa said, "come with me."

As they drove from the office to Hutchinson Island, Lisa had a thought, "you know Jo, we probably should've called ahead to see if Matt Arroyo was home."

"All taken care of, Lisa," JoJo replied, "I called him before we left, and he's looking forward to meeting us."

"Good thinking."

"And, by the way," JoJo added, "I found the file on the Jimmy Foster case, and I've got it with me if Arroyo needs to refresh his memory."

"Thanks!" Lisa said.

"You see, Lisa, I'm not just a flakey hat lady" JoJo said, "I'm a real detective, and I take my job just as seriously as you do."

"So," Lisa said sheepishly, "you heard me talking to the boss yesterday?"

"Like I said, partner, the walls are real thin."

"I didn't mean anything bad, Jo," Lisa explained, "I get it, Lisa, you and Dan Torres were a great team and you weren't happy that Davis split you up."

"That's true, but…."

"And I know I don't look like the typical police detective."

"No, you certainly don't!" Lisa replied, "I guess it's the clothes that throw me off a little."

"I've always had nice clothes, even when I was young and couldn't afford them. I used to put clothes on layaway and pay them off a few dollars a week. Then I could pick out something else to put on layaway!"

"Clothes were never important to me," Lisa said, "I used to make fun of girls like you!"

"I understand, Lisa, I really do. I still get laughed at a lot."

"So how many hats do you have, JoJo?"

"I dunno, Lisa, I lost count at three hundred!"

"You think people underestimate you because of the way you dress?"

"Oh, they sure do!" JoJo replied, "it's always been that way. They look at the frilly clothes and hats and they have no idea how tough I can be when I need to."

"I can believe that," Lisa replied.

"Even my name," JoJo continued, "my real name is Joanne but everyone calls me JoJo instead. That's like a little girl's name!"

"Geez, I didn't know you felt that way, partner," Lisa said, "I won't ever call you JoJo again!"

"No, that's fine with me. I'm used to it by now and I use it to my advantage."

"Really, how?"

"Men, and women too, but especially men, they talk to me about a lot of things because they think I'm just a cute and harmless JoJo," JoJo said quietly, "they tell me things, important things about cases, things I might not have learned any other way."

"I get it."

"And the more I learn the better I am as a detective."

"Tell me, though, how come you're always the one baking cookies and collecting money for presents for people?" Lisa said, "I've never seen another detective do that, only you."

"I just love making people happy, Lisa, it's just who I am. When I was two years old my mother used to dress me up and take me to hospitals and nursing homes to cheer up the sick people. So I guess I was always like this!"

"I'm really glad we're having this conversation, Jo," Lisa added, "is there anything else I should know about you?"

"Just that I teach a martial arts self defense class for women at the Civic Center on Monday evenings," JoJo replied, "so you can always count on me to have your back."

"That's really good to know." Lisa said.

"Look," JoJo said quietly, "all I'm asking for is a chance to prove to you that I can be as good a partner for you as Danny was."

"That's fair," Lisa replied.

"But, guess what, Lisa?" JoJo said with a grin, "you have to prove yourself to me, too!"

"That sounds fair, too!" Lisa replied with a smile.

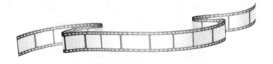

CHAPTER 5

NOVEMBER 15, 2018, 11:00 AM
THE HOME OF RETIRED DETECTIVE MATT ARROYO
HUTCHINSON ISLAND, FLORIDA

"It's funny that they call that new development Serenity," Matt Arroyo said, as he handed a bottled water to Lisa and JoJo, "come with me and I'll show you real serenity!"

The two detectives followed Matt as he led them onto the screened deck of his Hutchinson Island condo. They were immediately treated to a breath taking view of the Atlantic Ocean.

"I sit out here every morning, drink my coffee, and watch the sun rise on a brand new day," Matt said, "there's nothing more serene than that!"

"I can certainly see why you say that, sir," Lisa said, "and I really appreciate you taking the time to talk with us today."

"You, know," Matt said softly, "my wife died four years ago, and ever since then I've been alone most of the time. When you called and asked to see me it was the highlight of my day."

Matt Arroyo was tall and slender, in great shape for an eighty-one year old. He had a full crop of silver hair, a white mustache, and a tan that made it clear to anyone that he was a beach lover.

"It was February 8, 1995," Matt said, as the three sat in chairs on the deck.

"That was the day Jimmy Foster disappeared?" JoJo asked.

"That was the day we got over fifty calls from angry people," Matt replied, "every one of them said the same thing. They had given Jimmy Foster a deposit for a house he was gonna build and then, all of a sudden, his phone was disconnected and his office was empty."

"This was the Dreamland Estates project," JoJo asked, "right?"

"That's right," Matt said, as he opened a thick folder, "I kept the brochures. Quite an amazing place this was supposed to be."

JoJo examined the brochure. It was a full color rendition of what was going to be built in Dreamland Estates.

"Very impressive," she said, "look at all the fountains!"

"This place was way ahead of its time," Matt replied, "it was gonna have everything that any retired person could ask for in a neighborhood."

"Now we have a bunch of communities like this," Lisa said as she examined the brochure.

"That's true, today," Matt replied, "but twenty some years ago this was a brand new concept, at least in this part of Florida."

"So, tell us what happened with the money," JoJo said.

"Well, first of all, Jimmy Foster was the most amazing salesman you ever saw," Matt said, "He was tall and handsome and all the ladies loved him."

"Okay."

"And his sales manager was just as slick."

"Sales manager?" Lisa said, "what was his name?"

"Cary," Matt replied, "Cary Garnet, but he was so handsome and smooth everyone called him Cary Grant!"

Matt then removed a photo of Jimmy Foster and Cary Garnet together and showed it to JoJo and Lisa. JoJo studied the photo carefully.

"Two handsome gentlemen!" she said.

"That's right," Matt commented,"and everybody knows that it's the women who choose where couples live."

"So these two were selling more than just houses, huh?" JoJo said with a grin.

"These guys were selling a lifestyle," Matt responded, "and they were two hustlers who could charm the pants off anyone!"

"So tell us about Jimmy," Lisa asked.

"Jimmy Foster was born in 1956 in Teaneck, New Jersey, the only child in a middle class family," Matt began, "after high school he went to the University of Miami."

"So, that's what brought him to south Florida," Lisa said.

"Yes," Matt replied, "and his parents were killed in a car accident when he was in college."

"Sad," JoJo said, "so he stayed in Florida after he graduated?"

"Right, and after he graduated from Miami he went to work selling houses for Prentice Builders in Boca Raton."

"So, he started right out in the real estate business," Lisa said.

"Yes," Matt replied, "that's where he met Cary Garnet, and one of the people he sold a house to was a wealthy lawyer named Sidney Schwartz."

"Okay."

"Schwartz had a daughter named Louise," Matt continued, "and Jimmy ended up marrying her."

"So, how did Jimmy go from being a salesman to a developer?" JoJo asked.

"In the early 90's there was a crash in the real estate market in Florida," Matt explained, "and that's when Jimmy convinced his father-in-law to lend him the money to buy land in Port St. Lucie."

"We lived in Deerfield Beach back then," Lisa said, "nobody ever heard of Port St. Lucie."

"That's absolutely right," Matt replied, "and that's why Jimmy was able to buy twenty-one hundred acres of land for two million dollars."

"So what happened next?" JoJo asked.

"Jimmy had seen what worked in Boca so he brought the concept to Port St. Lucie."

"But then he had to convince people to move here," JoJo said.

"That's right," Matt replied, "so Jimmy created these amazing brochures and he placed ads in newspapers and on TV stations all over south Florida."

"He convinced a lot of people to buy," Lisa said, "what was the secret?"

"Jimmy masterminded a plan to create demand for his houses," Matt said, "First of all, his prices were 40% below Boca prices."

"Smart move," JoJo said.

"Yes it was," Matt said, "then Jimmy invited people to come to a party in a large tent, and he told them that they had to give him a $500 deposit just to attend this party. "

"Why would anyone do that?" JoJo asked.

"If they didn't buy they'd get their deposit back," Matt replied. "but most people bought."

"Amazing!" JoJo said.

"Jimmy made people believe that if they didn't come to one of his parties they'd be missing out on something really special," Matt continued, "he had a party every morning and every afternoon for two full weeks. Each one had live music and a full buffet, omelets, bagels, danish, shrimp, salads, and even a full bar."

"So the deposits and the parties were his way of greasing the skids for people to buy," JoJo said.

"Oh yeah," Matt replied, "and Jimmy was the master salesman. People say it was like the greatest show on earth."

"Impossible to resist," Lisa said, "even my parents got caught up in it."

"He set up a lottery system," Matt continued, "each buyer got a number when they registered and there were drawings to see who got what choice of lots in the neighborhood. It was amazing!"

"So, it sounds like Jimmy convinced people that they had to act right away or they'd be left out." JoJo said.

"Yes he did," Matt added, "together, he and Cary Garnet sold over 500 houses in just two weeks!"

"Wow!"

"So what happened next?" Lisa asked.

"Each buyer then had to choose the lot and model they wanted and, depending on the price, they gave Jimmy a big deposit."

"How much were these deposits?" JoJo asked.

"The deposits ranged from twenty-five thousand to forty thousand. Once they picked a lot they had two weeks to come up with the deposit money, and they did!"

"That's a lot of money he collected!" Lisa said.

"Jimmy collected around eighteen million in deposits, plus he had a twelve million dollar loan from St. Lucie Bank and Trust."

"So that's thirty million total," Lisa said, "quite a haul."

"So then what?" JoJo asked, "he just disappeared?"

"Yep, he just closed his office one day, shut down his phones, and took off!"

"And he's never been seen again?" JoJo asked.

"We found his Lamborghini parked at the Palm Beach International airport."

"Did you dust it for prints?"

"No, we just returned it to Mrs. Foster. But we checked every flight manifest leaving West Palm Beach around that time, looking for signs of Jimmy.

"No luck?" Lisa said.

"No luck. We had a lot of reported sightings of Jimmy Foster, from Canada to Mexico, Argentina, even Europe, but nothing ever panned out."

"And the money?"

"Gone too," Matt answered quickly, "Jimmy was taking it in big chunks from the bank loan account, the entire twelve million was gone, and there was no paper trail to show how he spent it."

"What happened to the deposits people paid?"

"That eighteen million was in a separate escrow account. The escrow account is supposed to be used only for construction, but we know that the eighteen million was transferred from the escrow account to a foreign bank account right around the time Jimmy disappeared."

"Embezzlement?" JoJo asked.

"Clearly," Matt replied, "but we could never find the money."

"But what about Cary Garnet?" Lisa asked, "he must have been up to his eyeballs in all of this."

"Garnet was arrested," Matt answered, "but he always claimed that he knew nothing about what happened to Jimmy or the money."

"Did he go on trial?" JoJo asked.

"He was never charged," Matt replied, "the state's attorney said they didn't have enough evidence to convict him, so the case went cold."

"Any idea where Garnet is now?"

"Let's see, I retired in '99," Matt replied, "and the last I remember Cary Garnet was selling real estate in Ft. Lauderdale."

"Sir," Lisa said, "you know we have a skull that was uncovered last week, and it could possibly belong to Jimmy Foster. We can't do dental records because the teeth are gone. We have DNA, but we don't have anything to match it with."

"Is there any chance you had a DNA sample from Foster?" JoJo added.

"DNA wasn't such a big thing back then, I'm afraid," Matt replied, "so no, we don't have any samples."

"Any blood relatives we could go to?" JoJo asked.

"Yes, as a matter of fact," Matt replied, "Jimmy had a son, Jeffrey. He was eight years old back in 1995, so I guess he's in his early thirties today."

"Okay, and his wife, Louise," JoJo asked, "any chance you know where she is?"

"I know that, after Jimmy disappeared, Louise and Jeffrey went to live with her family in Boca," Matt said, "a group of home buyers tried to go after her for money, but she was sheltered by the Dreamland Limited Corporation Jimmy had set up."

"Sir, is there anything else you can tell us that might help us?" JoJo asked.

"Oh," Matt said, "there was an accountant involved too. I can't remember his name."

"Laber," JoJo said, looking at the file she had brought, "Louis Laber."

"Yeah, that's him," Matt replied, "a shifty little guy. I always thought he was involved somehow, but he claimed Jimmy took total control over the money. Maybe he'll change his story now that Jimmy's dead."

"Louis Laber is retired now," JoJo said, "He lives in Plantation."

"We definitely need to have a talk with Mr. Laber," Lisa said.

"Anything else, Matt?" JoJo asked.

"Jimmy had a lot of vices," Matt replied, "he liked fast cars, fast women, booze, drugs, and gambling. There were a lot of people who wanted to see Jimmy Foster dead. If that is his skull it'll make a lot of people happy!"

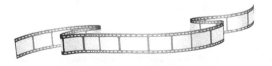

CHAPTER 6

NOVEMBER 16, 2018, 6:00 PM
THE HOME OF LISA AND RICK MARCH

Lisa walked through the front door and was immediately met by her husband Rick. He had two things for his wife, a big smile and a glass of Kendall Jackson Chardonnay.

"Hi hon," Lisa said, "I'm starving, what's for dinner?"

"Well," Rich said sheepishly, "I found a recipe on YouTube for meat-loaf."

"That sounds great! I haven't had that in years!"

"Well, Lisa," Rick replied sheepishly, "you're not having it tonight, either."

"Troubles, Rick?" Lisa asked with a smile.

"I did everything right except the oven temperature," Rick said, "I thought it said five hundred and fifty degrees, but it really said three hundred and fifty."

"So, what happened?"

"Let's just say we almost ate a football tonight!"

"Oh geez."

"But I saved the day, Lisa."

"Pizza Delight?"

"Should be here any minute!"

"Well, babe, thanks for trying."

"Lexie called today, Lisa."

"And what did our darling daughter need?" Lisa said with a grin, "or should I say how much did our daughter need?"

"Only two hundred this time," Rick replied, "a sorority thing, she said."

"I can't wait for that girl to graduate so she can start spending her own money, Rick!"

"She promised she won't ask again this semester."

"Yeah, sure she won't!"

Just as the pizza was delivered Lisa's phone buzzed. She could see that the call was from JoJo.

"What's up, Jo?"

"Hey, Lisa, I found thirty-three Jeffrey Fosters between Orlando and Miami."

"Oh, so you've been busy. Any one of them our guy?"

"Only four of them were in the right age range, and I called each one of them."

"And?"

"No luck. None of them were the son of Jimmy Foster."

"I guess he moved out of Florida, JoJo." Lisa said, "or he could be dead."

"Actually," JoJo replied, "I took a different path."

"What path was that?"

"I figured that a lot of times when people are caught up in a family scandal they change their last name to avoid having to deal with people bugging them."

"I've heard of that too," Lisa replied.

"Yeah, so I searched the Palm Beach County records for 1995 through 1997 and guess what I found?"

"What?"

"On April 13, 1996 Louise Foster was granted an uncontested divorce from James Foster."

"Well, that certainly makes sense," Lisa replied, "he wasn't around to contest it."

"For sure," JoJo said, "and Louise also petitioned to have her name changed back to Louise Schwartz."

"Smart move!"

"And, guess who else's name got changed at the same time?"

"Her son?"

"Yep. Jeffrey Foster became Jeffrey Schwartz!"

"Super work, JoJo!" Lisa said, "so now we have to find a thirty something named Jeffrey Schwartz."

"Already done, Lisa!" JoJo said proudly.

"You found him?"

"I found him!"

"Fantastic!" Lisa shouted, "let's go talk to him."

"I've got his address and he's agreed to meet us at 10 a.m. tomorrow, partner."

"Okay, JoJo," Lisa said, "great work. I'll see you in the morning."

As Lisa ended the call she turned to her husband.

"Rick," she said, "I think maybe I was wrong about JoJo Worthington!"

"You know what they say, honey," Rick replied, "never judge a book by its cover!"

CHAPTER 7

NOVEMBER 19, 2018, 11:00 AM
THE HOME OF JEFFREY SCHWARTZ
BOCA RATON

Lisa was impressed with the beautiful home of Jeffrey Schwartz. It was moderated in size, but tastefully decorated in high end furnishings.

"I guess he didn't suffer too much when his father took off," she said to her partner.

"I think you're right, Lisa," JoJo replied, "remember, his grandfather was very wealthy, and that's where he and his mother lived after Jimmy disappeared."

"I suppose the grandfather passed away and left them both a boatload of money," Lisa added.

As they approached the front door they were met by a handsome man. He was tall and well dressed.

"Hi, I'm Jeff Schwartz," he said, as he ushered the two women into his house.

They entered the living room and were greeted by a very attractive woman.

"This is my wife, Jill," Jeffrey said, "please have a seat."

"Thanks for agreeing to meet with us, Mr. and Mrs. Schwartz," Lisa said.

"It's Jeff and Jill," Jeff said.

"You know, sort of like Jack and Jill," Jill added with a smile.

"And we're happy to help in any way we can," Jeff said.

"You said you may have found Jeff's father?" Jill asked.

"We really don't know that," JoJo replied, "what we found was a skull."

"Oh, that's really creepy!" Jeff said.

"Yes, it certainly is," Lisa responded, "and we haven't be able to identify who it is yet."

"All we know now is that it was a man about six feet tall and about thirty-five to forty years old," JoJo said.

"And we estimate that he died around twenty to twenty-five years ago," Lisa added.

"And you think it could be my father?" Jeff asked.

"We just don't know," Lisa replied, "the age and timeline fits your father, but the only way we can truly identify him is through DNA."

JoJo checked in her purse and removed a small DNA swab kit.

"Jeff," she said, "we were hoping you would allow us to compare your DNA to the DNA we have from the skull."

"Of course, it won't be an exact match," Lisa added, "but, as his son, your DNA should give us enough information to know for certain whether the person we have is or isn't Jimmy Foster."

"Sure, no problem," Jeff replied, as JoJo demonstrated how he should use the swab to collect and store the sample for them.

"How much do you remember about your dad?" Lisa asked.

"I was just a kid when he disappeared," Jeff answered, "everybody said he ran away, but I wouldn't believe it. I never thought he would walk away and never see me again."

"So, you were close?"

"I sure thought so," Jeff replied. "My dad was my hero!"

"How did your mom handle his disappearance?"

"Mom was devastated. At first she thought Dad would be coming back, but after a while she had to accept the fact that he ran out on both of us."

"Did she or you ever think that he might have been killed?"

"That was a possibility," Jeff said, "my grandfather hired a private detective to find out what happened to Dad, but he couldn't find anything. And since all that money was gone it was assumed by everyone that my dad ran off with it."

"So, eventually you and your mom had to accept the fact that he was gone for good," Lisa observed.

"That's true," Jeff said quietly, "Mom said we had to move on with our lives."

"And she changed your last name."

"The name Foster was hated by so many people that Mom had to do something to protect me."

"Jeff," Lisa asked, "is there anyone in particular you can think of who would have wanted to kill your father?"

"I'm afraid that list is too long," Jeff laughed, "he was the most hated man in Florida when he took off with all that money."

"Do you know where we might find your father's old partner, Cary Garnet?"

Jeff laughed again. "Of course I do," he replied, "Cary and I are business partners in real state and he's married to my mom!"

"Oh! Can we get his cell phone number, please?" JoJo asked.

"Here's one of his business cards," Jeff said, "and on the back I wrote my mother's cell phone number in case you want to contact her."

"Jeff, we can't thank you enough for everything you gave us today."

"I'm happy to help," Jeff said, "I've wanted to find out what happened to my dad for over twenty years."

"As soon as we get the DNA results we'll call you to let you know what we found."

"Hey thanks!"

As they entered their car and began the ninety minute drive back to Port St. Lucie, Lisa said, "that was quite an eye opener, huh JoJo?"

"How's this for a scenario?' JoJo replied, "the business partner kills Jimmy, takes all the money, frames Jimmy, and runs off with his wife!"

"I think we're getting way ahead of ourselves, Jo!"

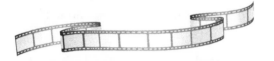

CHAPTER 8

NOVEMBER 22, 2018, 2:00 PM
THE HOME OF LISA AND RICK MARCH

"Happy Thanksgiving, Mom, Dad!" Lisa said with a smile, as her parents walked through the front door.

"I hope you didn't over cook the turkey, Lisa," Gloria Goodman dead-panned.

"No, Mom, it should be just right," Lisa said softly.

"Well," her mother continued, "I remember when we couldn't even eat it, it was so overdone!"

"That was ten years ago, Mom," Lisa shot back, "I think it's time to let that go!"

"Okay, honey," Gloria replied, "I'm just trying to help you."

Just then Lisa's father, Ernie, spoke up.

"Anything new on the skull case, Lise?"

"Nothing yet, Dad," Lisa replied, "we met with Jimmy Foster's son and he gave us a DNA sample."

"Was it a match?"

"We're still waiting on the results from the lab, but I really expect we'll get confirmation that the skull belongs to Jimmy Foster."

"Then the fun begins, huh Lise?"

"That's for sure, Dad," Lisa said with a grin, "There's a whole lot of people who wanted to see Jimmy Foster dead!"

Lisa's husband Rick walked in from the kitchen.

"By the way, honey," Rick said, "I just found out yesterday that my law firm represented a group of Jimmy's buyers who were trying to get their money back."

"That's right, I remember that," Ernie said. "It was the Simmons law firm that represented us."

"Us?" Lisa said, "You were part of that group?"

"I remember going to one meeting, Lise," Ernie said, "your mother refused to go, but I went."

"I've seen the file on that meeting," Rick said, "and there are still a couple of guys in the firm who were there back then."

"It was wild," Ernie said, "that's what I remember. People were crying and saying they lost their life savings. It was really bad."

"I heard there were a few men who swore they would find Jimmy Foster and kill him," Rick said. "One even brought a gun to the meeting."

"Oh yes," Ernie said, "now I remember it. When that stupid bastard showed the gun the place went nuts. People were running for the door."

"What happened next?" Lisa asked.

"Well, honey, since I was a cop I figured I needed to stop this guy from doing something stupid," Ernie replied, "so I calmly walked up to him and showed him my badge, and asked him to gently put the gun away and leave the meeting."

"Did he leave?"

"He started crying," Ernie said. "He swore the gun wasn't loaded, and he let me escort him out to his car."

"Always the hero, Dad!" Lisa said with a smile.

"But, you should get the names of the guys that were threatening to kill Foster," Ernie said, "who knows, maybe one of them actually did it."

"I've got the names, Lisa," Rick said, checking the notes he had brought home from his law firm, "Douglas Nucci, Stanley Cooper, and William Jardine."

"Thanks, Ricky," Lisa said, "this investigation is turning into a real family affair!"

Just then Lisa's cell phone buzzed.

"Hey, Jo, what's up?"

"I'm in the office, Lisa," JoJo replied.

"JoJo, you do know it's Thanksgiving today, don't you?"

"Yeah, but Stuart's watching football games with Billy, my daughter stayed at school for the holiday, and I was bored, so I came in to see if we got the DNA results."

"So, did we get them?"

"That's why I called, Lisa, no match!"

"No match?"

"No match, partner. I guess we're right back to square one."

"No match? Are they sure? I can't believe it!"

"That's what the report says, Lisa, no familial match between Jimmy Foster and Jeffrey Schwartz."

"Shit! Okay, Jo, I'll see you on Monday."

As she ended the call Lisa turned to her father and her husband.

"Our skull doesn't belong to Jimmy Foster," she said softly.

CHAPTER 9

When Lisa arrived she was not surprised to see JoJo already there, talking with coroner Stephanie Rogers. At six foot one, Stephanie towered over both detectives.

"Are we going on a safari today, JoJo?" Lisa laughed.

"Already been!" JoJo replied, as she twirled around in her leopard outfit with matching hat, shoes, and handbag.

Lisa quickly noticed that JoJo was also holding a large grocery bag.

"What's in the bag, Jo?"

"Oh, it's cookies. I baked them for everyone upstairs to celebrate Andy Spears' tenth anniversary with the department."

"How do you know all this stuff, Jo?" Lisa asked, "you're always bringing cookies for every special occasion."

"I guess people just like to talk to me, Lisa," JoJo replied with a wry smile.

"I hate to interrupt the safari and cookie exchange, ladies," Stephanie said sarcastically, "but I've got a busy schedule today."

"Okay, thanks Steph," Lisa said, "What 'ya got for us?"

Stephanie removed a sheet and uncovered the assembled skeleton.

"We've got all the pieces now," she said, "and we can release the construction crew to start their project again."

"Okay," Lisa said, "what do we know about the victim?"

"We know he's a caucasian male, about 35-40 years old, who died about 20-25 years ago."

"Cause of death?"

"Looking at the whole skeleton it appears that it was a single gunshot to the the mouth that exited through the back of the head," Stephanie said, "the only sign of trauma to any other part of the body are two fingers broken off on the right hand."

"That's weird," JoJo said.

"Not really," Stephanie replied, "it looks like the victim put his hand up to deflect the bullet and it ripped through two of his fingers before entering his mouth."

"Ouch!" JoJo said.

"Can you tell what kind of gun was used for the kill?" Lisa asked.

"Yes," Stephanie replied, "by the size of the entry and exit wounds we know it was a Glock 17."

"Thanks, Stephanie, that's good to know," JoJo said

"We thought we had a name," Lisa offered, "Jimmy Foster."

"I know," Stephanie replied, "but the DNA wasn't connected to Foster's son."

"Anything else you got that might help us?" JoJo asked.

Stephanie opened a large plastic bag.

"The crew recovered pieces of a blanket that we think the body was wrapped in when it was buried, and these clothes too," Stephanie replied, "they look like real expensive duds!"

JoJo looked closely at the charcoal gray pin striped jacket and pants. They were badly deteriorated but the inside label on the jacket read 'Hunter Brothers'.

"That's a two thousand dollar suit!" she exclaimed.

"Okay, so we know the guy had a lot of money," Lisa added.

"Did the clothes tell you anything?" Lisa asked.

"No bullet holes anywhere, so it appears the only shot he took was to the hand and mouth," Stephanie replied, "and we couldn't lift any fibers or DNA off the clothes because they were too far deteriorated."

"Why shoot somebody in the mouth?" JoJo asked.

"In my experience we call that a message shot." Stephanie replied.

"Message shot?"

"Apparently somebody thought this guy talked too much" Stephanie said stoically.

"Any chance he shot himself?" Lisa asked.

"The mouth is a popular place to shoot yourself," Stephanie replied, "but from the angle of entry and exit it looks like the shot came from a few feet away from his head and a foot below."

"Okay." Lisa said. "So the shooter was shorter than the victim, right?"

"Most likely."

"You know what?" JoJo added with a laugh, "in my experience people don't usually bury themselves after they commit suicide!"

"Oops, my bad!" Lisa said with a grin. "Okay, then, I guess that's it."

"One more thing," Stephanie said, as she reached into the large bag and opened a smaller plastic bag. She removed a gold band and held it up for the detectives to examine.

"This was with him."

"It looks like a wedding ring," Lisa said.

"I'm amazed it stayed on his finger all this time," JoJo commented.

"It didn't," Stephanie replied, "we found it in the pocket of his pants."

"That's strange," Lisa said, "why would he put the ring in his pocket?"

"There's only one reason a man does that, honey," JoJo laughed, "and that's cause he didn't want anyone to know that he was married!"

"Are you speaking from experience, JoJo?" Stephanie asked with a grin.

"Before I met Stuart I used to hang out at South Beach," JoJo replied.

"That's a wild place!" Lisa said.

"It sure is, honey," JoJo grinned, "and in my younger days I was pretty wild myself. They once hired me on St. Patricks day to dress up as a leprechaun and flirt with all the guys!"

"I'm shocked to hear that!" Lisa joked, feigning outrage.

"Anyway, I was there all the time, and at least once a night I'd get hit on by a married guy who was hiding his ring in his pocket," JoJo continued, "the morons couldn't see that they had a tan line where the ring used to be!"

"Maybe some of the women didn't care if they hooked up with a cheating bastard!" Stephanie said.

"Okay, so we know our victim was a caucasian male, six feet tall, around forty years old, and a cheating bastard!" Lisa laughed.

"Maybe he got what was coming to him," JoJo replied, "maybe it was a jealous husband that shot him."

"Take a look at this," Stephanie said, as she gently placed the ring under her microscope, "the ring is engraved on the inside."

Lisa and JoJo took turns looking into the microscope.

"It says W E E Z E E 7/25/82," JoJo said, "I wonder if that's the husband and wife's initials and the date of their wedding. Wendy Elizabeth Everly married Zachary Edward Everly on July 25, 1982!"

"Wasn't he one of the famous Everly brothers?" Lisa joked, "he even wrote a song about Wendy."

"There you go!" Stephanie said with laugh, "Case closed!"

"Actually I think that was the Beach Boys," JoJo said, still smiling.

"Nice try, Jo," Lisa added, "but I think you're probably right about those being the married couple's initials."

"Could be," JoJo replied, as she snapped a photo of the ring engraving, "I'll text this to you, partner. At least this gives us something to work with."

With that the two detectives thanked Stephanie and headed upstairs to their office.

"How many couples do you figure got married on July 25, 1982?" Lisa asked.

"If we're right, and their last name starts with E, then that narrows down the field considerably," JoJo replied, "I'll start researching it right away."

"Okay, Jo, but we have no idea where this wedding took place," Lisa said, "it could have been anywhere in the world!"

"Well, that just means it'll take me a little longer to find it, partner!"

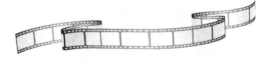

CHAPTER 10

Lisa and Rick had just finished dinner when the doorbell rang. Lisa opened the front door and was surprised to see her parents standing outside.

"Mom, Dad!" she said with a smile. "What brings you here tonight?"

"Happy Hanukkah!" Gloria shouted, "we wanted to light the menorah with you."

"Oh sure, Mom," Lisa replied, as she frantically searched her brain to remember where she had stored the menorah after Hanukkah ended last year.

Just then Rick came to the rescue. He was holding a menorah and two wax candles to light.

"I'm glad you came, folks," Rick said. "We were just getting ready to light!"

And that's why I love this man so much, Lisa thought. I'm the Jew in the family and he's the one who knows where the menorah is.

The candle lighting went smoothly and, as they backed away from the menorah, Lisa asked, "so, you want to stay for a little while?"

"Ask your father," Gloria Goodman replied with a grimace.

"Dad?"

"Your father wants to help you solve this skull thing!" Gloria said, with more than a hint of sarcasm, before her husband could respond.

Now Lisa understood the real reason for her parents sudden visit. It had been many years since Ernie Goodman had retired from the police force, but he had never lost the curiosity and determination that had made him a great detective for so many years.

"That's great, Dad," Lisa said, "we're spinning our wheels on this case right now."

"Where are you, Lise?" Ernie asked.

"We know the victim is a Caucasian male, six feet tall, about forty, who was killed by a single gunshot wound to the mouth about twenty to twenty-five years ago."

"I know all that, Lise, but didn't you find out that he's Jimmy Foster?"

"We thought so, but the DNA didn't match Jimmy's son."

"That sucks," Ernie said, "so, are you dead in the water?"

"Well, Dad," Lisa replied, "we found an expensive suit they guy was wearing."

"Gee, that sounds like Jimmy Foster," Ernie said, "he always dressed in expensive suits. I remember that."

"JoJo says the suit would cost two grand today."

"Sure sounds like Jimmy," Ernie said, "are you sure about that DNA?"

"They don't make mistakes, Dad," Lisa replied, "but we do have another lead that JoJo's following up on."

Lisa picked up her cell phone and showed Ernie the photo of the engraving on the ring.

"This wedding ring was in the vic's pocket," she said, "take a look at the engraving."

"W E E Z E E 7/25/82," Ernie read aloud, "that looks like his wedding date."

"And we think those are the bride and grooms initials."

"You do?"

"Yes, Dad, so JoJo is looking at weddings on that date where the last name of them married couple starts with the letter E."

"W E E Z E E," Ernie read the letters again, "have you tried sounding it out?"

"Huh?"

"You've been spelling the letters out like they're somebody's initials," Ernie said, "but, what if it's just one name, Weezee?"

"Weezee?" Lisa said. "Who has a name like Weezee?"

"You're too young to remember, but in the late seventies and early eighties there was a popular show on TV called *The Jeffersons*."

"I think I remember that," Lisa said, "I was just a kid."

"Anyway," Ernie said, "the husband on the Jeffersons was George and he always called his wife Weezee."

"So, how does that help us?"

"The wife's real name was Louise."

"Damn, Dad, that was Jimmy Fosters' wife's name!"

"If they were fans of *The Jeffersons* he might have called her Weezee," Ernie said. "I think a lot of people used that nickname back then."

"Wow, Dad, that's really good!"

"What'll you bet Louise and Jimmy Foster were married on July 25, 1982?" Ernie added.

Lisa picked up her cell phone and speed dialed her partner.

"JoJo, how fast can you find out the date that Jimmy Foster married his wife Louise?" she said, "I'm guessing the wedding took place in Boca Raton or close by."

"I'm on it, partner," JoJo said.

"Dad, I think you could be right about this," Lisa said, "but that doesn't explain the DNA mismatch to his son."

"There's a simple explanation for that, honey."

"What's that?"

"It's not his kid!"

"Holy shit, Dad, this just keeps getting better and better!"

"Let me know what you find out, Lise," Ernie said, "now I'd better take your mother home before she drives Rick crazy!"

CHAPTER 11

Jimmy stared at his image in the full length mirror. He loved his new custom-made Hunter Brothers suit. Jimmy was tall, handsome, and in great shape, and the contoured suit fit him like a glove. Charcoal gray with pinstripes is just the right look for today's graduation ceremony of our Dreamland sales force, he thought.

He held up a red tie and a blue tie in front of the pale blue shirt he wore under the jacket.

"Weezee," he said loudly, "I need your opinion on what tie to wear."

Just then Louise Foster walked into the bedroom. She saw her husband standing in front of the mirror.

"I see you're looking at your favorite person!" she said with a smile.

Louise was the perfect match for her husband. She was also tall, and with her blond hair and makeup she was a truly stunning woman. Louise and Jimmy Foster turned heads every time they entered a room together.

"What d'ya think, Weezee," Jimmy asked, "red tie or blue?"

51

"I like the blue, Jimmy," she replied, "it matches your eyes!"

"Then blue it is, babe."

"Cary's downstairs waiting for you. He's got a briefcase for you."

"Okay, good, tell him I'll be right there."

"Good luck, today, honey!"

"Thanks, babe. Cary says this is the best sales team he's ever put together."

"I bet you can't wait to give them the Jimmy Foster speech!"

"We'll get them charged up for the next two weeks, that's for sure!"

Jimmy put the finishing touches on his outfit, checked his hair, and went downstairs to meet with his sales manager, Cary Garnet.

Cary was waiting in the kitchen talking with Louise and eight year old Jeffrey. Cary was six foot three, with blond hair and green eyes. He was single, but never spent a weekend without an attractive woman by his side.

Jimmy and Cary had first met as sales associates for Prentice Builders, the largest housing developer in south Florida. They were often referred to as Butch Cassidy and the Sundance Kid. The two best friends took turns, month after month, as the first and second place sales associates for the entire company.

So, it was no surprise to anyone when Jimmy asked Cary to be his sales manager for the Dreamland project.

"You got the cash?" Jimmy asked.

"Right here," Cary replied as he showed Jimmy the small brief case.

"I bet that'll get the crowd worked up!" Jimmy smiled.

"My friend," Cary replied, "You could work up a crowd in the cemetery! I'll meet you over there."

As Cary left the house Jimmy's son Jeffrey walked up to his father.

"You coming home later, Dad?" Jeffrey asked.

Jimmy gave his son a hug. "I'm gonna take you out for dinner tonight, Jeffy," he said with a smile, "just you and me. So you start thinking about where you want to go."

"McDonalds!" Jeffrey yelled.

"Keep thinking," Jimmy replied, "I'll see you later, bud."

Jimmy kissed Louise and walked outside to his awaiting Lamborghini Diablo.

CHAPTER 12

Lisa walked into the office and, once again, she found JoJo at her desk. This time she was on the phone. Today's outfit was lavender. Within one minute JoJo ended her call.

"Bingo!" JoJo exclaimed in a loud voice.

"What's that all about, Jo?" Lisa asked.

"July 25, 1982, The Boca Club."

"You found it?" Lisa said excitedly.

"The wedding of Louise Elizabeth Schwartz to James Edward Foster," came JoJo's reply, "it is him!"

"How'd you find it, Jo?"

"You know, partner, just a lot of grunt work on the phone and the internet," JoJo replied, "I love that kind of stuff, especially when it pays off like this!"

"So I guess now we need to talk to Jimmy's widow," Lisa said.

"She's expecting us at two this afternoon, partner," JoJo replied, "and I've got the address plugged into my GPS."

"I guess we need to leave around twelve thirty, then."

"I can't wait to show her that ring," Lisa said as she checked her phone, "I bet she recognizes it."

"I think she's the key to finding out who killed Jimmy."

"What makes you say that, Jo?"

"Because the wife always knows, Lisa, trust me on that one!"

"I think you're right about that, Jo," Lisa replied, "but I'm not so sure she'll be willing to tell us the truth about her husband. From what we've learned so far he was a really shady character."

"And not the best husband either."

"I'm interested to see if she defends him or attacks him."

"Hey, Lisa, I have to leave for about an hour this morning, but I'll be back before we have to leave for the trip to Boca."

"Sure no problem, Jo," Lisa replied, "anything I can help you with?"

"Thanks, Lisa. I've got a meeting with one of my son's teachers at eleven."

"Okay, I'll be prepping for this afternoon's meeting with Louise Schwartz."

"Great," JoJo replied, "I sent you a text with a list of suggested questions to ask her, and we both have the ring photo on our phones."

With each passing day Lisa was more and more impressed with JoJo Worthington.

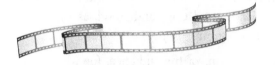

CHAPTER 13

JANUARY 11, 1995, 10:00 AM

DREAMLAND

PORT ST. LUCIE, FLORIDA

Jimmy parked his Lamborghini and waited outside the tent as Cary warmed up the assembled group of sales associates. He listened as Cary spoke to the group.

As he waited Jimmy looked around at what he was about to create. Dreamland Estates was going to be the greatest community to ever be built in South Florida. He was certain of that.

The huge tent, which today was occupied by forty young and eager sales associates, would soon be filled with buyers ready to purchase a home in this amazing new community.

Jimmy could hear Cary warming up the crowd, congratulating them for completing their sales training and promising them an exciting two weeks to come. He knew that the forty thousand dollars in cash he was holding in his briefcase would be a great symbol of the potential that lies ahead for the young sales force.

Just then Cary stopped talking and the music began to play. As planned, the voice of Freddie Mercury and Queen filled the room with the words, *"We are the champions, my friend!"*

That was Jimmy's key. He opened the tent door and bounded into the room with a huge smile on his face. As soon as he entered the audience jumped to their collective feet and erupted in cheers as they reveled at this opportunity to meet the great Jimmy Foster.

Jimmy danced his way to the front of the room in perfect harmony with the song. He hugged Cary and stood, as the crowd continued to worship him. To this group, Jimmy Foster was a rock star.

Jimmy stood in front of the audience, for what seemed an eternity, until finally they settled down back into their seats to hear him speak. He smiled at the assembled group. They were all young and attractive, the perfect combination to sell houses.

On cue the music stopped cold.

"Cary tells me this is the best sales team ever assembled," he began, "is he right?"

"Yes!" A few from the crowd answered quietly.

"I can't hear you!" Jimmy yelled, "is he right?"

"Yes!" came the roar of the crowd.

"Yes?" Jimmy yelled again.

The crowd was on their feet yelling "Yes!"

"Yes, yes, yes you are!" Jimmy screamed.

The group was now worked into a frenzy. "Yes we are!" they all screamed. "Yes, yes, yes we are!"

Jimmy paused and waited for just the right moment to continue. He opened the brief case and wildly tossed the forty thousand dollars in cash on the table in front of him.

"Who wants forty grand?" he yelled.

"I do!" was the loud reply.

"Do you?"

"Yes!"

"Do you?"

"Yes!!"

"Good," Jimmy said quietly, bringing the group with him as they hung on his every word, "because each and every one of you is gonna have the opportunity to walk away with this much money, or even more, over the next two weeks. How's that sound to you?"

"Great!" Cary yelled from behind Jimmy.

"Sounds good?" Jimmy smiled.

"Yes!" came the roar from the audience.

Jimmy calmly stepped in front of the table, closer to his audience. He pointed to an attractive young woman wearing the name tag 'Becca'.

"Hi Becca, where are you from?"

The young woman quietly responded "West Palm Beach."

"Welcome to Dreamland, Becca," Jimmy said, 'let me ask you, have you ever made forty thousand dollars in two weeks before?"

"No sir!"

"Neither had I, Becca," Jimmy replied, "not until I started selling real estate. And the reason I love this business is because we are able to make a lot of people happy while we make a lot of money doing it. How's that sound to you Becca?"

"Sounds great!" Becca replied.

"So here's the deal," Jimmy said calmly, "for you, Becca and for every one of you in this room today. Each of you is gonna meet at least thirty highly motivated buying couples over the next two weeks. If you can sell homes to ten of them you'll walk away with twenty thousand dollars in your pocket. Sell to twenty of them and you'll make forty grand! Sound good, Becca?"

"Sounds better than good!" Becca replied.

"How's it sound to the rest of you?" Jimmy said, as he challenged the audience to respond.

"Great!" came the collective reply.

"Raise your hand if you're gonna make at least twenty grand!" Jimmy shouted.

Everyone in the room stood on their feet with their arms held high.

"Now raise your hand if you're gonna make forty!"

Once again every hand went up.

"Are you gonna do it?" Jimmy shouted, pointing at one young man in the crowd.

"Yes! I'm gonna do it!" the young man shouted.

Jimmy pointed to an another young woman. "How about you?"

"Yes I am!"

"Are you all gonna do it?" Jimmy screamed.

"Yes!" The crowd yelled.

"Yes you will!" Jimmy shouted. "Yes you will!"

"Yes we will!" The crowd roared, over and over again. "Yes we will!"

"You're gonna make your twenty, right?"

"Yes!"

"And then you're gonna make forty, right?"

Jimmy cupped his right hand and held it up to his right ear like pro wrestler Hulk Hogan. With his left hand he waived the crowd to respond.

"Forty, forty forty!" they screamed.

"I can't hear you!" Jimmy yelled.

"Forty, forty, forty!" The sound was deafening.

On cue the music began *"We are the champions!"* The entire audience began to sing along with Freddie Mercury's voice. They were worked up into a frenzy.

Jimmy gathered up his money in the briefcase and walked out of the room, slapping palms with audience members as he walked by. The master motivator had done it again. He had accomplished his mission.

As he exited the tent and walked toward his car a familiar man was waiting for him. He was a very large man with a menacing face.

"He wants his money today, Jimmy," the man said sternly.

"I know, Dominic, I know" Jimmy replied, "I don't have it today, but I will have it in two weeks."

"Today is the deadline, Jimmy," the man replied, "and you know he doesn't take kindly to being told no."

Jimmy was shaken. He handed the briefcase to Dominic. "Look, there's forty grand in here. Tell him I'll have the rest in two weeks."

Dominic opened the briefcase and examined the contents. "This is chump change compared to what you owe, Jimmy. Somehow you found the money to buy this Lamborghini, didn't you?"

"It's leased Dominic. Look, I promise you I'll have the whole amount in two weeks. I swear!"

"I'll pass that message on, Jimmy," Dominic said, "but I know he ain't gonna like it."

As the man disappeared into the night Jimmy sat inside his Lamborghini. These kids better sell a lot of houses, he thought.

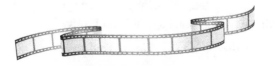

CHAPTER 14

"How do I get to live in a neighborhood like this?" JoJo asked, as the two detectives drove up to the guard house of Louise Schwartz's estate home in Boca Raton.

"I thought you had a rich husband who bought all your clothes, Jo," Lisa replied.

"Stuart does fine, Lisa, but down here we're looking at serious money!"

"Serious money?"

"Stuart says serious money is when you've got so much you don't even know how much you're worth."

"I guess that ship has sailed for us then, JoJo."

"I dunno," JoJo mused, "Stuart says I should come to Boca wearing a bikini and find a serious money guy to take care of me after he dies."

"Dies?" Lisa replied, "Stuart's like what, fifty?"

"Fifty-three, and he's not dying anytime soon, I hope," Lisa replied, "but he says maybe I should start looking now and maybe the guy will take care of him too!"

The two partners laughed as they flashed their badges at the security guard. Within minutes they were inside the home of Louise Schwartz.

Louise was a stunning woman. At sixty she was still a head turner, tall, blond, and slim. She welcomed the detectives into her mansion and sat down with them in the massive living room. Lisa was enthralled by the huge pool in the back yard that featured a large rock waterfall.

"You have a beautiful home," Lisa said.

"Thanks," Louis replied, "It belonged to my parents. After my mom died I just didn't have the heart to sell it, so I moved in."

"Did your dad also pass away?" JoJo asked.

"No, Dad is living in a nursing home in Jupiter," Louise replied. "He's ninety-two and suffers from Alzheimer.

"I'm sorry," JoJo said softly.

"No need to be sorry," Louise grinned, "he's still a handsome devil and he's got two girlfriends fighting over him! They always bake him chocolate chip cookies and then they argue over which ones he likes the best."

"It sounds like he's happy," Lisa said.

"Yes," Louise added, "I just wish he knew me when I visited him. He's like a stranger." She grabbed a tissue and wiped a tear from her eyes.

"We met Jeffrey," JoJo said, hoping to lighten the mood, "what a nice young man."

Louise smiled, "Yes he is. I'm very proud of him. He looks a lot like my dad."

"Louise," Lisa began, "as you know, the reason we came to talk to you today is because we found what could be the remains of your husband, Jimmy Foster."

"Yes I know that," Louise said, "where were these remains found?"

"A skeleton was unearthed by a construction crew up in Port St. Lucie," Lisa replied.

"That's where Jimmy was building Dreamland." Louise said. "so how can you be sure that it's really Jimmy?"

"That's just it," JoJo said, "we're not sure if it's him and we were hoping you could help us."

"Sure, how can I help?"

Lisa reached into her purse and removed her cell phone. She quickly brought up the photo JoJo had taken of the engagement ring. "This ring was found in the clothing of the recovered body."

Louise held the phone as she grabbed her reading glasses. She looked carefully at the ring and sat quietly for several seconds before she spoke.

"Let me show you something," Louise said softly.

She got up from her chair and walked out of the room. In two minutes she returned with a a gold band that looked exactly like the ring in the photo. She handed the ring to Lisa.

"This was the ring Jimmy placed on my finger the day we got married," she said, "it's engraved 'JIMMY 8/25/82'.

"And the other ring is the match to it?" JoJo asked.

"Yes," Louise replied with a tear, "Jimmy always called my Weezee."

Lisa waited a few minutes as Louise collected herself from the emotion of the moment.

"Tell us about Jimmy."

Louise collected her thoughts for a moment. Her tears subsided as she began to speak. "I met Jimmy for the first time when he sold this house to my parents. I thought he was the most handsome man I had ever seen. I knew the first day I met Jimmy that I was going to marry him."

"So you guys were married for thirteen years," Lisa said.

"Yes, we were, almost thirteen."

"And you had one son, Jeffrey?"

Lisa was surprised to hear that question come from JoJo. They had decided they wouldn't mention the DNA test results from Jeffrey unless it was critical to solving the case.

"Yes we did," Louise respond with a smile. "Jeffrey was our miracle baby."

"Miracle baby?"

"We tried for four years to get pregnant with no success," Louise replied, "and then we found a fertility clinic that helped us have Jeffrey. So we always called him our miracle baby."

"Louise," JoJo said, "may we call you that?"

"Of course."

"Louise, can you tell us about the last time you saw your husband."

"It was a long time ago but I'll never forget it," Louise replied, "February 3, 1995, a Friday night. Jimmy was going out with his sales staff to celebrate their five hundredth Dreamland house sold. He said it would be a very late night and he was gonna stay at the hotel for the night."

"Where was he going to celebrate?" Lisa asked.

"It was at The Breakers in Palm Beach. Jimmy always liked to go first class in everything he did."

"So I guess he didn't come home that night?" Lisa asked.

"That's right. The next day I didn't see Jimmy at all, but I figured he was busy so it didn't concern me at all. He often stayed away for a couple of days at a time. It wasn't until Monday that I started to worry."

"So what did you do then?" JoJo asked.

"First, I called Cary," Louise replied, "I guess you know who he is."

"Yes we do." Lisa plied.

"So, Cary told me he hadn't seen Jimmy since they all left the dinner party Friday night."

"Did you call the police?"

"I called my father first. He said not to call the police."

"Why was that?" Lisa asked.

"He said Jimmy was probably off on a binge of some sort and he didn't want to create a scandal that would cause the Dreamland buyers to panic."

"Binge?" JoJo said.

"Jimmy lived a fast life," Louise said quietly. "He loved to indulge in things that weren't always good for him. I thought I would be able to tame him after we got married, but I never was able to. He was a good man who had flaws."

"So, what kind of things did he indulge in?"

"He loved to gamble, and when he gambled he drank a lot and sometimes did other things."

"Where did he go to gamble?"

"He usually went to the Backroom Casino. He loved to play blackjack, and he was good at it too!"

"He was good?" JoJo asked.

"He always said he won money, I guess they all say that, though."

"Did you find out if he went there that night?"

"My father hired a private detective to find out what happened to Jimmy but he couldn't find him. The Backroom is very private and they refuse to talk about who goes there."

"And when did the police get involved?" Lisa asked.

"The police got involved the next week after the buyers realized that the office was closed and their money was gone. I guess a lot of people were angry at Jimmy for stealing their deposits. I don't blame them for that."

"Did you believe Jimmy ran off with the money?" JoJo asked.

"At first I didn't," Louise replied, "I refused to accept the fact that Jimmy would leave me and Jeffrey like that."

"So, what changed your mind?"

"When my father found out that the money was gone we realized that Jimmy had run off with the it. He was the only one who had access to the money other than his accountant. My father said he thought Jimmy might have had a second family somewhere. That's when I finally accepted the fact that he left me and Jeffrey."

"Louise," Lisa said, "now that we know Jimmy was killed do you have any idea who could have done it?"

"A lot of people were mad at Jimmy for stealing their money," Louise replied, "but that was after he disappeared."

"So, who else would have wanted to kill him?" Lisa asked.

"I just don't know," Louise sighed, "my father spent a fortune trying to find out what happened and he just couldn't do it."

"Did he find that second family?"

"No, they found no trace of Jimmy anywhere. Over the next several years my father kept trying to track Jimmy down, but he never succeeded."

"Do you have the name of the private investigator your father hired?"

"His name was Bannister, John Bannister. I heard he died a few years ago."

"Okay thanks, Louise," JoJo said, "I have one more question for you. The ring we showed you, it was found in the pocket of Jimmy's pants. Do you have any idea why Jimmy would have the ring in his pocket instead of on his finger?"

Louise paused, as if she were searching for the correct words to say. "As I said, Jimmy liked to in indulge in things that weren't always good for him."

"Like other women?" JoJo asked.

"Like other women," Louise replied, "he thought I didn't know about it, but I did."

"How did you find out about the other women, Louise?"

"My father never trusted Jimmy, so he had Bannister follow him around constantly."

"But wasn't it your father who lent Jimmy the money to buy the land for the Dreamland project?" Lisa asked.

"Yes, he did that," Louise responded, "he told me it was a good investment and it would keep Jimmy busy too."

Lisa stood up as if to leave, but she stopped and spoke instead. "How long have you and Cary been married?"

"We've been officially married for twelve years," Louise replied, "but we were together almost eight years before we decided to get married."

"Tell us about that," JoJo said.

"After Jimmy left, Cary and I spent a lot of time together. He was my shoulder to cry on, and I was his. A lot of people blamed Cary for the money being gone, and some even blamed me. So we were all we had."

"I see."

"Both of us lost our best friend and our reputations at the same time."

"So when did the romance begin?" JoJo asked.

"I guess it was about three years after Jimmy disappeared. I had filed for divorce and changed my name, so I felt that it was time to move on with my life."

"And Cary was there for you,"

"And Cary was there for me, yes."

"We'd like to talk with Cary," Lisa said.

"He's working right now," Louise replied, "but I'll have him call you as soon as he gets home."

Lisa and JoJo thanked Louise for her time and walked back to their car for the ride up to Port St. Lucie.

"Something just doesn't seem right to me, Lisa."

"I was thinking the same thing, Jo."

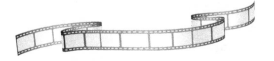

CHAPTER 15

DECEMBER 5, 2018, 8:00 AM
THE HOME OF LISA AND RICK MARCH

"Lexie called while you were in the shower, babe," Rick said calmly to his wife.

Lisa sipped her morning coffee. "So early?" she said, "let me guess, she needs money!"

"Actually no, not this time Lisa. She said she needs to speak to you."

"She needs to speak to me but she calls you. Now does that make sense?"

"She always calls my phone, even when she wants to talk to you. I told her you were in the shower and you'd call her back as soon as you got dressed."

"Any hint as to what she needs?"

"She said her roommate didn't come home last night."

"Oh no!" Lisa grabbed her cell phone and called her daughter. She was taken right to voicemail.

"Hey Lex, it's Mom. Call me as soon as you get this message. Okay bye."

"Maybe the roommate is back home by now, Lisa."

"I hope so."

"Speaking of missing persons, how's your case going?

"We met Louise Schwartz today."

"Refresh my memory Lisa, who is she?"

"Oh, she's the ex-wife of Jimmy Foster."

"The dead guy?"

"Yes, the dead guy. And now we're certain it's him because she recognized his wedding ring."

"So, what's next, Lisa?"

"Now all we have to do is figure out who killed him!"

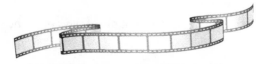

CHAPTER 16

DECEMBER 5, 2018, 9:00 AM
PORT ST. LUCIE POLICE HEADQUARTERS

Lisa arrived to find her partner hard at work as usual, this time dressed in a black and white outfit, with matching hat.

Captain Davis walked by the desk where the two women were talking.

"Captain," Lisa said, "can I see you in your office for a minute?"

As they entered the office, Captain Davis said, "what's up March?"

"I need a big favor," Lisa replied.

"What kind of favor?"

"I need a couple of days off. If I can take off today and Friday I'll be back on Monday."

"What's on your desk," the captain asked, "anything hot?"

"We're working on the Jimmy Foster case from twenty-four years ago, boss," Lisa replied, "I'm sure it can wait a couple more days to get solved."

"Okay Lisa, anything I can do to help?"

"Thanks, boss. I've got to drive up to Tallahassee to help my daughter."

"Okay Lisa, let me know if you need anything."

"Thanks, Captain!"

"One more thing, Lisa."

"Sure, what's that, boss?"

"It looks like you and Worthington are working great together!"

Lisa grinned and walked out of the office. She was met immediately by JoJo.

"Everything okay, Lisa?"

"I'm not so sure, Jo. I'm taking a couple of days off to help Lexie up at FSU."

"Lexie goes to FSU?" JoJo responded, "I didn't know that. My daughter Madison is a freshman there. Aren't they all scheduled to come home for winter break this weekend?"

"Yes they are," Lisa replied, "but Lexie has a serious problem she's facing, so I'm gonna try and help her.

"Anything I can do to help, partner?"

"Actually I don't even know if I can help. Lexie's roommate, Carly Adams, didn't come home last night, and I'm gonna see if I can help find her."

"Are they sure she didn't just leave early for break?"

"That's the first question I asked, but Lexie says Carly wouldn't leave without saying goodbye."

"When did Lexie last see her?"

"Lexie said Carly had a date last night with a new guy, somebody Lexie hadn't met. She left the apartment about seven, and that's the last time anybody has seen her."

"So I suppose they tried calling her several times."

"When Lexie woke up this morning, and Carly wasn't there, she tried calling her, but every time the call just went to voice mail."

"Did she call the cops?"

"The campus police are supposedly looking into it, but I don't have much confidence in them. That's why I'm going up there right away."

"Did they find the guy she had the date with?" JoJo asked.

"Nobody even knows who he is!" Lisa replied.

"Let me come with you, Lisa. We're a team, and this will give me a chance to drive Maddie back home for the holidays."

"But, I'm leaving this afternoon and taking the next two days off work."

"Well then, so am I, partner!"

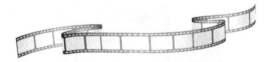

CHAPTER 17

JANUARY 18, 1995, 9:00 PM

SUITE 1201, THE BREAKERS

PALM BEACH, FLORIDA

Jimmy Foster was seated at the conference table along with his sales manager, Cary Garnet and the Dreamland accountant, Lou Laber.

"Okay guys," Jimmy began, "we're halfway through the big sales push, so let's take a look at how we're doing."

Cary opened a folder and proudly read the results of the first week of sales. "I'd say we're on track to sell 500 units. We might even get to the max sellout of 523!"

Jimmy leaned back in his chair and smiled. "That's what I wanna hear, Cary! Sounds like your sales team is doing a great job."

"We've had fourteen sales parties this past week with an average of 50 couples per party," Cary said. "And so far we've received deposits on 312 houses. That's about a 45% sales ratio!"

"That's a damn good sales rate," Jimmy added, "so how much have we collected so far?"

Lou Laber, a smallish man in his early fifties, spoke softly.

"We've collected full twenty percent deposits on 172 houses and partials on 150. In total we've collected a little over seven million."

"How do the partials look?" Jimmy asked.

"That's always tricky," Cary replied, "my experience is that about half of them get cold feet and ask for their deposits back."

"I think you're right," Jimmy replied, "so realistically we've got about 250 solid sales."

"Right on target, with another week to go," Cary added, "and we've got another 620 potential buyer couples lined up for those parties."

"And where are the deposits right now, Lou?" Jimmy asked.

"They're safely tucked away in our escrow account at Saint Lucie bank." Lou replied. "We can't touch those funds until we start construction of houses."

"I know," Jimmy answered abruptly.

"Almost all of the twelve million loan money is gone, Jimmy," Lou said, "We're gonna have to start tapping into the escrow account soon."

"How'd we spend all the loan money, Jimmy?" Cary asked.

"Look Cary, the things we're doing aren't cheap, okay?" Jimmy replied curtly, "you just leave everything to me."

"Okay, boss," Cary replied.

"It's not that simple, Jimmy," Lou Laber said, "the bank is gonna audit us and they want receipts for every dime of that twelve million you spent. I told you that when we got the loan!"

"Don't lecture me, Lou!" Jimmy yelled.

"You hired me to be your accountant, Jimmy," Lou said firmly, "you need to let me do my job."

"I hired you to do what I tell you to do," Jimmy shot back, "not what the fucking bank says!"

"We need receipts, Jimmy!"

"I'll get your damn receipts, and I want you to get me the bank account information on the escrow money, Lou."

"Okay, Jimmy," Lou replied, as he handed Jimmy the bank account number and password for online banking, "Please put this in a secure place."

"Thank you Lou, I'll take good care of it," Jimmy said with a grin.

"And remember, we can't touch that money until we start construction on the houses. You gotta listen to me, I'm trying to protect you."

"Lou," Jimmy answered, as he collected himself and allowed a calmer tone to his voice, "I'm not questioning your ability or your integrity. I just want access to my money. Is that okay with you?"

"Whatever you say, Jimmy," Lou replied with a sigh.

"Cary, you told me one woman has been our best sales associate."

"You remember the girl you singled out in the tent, Becca Raymond?"

"Oh yes," Jimmy smiled, "she's a cutie!"

"That she is!" Cary replied, "And she's a great salesman too! She's met with fourteen potential buyers and sold twelve!"

"That's one hell of a record," Jimmy said. "Just like you and I used to do!"

"It's fantastic," Cary replied, "the next best associate only has nine sales."

"I want to meet with her, Cary."

"I figured you'd say that, Jimmy, so I invited her to join us here tonight." Cary said, "She's waiting down in the lobby."

"Great! On your way out, send her up."

"You want a private meeting? Up here in this room?" Cary grinned.

"Very private!" Jimmy replied as he glanced at the king sized bed in the room. He carefully removed the wedding ring from his finger and placed it in his pocket.

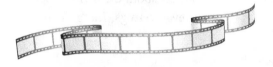

CHAPTER 18

DECEMBER 5, 2018, 3:00 PM

INTERSTATE 75, FLORIDA

Lisa waited for JoJo to finish reading emails on her cell phone.

"So, how did your meeting go yesterday at your son's school, Jo?"

JoJo hesitated for a moment to collect her thoughts.

"Billy has Down's Syndrome," she said quietly.

Lisa was taken aback, and not sure how to respond.

"Oh, I'm sorry," she said, the words barely escaping her lips.

JoJo took her partner's right hand and smiled.

"Thank you," she said, "but there's no reason to be sorry, really."

Lisa was embarrassed. "I didn't know what to say, JoJo."

JoJo held Lisa's hand. "It's okay, really," she said, "I know you meant well."

"I guess I'm not the first person to say that to you."

JoJo chuckled. "If I had a dollar for every time someone said that to me I could buy a new car!" she said, "but I know that people mean well and that's what really matters."

"Well, then," Lisa replied, "thanks for letting me off the hook."

"You know, when we found out that Billy had Down's Syndrome we were devastated. Stu and I kept asking why God would do something like this to us. Our first child, Madison, was perfect, and now we had to face a life of misery, we thought."

"That must have been very difficult, Jo."

"It was. But then we learned about a Down's support group through our church, so we went to a few meetings. That's when our whole perspective changed."

"What made that happen?"

"We realized that every parent with a special needs child feels like we did, but most of them came to accept that they were chosen by God to raise one of his children. We know that God would never have chosen us if he didn't think we were up to the task."

"So, what has it been like for you, raising Billy?"

"Billy has given us challenges. Lisa, but what child doesn't?"

"You're right about that!"

"But Billy is the sweetest, kindest person I have ever met."

Tears welled up in Lisa's eyes. "That is wonderful, Jo!"

"Billy's sixteen now, and he has brought us more joy than we could ever ask for!"

"What school does he go to?"

"Billy has learning issues, of course, but we found a wonderful private school that specializes in mainstreaming special need students. Billy absolutely loves it there. He's even on the football team!"

"Football? Aren't you worried that he might get hurt?"

"He loves football, Lisa, and he kept begging Stuart and me to let him try out for the team. So we talked to the coach, and he's a wonderful, supportive guy. He said he would be happy to have Billy on the team, and that while Billy might get a few bumps and bruises like the other players, he would make sure that he didn't get hurt badly. That was good enough for us."

"So, does he play in the games?"

"Mostly he just stands on the sidelines wearing his uniform and cheering for his teammates. He loves that uniform! He would wear it every day if I let him!"

"And his teammates? How do they treat Billy?"

"These kids are great, Lisa. Going to that school, they're used to being with special needs kids. They love Billy and he loves them. Football was the best thing we ever did for him."

"So, did he ever get to play in a game?"

"That's an amazing story," JoJo replied. "one time the team was losing by a lot with only a minute left in the game. I saw Billy's coach talking to the other coach, and then he sent Billy into the game."

"Really?"

"When they announced Billy Worthington's name over the loud speaker everyone in the stands went nuts. They were cheering for my son and I was crying like a baby!"

"I'm crying now!" Lisa said, wiping tears from her eyes.

"On the next play the quarterback handed the ball to Billy and he ran all the way down the field for a touchdown. The other team made fake attempts to tackle him but it was obvious what was going on. When Billy got to the end zone his teammates picked him up and carried him off the field on their shoulders. It was the happiest day of my son's life!"

"I bet he'll never forget that day," Lisa said, still wiping her eyes.

"Here's the best part, Lisa," JoJo continued, "a few days later we were talking about that play and we were telling Billy how proud we were of him, he said something that I'll never forget."

"What was that?"

"He said 'Mom, I know the other team let me score that touchdown but I'm still happy because everyone was so nice to me! That was more important to me than the touchdown!'"

"Wow, what an amazing kid!"

"That's my son," JoJo said with a smile, "and the last thing in the world I am is sorry!"

Lisa was speechless.

"Okay," JoJo said, "enough of that. Wanna hear a blonde joke?"

Lisa was happy to lighten the mood. "Sure, tell me your favorite one."

"This guy walks up to a blonde and says 'I bet I can tell you the exact day you were born just by feeling your boobs.'"

"She looks at him and says 'no way you could do that'"

"He says 'I'll bet you twenty bucks I can.'"

"She says 'your on', so he grabs her boobs and fondles them for a couple of minutes. Finally, she says 'that's enough, so tell me the exact day I was born.'"

"The guy hands her the twenty bucks and says 'yesterday!'"

Their laughter stopped only when JoJo's phone rang.

"Maddie! Hi honey."

"Where are you, Mom?"

"We're on our way, Mads. Where are you?"

"I'm in Lexie March's apartment, Mom."

"You are? Geez, I didn't even know you two knew each other."

"Actually we met when I first came to campus, back in August. Lexie's a junior and she was part of the freshman orientation team. They paired her with me because we're both from Port St. Lucie."

"Oh that was nice," JoJo replied. "So I guess you must have been surprised when you realized that your mothers are both detectives in the same department, huh?"

"Actually, the subject of our mothers never came up."

JoJo could hear the sound of her daughter rolling her eyes as she answered that question. "Oh, ah, okay, so what's going on right now Maddie?"

"There's a young campus cop here, Mom, but he acts like he doesn't know what to do."

"Okay sweetie, we'll help him as soon as we get there."

Just then Lisa's cell phone rang. Since she was driving she answered on speaker phone. The call was from her daughter, Lexie.

"Mom, the campus police are here," Lexie said, "how far away are you?"

Lisa glanced at JoJo, who held up two fingers.

"We're about two hours away, honey, can you put the campus police officer on the phone please?"

In the background Lisa heard Lexie asking the campus police officer to take her cell phone. At first he was reluctant but eventually he gave in and took the phone.

"Hello, this is Officer Colin Ryan, to whom am I speaking."

"Good morning Officer Ryan, my name is Lisa March, and that is my daughter you just spoke with. I'm on my way to see my daughter and you're on speaker phone with me and Joanne Worthington."

"Uh huh."

"Mrs Worthington and I are detectives in the Port Saint Lucie police department, and both of our daughters are there with you now. We would like to help you in any way possible"

"Uh huh."

"Officer Ryan, we have a few questions to ask about your investigation."

"I'm sorry ma'am, I know you want to help but I can't divulge anything to you at this time."

"Are you on this case by yourself?"

"Yes I am. But I can't talk to you about it."

"We get that, officer, so let me just talk and you can just listen. You don't have to tell me anything."

"Okay."

"I'm assuming that you haven't found the missing student yet, and I'm assuming that you haven't been involved in a lot of missing persons cases. Detective Worthington and I have."

"Uh huh."

"Officer Ryan, in missing person cases time is of the essence. The young lady has already been missing for almost twenty-four hours so it's critical that you act fast."

Just then JoJo motioned to Lisa to let her speak. She ended the call with her daughter and spoke to the officer.

"Officer Ryan, this is detective Worthington."

"Uh huh."

"Here are two things you need to do right away. Number one, you need to trace the missing girl's cell phone to see what towers it's connecting to."

"Yes."

"Good, and here's the next thing you need to do. Find out if she has a debit card, you probably need a warrant but you need to find out if the card has been used to withdraw money in any ATM machines."

Lisa chimed in, "And see if she has a credit card. You can find out if it's been used since she went missing."

"We'll be there in less than two hours, officer Ryan. I know we can't officially get involved but we'll do whatever we can legally without jeopardizing your job. Okay?"

"Okay, thanks."

As she ended the call Lisa said, "I think this poor guy is in way over his head."

CHAPTER 19

Jimmy was awakened by the sound of the shower in his hotel room. He glanced at the pillow beside him to see that his sleeping partner for the night had left the bed. In a few minutes young Becca Raymond emerged from the bathroom, wrapped in a towel.

Becca was small, blonde, and well built, about twenty-five, Jimmy guessed. She was by far the prettiest sales rep in the Dreamland group.

"I've gotta get back to Dreamland for our next set of buyers this morning," she said, as she unwrapped the towel and began to get dressed. "I enjoyed getting to know you."

As soon as the towel dropped Jimmy motioned to the bed, "You can be a few minutes late today, Becca," he said with a grin, "you have permission from the boss!"

Jimmy reached out to the young woman, but she backed away and continued putting on her clothes.

"That's real nice of you, boss," she said, "but if I'm late I might miss a sale and that would cost me two grand in commission. I mean, you're great and all, but you're not worth two thousand bucks!"

Jimmy laughed. He wasn't used to being rejected by females but he had to admire her determination to sell houses in Dreamland.

"Okay, babe," he smiled, "let's do this again after you get your forty grand!"

"Maybe," Becca replied, as she exited the hotel room.

A few minutes later Jimmy left the hotel. He remembered to place the wedding ring back on his finger.

On his way back to his car he was stopped by the man named Dominic. Jimmy hated the sight of this menacing man.

"You've got one more week, Jimmy," Dominic said sternly, "and the clock is ticking."

"I know, Dominic," Jimmy replied nervously, "tell him everything is working out, and I'll definitely have his money."

"Talk is cheap, Jimmy."

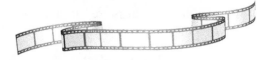

CHAPTER 20

DECEMBER 5, 2018, 5:00 PM
THE APARTMENT OF LEXIE MARCH
FLORIDA STATE UNIVERSITY

Lisa and JoJo burst into Lexie's apartment, where they found Lexie, Madison, and officer Ryan. The officer looked not much older than the students.

"We found her!" Officer Ryan said with a smile.

"You found her?" Lisa said, "Where, how?"

"Actually she found us is a better way to put it," Lexie said, "she called me five minutes ago and said she was okay. She left early for winter break."

"And she just disappeared for twenty-four hours?"

"She said she was with a guy and they were driving to Alabama. I could hear him whispering in the background."

"Boyfriend?"

"I didn't even know she had a boyfriend, Mom," Lexie said.

"Lexie, are sure it was her?"

"Yes, I'm sure."

"And she didn't sound like she was in distress?" JoJo asked.

"Uh, no, I don't think so," Lexie answered, "she just said she was driving home to Alabama."

"Let me have your phone," Lisa said.

As soon as her daughter complied with her request Lisa checked the most recent number received on the phone. She immediately redialed that number. After several rings the call ended.

"I think someone saw the call, answered it, and then immediately ended the call."

"What does that mean, Mom?" Lexie asked.

"I don't know what it means, honey, but it doesn't sound good."

Lisa then turned to Officer Ryan. "Did you get someone to track her cellphone?"

"My boss is looking into it," he replied. "She said she'd get back to me in an hour."

JoJo turned toward Madison. This was the first time she had seen her daughter since school had started back in August. She walked toward Madison and gave her a hug.

"How's Billy, Mom?" Madison asked.

"He misses his sister."

"I miss my brother too, Mom."

As JoJo backed away from the hug she noticed a bruise on her daughter's face.

"What's this, Maddie?" she asked.

"Oh it's nothing," her daughter replied, "I just fell."

JoJo examined the bruise carefully.

"That's not from a fall, Maddie," she said forcefully, "that's from a fist!"

"No, Mom!" Madison pleaded.

"Yes it is, Maddie. Now tell me who did this to you."

"Mom," Madison pleaded, "just let it go!"

"Tell me who did this Maddie, right now!" JoJo was seething with rage at the thought of someone hurting her daughter.

"Was it a guy?"

"Tell her, Maddie," Lexie pleaded, "you need to tell her."

Madison hesitated for a moment and then began to speak. "His name is JT."

"JT what?"

"It's JT Flanagan, Mrs. March," Lexie added. "He's a huge football player and this wasn't the first time he hit Maddie. I told her to report it but she wouldn't do it!"

"He's my boyfriend, Mom," Madison said softly, "and I didn't want to get him kicked off the football team."

"Jesus Christ, Maddie, he hit you!"

"At first he would punch me playfully. But then the punches got harder and harder any time I disagreed with him. I told him he had to stop, but he kept hitting me. He said he knew that I liked it!"

"Son of a bitch!" JoJo screamed. She was in a rage. "Where is he?"

"No Mom," Madison pleaded, "it's okay now, we broke up."

"But he keeps calling you and sending you threatening message, Maddie!" Lexie said.

"Where does he live?" JoJo demanded.

"No, Mom!"

"Madison Worthington," JoJo screamed, "you tell me where this man lives, now!"

"Champions Hall, room 16," Madison replied, "but, Mom!"

JoJo did not stop long enough to hear the rest of what her daughter had to say. In a flash she was out the door and on her way to Champions Hall.

Two minutes after JoJo left, Lexie's cell phone buzzed. She answered and was thrilled to hear her roommate's voice again.

"Carly, are you okay?" Lexie asked.

"Yes, I'm fine Lex," came the voice on the other end. "I'm sorry I left without telling you. I hope I didn't cause too many problems there."

"We were just worried about you, Carly, that's all."

Lisa motioned to her daughter to give her the phone.

"Carly, this is Lisa March, Lexie's mom."

Carly did not respond.

"Carly, I want to make sure that you are okay and not being held against your will."

"Okay."

"So here is what I want you to say," Lisa commanded. "If you are okay say 'I'll talk to you tomorrow'. And if you are not okay say 'I'll talk to you next week'. Do you understand?"

"Okay, I'll talk to you next week!" came the reply, and immediately the phone went dead.

"Call the Tallahassee police," Lisa said firmly, "this girl was abducted."

"I talked to my boss about that before you came," officer Ryan said, "she says the local police won't get involved until a formal missing persons report is filed by a family member, and they have to wait the full twenty-four hours before they can file the report."

"We don't have time for that," Lisa shot back, "that girl is in grave danger!"

Lisa reached for her purse and found the business card of Agent Robert Elliott of the Florida Bureau of Criminal Investigations. As she waited for Elliott to answer she turned to Officer Ryan.

"I'm calling a friend. If anybody can help us he can."

Bob Elliot was a no nonsense agent for the BCI. Earlier in the year he had proven to be a big help to Lisa as she cracked the Pickleball murder case.

"Elliott," came the powerful voice.

"Agent Elliott," Lisa began, "my name is Lisa March from Port St Lucie. I hope you remember me."

"Of course I remember you, March!" Elliot replied, "the Pickleball case, right?"

"Yes, that's me."

"How'd you get my number?"

"You gave me your card, remember? You said if I ever needed anything I should call, so here I am."

"Sure, no problem," Elliott said, "I'm actually with the FBI now, but I've got the same cell phone."

"FBI?" Lisa said, "Oh, that's prefect!"

"What can I do for you, detective?"

"I'm in Tallahassee at FSU and I'm working on the case of a student that was abducted."

"Okay."

"I need your help to find her."

"I'm all over it Lisa," Elliot replied, "just give me the particulars and we'll find her."

"She was last seen in Tallahassee last night and I'm afraid she might have left the state by now."

"That's no problem. We've got agents everywhere."

Lisa spent the next ten minutes telling agent Elliott everything she had learned about the missing girl.

"I'll get back to you this evening, Lisa."

"Bob," she replied, "I can't thank you enough."

"Don't thank me yet," Elliott mused, "we haven't found her yet."

"But I know you will, Bob. I know you will."

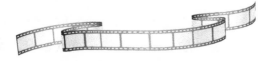

CHAPTER 21

DECEMBER 5, 2018, 5:30 PM

CHAMPIONS HALL

FLORIDA STATE UNIVERSITY

JoJo marched through the entrance and into the lobby of the building that housed the Florida State football team. As soon as she entered she reached into her handbag and turned on the recorder that rested inside.

Several players were milling around the lobby and, when they noticed JoJo, they reacted.

"Hey, Mama," a large man said with a big grin, "you come to see me?"

"Where's room 16?" JoJo shot back without a hint of friendliness. She was in no mood for small talk.

Another player, taller and thinner, joined the conversation. "That's JT's room. I didn't know he was dating a MILF."

"You know what a MILF is, Mama?" still another player added, "it's a mom I'd like to... you fill in the rest honey!"

Again JoJo had no response other than to demand, "Room 16, where is it?"

The largest player pointed toward a hallway behind him, "half way down the hall on the right."

JoJo walked quickly down the corridor and stopped in front of a door with the number 16 on it. She knocked several times and yelled, "JT Flanagan?"

As she was about to start knocking again the door opened. JoJo looked up to see a giant of man, well over six foot five and 250 pounds. He had a big smile on his face.

"I'm JT honey," he said with a grin, "what can I do for you?"

JoJo walked through the door, looked straight at JT, and said, "my name is Joanne Worthington. I'm Maddie Worthington's mother."

JT smiled. "I can see where Maddie gets her good looks, sweetheart!"

"I'm not here for small talk or flattery, Mr. Flanagan. I'm here to talk to you about you hitting my daughter."

JT grinned. "Why, you want a piece of me too, honey?"

JoJo was incensed by the lack of respect she was getting from this over-grown boy.

"You think it makes you a big man to beat up a girl half your size?"

JT smiled again, which made JoJo even angrier. He puffed out his massive chest and spoke. "Well, honey, you shoulda taught your little girl to listen better, then I wouldn't need to discipline her!"

"Let me tell you something you arrogant piece of shit," JoJo screamed, "you go anywhere near my daughter again and you'll regret it for the rest of life!"

The big man looked down at JoJo and let out a loud belly laugh. "Honey, every day I go one on one with 300 pound lineman, and you think I'm afraid of a little old bag like you?"

JT raised his large fist. In an instant JoJo yelled, "get your hands off of me!"

Suddenly she let off a fierce kick that found it's mark in JT's groin. He doubled over in pain. As he crouched, she twirled around a landed a roundhouse kick to the side of his head, knocking him to the ground. Then she jumped on top of him and locked him a choke hold. Within seconds he was gasping for breath. She held the choke hold for several seconds as the life began to slip away from JT Flanagan. His face was turning bright red and, in the mirror, she could see the look of panic and mortal fear in his bulging eyes.

At just the right moment, however, JoJo released the hold and stood up over JT. He was on the ground, curled up in the fetal position, wheezing and coughing.

"You're lucky I didn't kill you today, you worthless piece of shit!" she screamed. "Now open your eyes and look at me."

JT's eyes remained closed.

"I said look at me!" JoJo screamed twice until he complied with her command.

"Big man," she said as she stared at him, "you just got the shit kicked out of you by a woman less that half your size. You know what that makes you?"

No response came from JT.

"That makes you a big pussy!" JoJo yelled. "You think you're a big man because you're on the football team, but now everybody's gonna know the truth. You're nothing but a big pussy! You hear me?"

From his position below her the big man nodded. He could hardly speak. JoJo was in a frenzy by now.

"Now you listen to me, JT Flanagan. If I find out that you came anywhere near my daughter, or that you called her, or texted her, or sent her an email, or even so much as looked in her direction I will be back. And I can assure you the next time I won't be so easy on you. Next time will be a lot worse, and you'll never play football again. I can guarantee you that!"

JT nodded.

"Is that clear!"

"Yes ma'am," he mumbled.

With that JoJo calmly walked out of the room and back through the lobby. A large crowd of football players had gathered, and most them had overheard the tumult coming from room 16. As JoJo walked out the door not one player said a word to her.

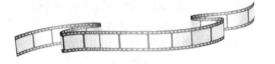

CHAPTER 22

Sam Mays loved his job as head of hospitality for the Backroom Casino. He especially liked it when the biggest gamblers, the 'whales' they were called, came in and had a table set up just for them. Tonight Sam was being shadowed by twenty-two year old Adrian Burkett, the son of Backroom Casino co-owner Jerry Burkett. Sam was showing young Adrian the ropes.

One of the whales had just arrived, and Sam was there to make sure that he was comfortable. The Penthouse suite was being readied and a beautiful young lady was waiting there whenever it suited the pleasure of the whale, Mr. Jimmy Foster.

Sam greeted Jimmy with a hug and a glass of Johnny Walker Black. He introduced Jimmy to Adrian and stepped back as a tray of one and five thousand dollar chips was brought to Jimmy's table. Jimmy reached into the pile of chips and handed the dealer a $1,000 chip.

"The only game Jimmy plays is blackjack," Sam whispered to Adrian as the card shuffle began. "He typically gambles $25,000 per hand and has four hands dealt each time."

"Is he a big winner, Sam?" Adrian asked.

"Over the years Jimmy's won and lost millions in the Backroom but the past six months have been a disaster for him."

"Where does he get the money to lose?"

"Jimmy married into a rich family, and that's what he used to get started here," Sam replied, "he had a long line of credit with us but then that dried up. I heard he was tapping into a bank loan that was supposed to be used for a construction project he was working on."

"Isn't that illegal?"

Sam laughed. "Adrian," he said, "do you know the difference between ignorance and apathy?"

The younger man thought for a moment. "No."

"I don't know, and I don't care!" Sam answered with a belly laugh.

It took Adrian a few minutes to get the joke.

"I heard that Jimmy blew all the construction money and then he was forced to borrow money from a loan shark named Mr. Black."

"Mr. Black?"

"That's the guy, no nonsense. You pay on time or you lose a finger, that kind of guy."

"I get it."

"But Jimmy still comes here a couple of nights a week. He's always hoping for the big score that will make things right for him."

"Sad situation," Adrian said quietly.

"Yes it is, Adrian," Sam replied, "and it's the same routine every time. He gambles until two a.m. and then goes up to the penthouse to have sex with one of our girls. Then he wakes up the next morning and leaves."

"But he keeps losing?"

"Not every time, but overall, yes he keeps losing."

"How much, Sam?"

"In total he's lost close to twenty million, son."

"Holy shit, Sam!"

"Hey Adrian," Sam laughed, "he paid for your braces, your college tuition, your first car, everything!"

"Yeh, but how's he gonna pay back that Mr. Black guy?"

"Ignorance and apathy, Adrian, ignorance and apathy!"

CHAPTER 23

"You have to eat, Lex," Lisa said as she watched her daughter move food around her plate without ever placing it in her mouth.

"I can't eat, Mom," Lexie replied, "I mean, what if Carly's dead?"

"We've got the right people looking for her now, thanks to your mom," JoJo offered.

"I'm hoping Bob Elliott will call me tonight or no later than first thing in the morning," Lisa added, "He's the best in the business, so if he says he's gonna call you can take it to the bank."

"I'm just afraid of what he might tell us!" Madison said.

"Me too!" Lexie added.

"Look, I know how upsetting this is, girls," Lisa said quietly, "but right now there's not a thing we can do other than wait. So let's talk about something else."

"Like what," Madison offered, "like how you beat up a football player?"

"Oh, you know about that, Maddie?"

"The whole school knows about it, Mom! They say you went into his room and nearly killed him!"

"How'd the word spread so fast?" JoJo asked.

"Ever heard of Twitter?" Madison responded.

"And Facebook," Lexie added.

"And Instagram, and Snapchat…" Madison continued.

 "Okay," JoJo conceded, "I get it!"

"I think we might get a visit from the campus police," Lisa said.

"That's okay," JoJo replied, "JT admitted hitting Madison and then he tried to hit me, so I took care of him. It was self defense."

"Can you prove it, Jo?" Lisa asked.

JoJo smiled and removed the recorder from her purse. "I recorded the whole thing, partner."

After listening to the recording Lisa was relieved. "Smart move, partner. This school isn't gonna want this recording to be heard anywhere!"

"I told you I wasn't just another dumb blonde!" JoJo said with a grin.

"Mom," Madison said, looking at her cellphone, "they're calling you Wonder Woman!"

"Actually I have a Wonder Woman costume at home!" JoJo laughed.

"I know, Mom, I know."

"I gotta see that!" Lisa said with a grin.

"When I was little, " Madison said, "Mom would dress up and entertain at all my friends' birthday parties."

"I was Snow White, Cinderella, Sleeping Beauty, Jasmine," JoJo added, "whatever character the kid wanted. I even had a Little Mermaid costume."

"That was always the dads' favorite costume!" Madison added with a grin.

"I'm concerned that this guy JT is gonna do this again to another girl," Lisa said.

"If he does it won't be here at FSU, Mom," Lexie chimed in.

"Now every girl on campus knows what he did to Maddie and what you did to him. They won't go near him with a ten foot pole."

"Everyone's saying he should get kicked off the football team," Madison added.

"I don't think he'll ever come back to school here after the Christmas break," Lexie said.

Just then Lisa's cell phone buzzed. She looked to see that it was agent Bob Elliott. Her heart raced as she answered.

"Agent Elliott!"

"Detective March, we found the missing girl."

"Is she okay?"

"She's fine."

"Oh thank God! How'd you find her so fast?"

"We were watching her cell phone ding off towers as she was heading west," Davis explained, "and we got a hit on her ATM card at a convenience store in Pensacola."

"That's great," Lisa replied, "I'm here with my partner and our daughters. Do you mind if I put you on speaker so they can hear this?"

"Sure, no problem."

Lisa hit the speaker button and the narrative continued. "I got the Pensacola police to visit the convenience store and they had a surveillance camera that showed the girl using the card to withdraw three hundred bucks. They also showed her getting into a car with a man driving. They got the plate and chased the car down about an hour west of Pensacola."

"Was she taken against her will?"

"At first she said no, she was fine," Elliott explained, "but after she was separated and the man was cuffed she started to cry and told the whole story."

"What happened to her?"

"She said she had a date and got dropped off in front of her apartment building a little after midnight. This guy then grabbed her and forced her into his car."

"Any priors on the perp?"

"The guy is Wayne Frizzle. He's well known to us and we've been looking for him for a long time. He's a suspect in the rape and murder of three young women. In each case he abducted them on the street, raped them repeatedly, and then killed them. He was on the FBI's ten most wanted list."

"Oh my God!" Lisa said, "this girl could have been his next victim!"

"No doubt she would have been if it wasn't for you guys," agent Elliott replied, "you saved her life!"

"We can't thank you enough, agent Elliott," Lisa said.

"I think it's about time you called me Bob," Elliott replied.

"Okay, Bob," Lisa said, "and you can call me Lisa."

"Listen, Lisa, when you get home I want you to give me a call. I've got an important matter I need to discuss with you, okay?"

"Sure, agent, er Bob. I'll call you next week."

As Lisa ended the call JoJo said, "I wonder what he wants to talk about, Lisa."

"I don't have a clue, Jo!"

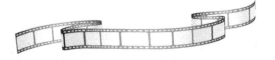

CHAPTER 24

Jimmy waited outside the ballroom until he heard Cary's introduction. He checked the mirror on the wall to make sure that his blue tie was straight and the pocket flaps on his favorite Hunter Brothers suit were outside the pockets and not tucked in. He tucked in the left pocket flap and knew then that the look was perfect. He held tightly to the briefcase he had brought from the office.

"And now," Cary declared to the assembled group of forty Dreamland sales associates. "Here's the man who made all of this possible, Jimmy Foster!"

As the music began blasting "We are the Champions" Jimmy bolted into the hall to thunderous applause from the group. They were seated at round tables, having just finished the lavish dinner Jimmy had paid for. As soon as Jimmy came in they were standing and shouting "Jimmy, Jimmy, Jimmy!"

Jimmy ran to the front of the room and soaked in all the affection. He cupped his left hand and placed it behind his left ear, and with his right hand he waved to group, egging them on to continue their display of adoration. Once again he had worked the crowd into a frenzy.

Jimmy waited until the group settled back into their seats. Then he paused until just the right moment to speak.

"Guess what folks?" he asked playfully, "anybody know why we're all here tonight?"

Jimmy glanced at Cary, who was standing in the corner of the room. That was Cary's key to unleash a large banner that dropped from the ceiling and rested just behind and above Jimmy. The banner read:

DREAMLAND

523 HOMES

SOLD OUT

THANK YOU!!!!

As soon as the banner appeared the crowd leaped to their feet and erupted again, "Jimmy, Jimmy, Jimmy!" they shouted.

"You did it!" Jimmy yelled as he pointed to the sales associates, "you, and you, and you, all of you!"

After the group settled down again Jimmy opened his briefcase. "Anybody wanna guess what's in here?" he asked with a grin.

"Commission checks!" A young man shouted.

"Smart guy," Jimmy replied as he pointed to the young man. He reached into the brief case and removed forty envelopes. Each envelope housed a commission check, one made out to each of the sales associates. They ranged from the smallest at $18,000 to highest check for $48,000 that went to Becca Raymond. In total the checks added up to just over one million dollars.

Jimmy handed the envelopes to Cary and watched as he called the sales associates one by one to come up and receive their commission check. Each name was met with applause from the crowd and each recipient shook Cary's hand. It looked like a college graduation, Jimmy thought.

"Hey," Cary said," before you all go, let's get everyone in a group photo! Come on, I've got the Breakers photographer here to do it!"

All the sales people then gathered around Cary and Jimmy for the group photo. Each one held their commission check and sported a giant smile, filled with the satisfaction of knowing that they had succeeded.

Jimmy never let on that the checks were worthless.

CHAPTER 25

DECEMBER 11, 2018, 11:00 AM

STARBUCKS

JUPITER, FLORIDA

Lisa and JoJo sat at a table in the rear of the coffee shop for five minutes before Cary Garnet entered the building to join them. He was a tall and handsome man, and several women stared as he walked by their tables. His gray hair was the only indicator that he was a man of sixty-five.

Cary stopped at the counter, ordered a coffee, and then made his way to the back of the room where the two detectives were waving to him.

"Thanks for meeting us, Cary," Lisa said as he sat down beside them.

"I'm Detective Lisa March and this is my partner, Joanne Worthington. May we call you Cary?"

"Of course," Cary answered with a smile. He held out his right hand to shake with the two detectives. As each of their right hands grasped his, he gently placed his left hand over the top, cradling the handshake.

This is a very seductive man, Lisa thought. They sipped their lattes and settled down for a long conversation.

"Cary," JoJo began, "as you must know, the skeletal remains of Jimmy Foster were discovered at a construction site in Port St. Lucie last month."

"I know," Cary said softly.

"You and Jimmy were long time friends?" JoJo asked.

"We met back in the seventies," Cary replied, "Jimmy was like a brother to me. He never had a brother and my only brother died of cancer when I was ten, so all we had was each other."

"How did you two meet?" Lisa asked.

"We both worked for Prentice builders. Every month either Jimmy or I was their top salesman."

"But you left Prentice to start Dreamland?"

"Actually, Jimmy got fired, so that's why he left."

"Top salesman gets fired?" Lisa asked, "that seems a little strange."

"Jimmy and I sort of fancied ourselves as ladies men back then," Cary replied as he sipped his coffee, "I'm not proud of it, but we saw every attractive woman as a conquest that was waiting for us."

"So, what happened that got Jimmy fired?"

"He had an affair with the boss's daughter-in-law, and he got caught."

"I guess that'll get you fired from any job!" JoJo mused.

"So, then you and Jimmy worked together on the Dreamland project?" Lisa asked.

"Yes, Dreamland," Cary responded, "I left Prentice in '94 to join Jimmy because I really believed in the project. It could have been the best development ever. But then Jimmy disappeared and the dream died."

"Did it surprise you to learn that Jimmy was murdered and didn't run away?" JoJo asked.

"Not really," Cary replied, "I never really thought Jimmy ran off with the money and I knew there were some bad people after him."

"Bad people?" Lisa said.

"Look, Jimmy had a bad gambling problem," Cary sighed, "he just couldn't stop. And the more he gambled the more he lost. Jimmy was always trying for that big winning streak that would wipe out all of his debts, but it never came."

"Debts," JoJo asked, "debts to who?"

Cary took a sip of his coffee and continued. "When he first started losing the casino gave him a line of credit, but when he reached his limit they cut him off."

"So, what did he do then?"

"Then he started borrowing from a loan shark. He called the guy Mr. Black."

"Did he ever win?"

"Once in a while he won but he would never know when to quit, so in the end he was a big time loser, like most gamblers I suppose."

"So how much did he owe this Mr. Black guy?" Lisa asked.

"I don't really know," Cary answered, "he never told me the exact amount, but I'm sure it was millions. He just told me they threatened him if he didn't pay it back."

"Is that why he took the Dreamland money," JoJo asked, "to pay back the loan?"

"I'm sure of that."

"Did you tell this to the police back then?" Lisa asked.

"I told them, yes, but I never said who the lender was. I said I didn't know his name."

"You never mentioned this Mr. Black guy?" JoJo asked, "why not?"

"Because I was afraid."

"Afraid?"

"Jimmy told me that one of Mr. Black's henchmen approached him and threatened to kill Jeffrey if Jimmy didn't pay up," Cary said quietly.

"Jeffrey?" Lisa said, "Jimmy's son, Jeffrey?"

"That's what he told me. So, after Jimmy disappeared, I figured that Mr. Black was involved. I don't know who this guy Mr. Black is, or was, but I wasn't gonna say or do anything to piss him off, so I just kept my mouth shut when I talked to the cops."

"Okay, I get that," JoJo said, "But it seems that Louise's father spent a lot of money trying to find Jimmy."

"Sidney hated Jimmy from the day he started dating Louise, Sidney's daughter."

"Why was that?" Lisa asked.

"Sid always said Jimmy was a player," Cary replied, "he thought Jimmy seduced his daughter just to get a piece of Sid's money. He was loaded and he didn't want Jimmy to get his hands on that money."

"But it was Sidney that gave Jimmy the money to start Dreamland." JoJo said.

"Louise begged her father to do it," Cary replied, "Sidney Schwartz was a tough son of a bitch, but his one weakness was his little girl. He could never say no to Louise."

"Sidney's in a nursing home now?" JoJo asked.

"He's at the Gatlin Home," Cary replied, "he has Alzheimer's really bad. He doesn't even know his daughter any more. It's sad."

"But, when Jimmy disappeared, Sidney hired a private detective to find him, right?" Lisa asked.

"John Bannister was Sidney's right hand man," Cary said, "he did a lot for Sidney."

"But nothing came up?" JoJo added.

"That's what Sid told everybody," Cary replied, "but I think he knew exactly what happened to Jimmy.

"Really," Lisa asked, "why do you say that?"

"I honestly don't have any proof, but it always seemed strange to me that Bannister found nothing," Cary said, "at least that's what we were told."

"So you think they knew Jimmy was dead and Mr. Schwartz didn't say anything?" Lisa asked.

"I can't prove it," Cary responded, "Sid Schwartz is incoherent and I heard Bannister died a few years ago, but it just makes sense that, no matter how tough Sid was, he wasn't gonna mess with this guy Mr. Black any more than I was."

"But you have no clue as to who Mr. Black is?" Lisa asked, "even now, you don't have any suspicions?"

"I don't know, really," Cary said stoically, "and to be honest I really don't want to know. Nothing will bring Jimmy back, anyway."

As they left the coffee shop and entered their car, Lisa said, "that is one handsome man!"

"I know. It was hard to focus on what he was saying," JoJo replied, "but I think the only way we solve this murder is to find this guy, Mr. Black."

As they drove back to Port St. Lucie JoJo turned to her partner. "Did you ever call that FBI guy, Lisa?"

"I did."

"And?"

"He asked me not to say anything, Jo."

"Lisa, I'm a detective just like you. You know I'm not gonna settle for that answer, so let's have it!"

"His name is Bob Elliott, He was with the Florida state police but he recently took a job with the FBI in their Melbourne field office."

"Uh huh."

"He said they have another opening and he wants me to fill it."

"Holy shit, partner, the FBI wants you!"

"Be careful how you say that, JoJo, " Lisa laughed, "if I'm wanted by the FBI it better be for a job!"

"So, are you gonna take it?"

"Well, first of all, it hasn't been officially offered to me yet."

"Sounds like just a formality to me."

"I'm not sure, Jo. Elliott said they were gonna send a formal letter to Captain Davis asking to interview me."

"Do you want the job, Lisa?"

"It's hard to say no to the FBI, Jo. I heard the pay is a lot higher than what we make here, but it means I have to move to Melbourne, I guess."

"How does Rick feel about that?"

"Rick is always supportive of me. His office is in Ft. Pierce so he says we could get a house in Vero Beach and we'd only be a half hour away from both jobs."

"He's a good man, Lisa. Hang on to him!"

"So, first I have to wait for the letter to come to the captain and then we'll go from there."

"I guess that means I have to break in another new partner, Lisa!" JoJo laughed.

"We'll see about that, Jo," Lisa chuckled.

JoJo then reached into her purse and removed a plastic zip lock bag.

"What you got there, Jo?" Lisa asked.

"I took Cary's coffee cup," JoJo replied, "I'm gonna send it to the DNA lab"

"What's on your mind, partner?"

"I'll bet you ten cents it matches Jeffrey Schwartz!"

CHAPTER 26

Jimmy stood by the exit from the ballroom and shook the hand to congratulate each sales associate as they left. At the very end of the line was Becca Raymond.

As Becca reached out her hand, Jimmy held it tightly. "I think this calls for a celebration, don't you?" he said with a grin.

"I sure do!" Becca replied with a smile.

"I'm in room 1177," Jimmy said, squeezing Becca's hand again.

"Sorry, Jimmy," Becca responded, "My boyfriend is waiting for me outside. We're going back to my place to celebrate."

"Well," Jimmy said, "you kids have fun."

"Thanks Jimmy," Becca replied, "thanks for everything. If you ever start another project look me up."

Jimmy watched as Becca began to walk away. He wasn't used to rejection but the sting only lasted a few seconds until he heard from Cary Garnet.

"Jimmy," Cary said with a solemn tone and look, "be honest with me. Do we have the funds to cover all of the checks we just gave out?"

"It's Friday Cary!" Jimmy replied with a grin, "the banks are closed all weekend, and by Monday I'll have the checks covered. I promise."

Cary moved very close to his friend. "How the hell are you gonna do that, Jimmy?"

"Trust me, Cary," Jimmy said, "I've got everything under control."

As he watched Cary walk away, Jimmy carefully removed the wedding band from his finger, placed it in his suit pocket, and headed down to the Breakers' bar. If Becca was busy tonight, he would just have to find someone else to celebrate with.

Jimmy took the elevator down to the lobby level. He entered the bar, sat at his usual stool, and ordered a Jack Daniels on the rocks. At the far end of the bar was an attractive young woman sitting alone. Jimmy asked the bartender to refresh her drink on his tab. She smiled and lifted her glass toward Jimmy.

Jimmy moved over to the bar stool next to her. She was one of the most beautiful women he had even seen.

"Jimmy," he said with a seductive smile.

"Sandra," she replied.

"You here alone?"

Sandra shook her head and glanced over her shoulder. Jimmy saw a very large man walking towards them. As a precaution Jimmy moved over one stool and began a conversation with the bartender. The last thing he needed tonight was a confrontation.

The large man kissed Sandra and she whispered something in his ear. He looked menacingly at Jimmy. This was not his night, Jimmy thought. He quickly finished his Jack Daniels, dropped a fifty dollar bill on the bar, and headed out to his car.

Jimmy sat behind the wheel of his Lamborghini and thought about how he was going to get out of the mess he was in. My only chance is to win big at the Blueroom, he thought. One good run and I'm home free.

Jimmy started the engine and drove a few hundred yards before he heard the sound of gun cocked behind his head. He began to turn back towards the gun when the gunman whispered, "don't turn around, Jimmy, or you're a dead man."

"What do you want?" Jimmy asked.

"Just drive, I'll tell you where to go."

John Bannister started his car and followed from a safe distance behind.

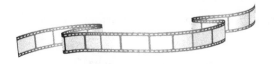

CHAPTER 27

DECEMBER 12, 2018, 9:00 AM

POLICE HEADQUARTERS

PORT ST. LUCIE, FLORIDA

As Lisa entered the office she noticed her partner sitting at her desk, smiling.

"Wait till you see what I've got for you today, Lisa!" JoJo said with a grin. She was holding a white envelope addressed to Captain Davis.

"Is that what I think it is?" Lisa asked.

"It's from the FBI, Melbourne field office!"

"How the hell did you get that, Jo?"

"Captain Davis is on vacation this week so I thought I might stop in his office," JoJo replied, "and while I was in there I just happened to see this letter on his desk."

"Holy shit, Jo. Did you open it, too?"

JoJo smiled and showed her partner the letter that had once occupied the FBI envelope.

Lisa grabbed the letter and said, "how the hell did you do that, Joanne Worthington?"

"Lisa, how many times do I have to tell you I'm not just a pretty face," JoJo responded with a big grin, "now just read the damn letter so I can put it back in the envelope and seal it up again. Captain Davis will never know the difference!"

Lisa read the letter carefully. "They want me to come for an interview next week," she proclaimed proudly.

"I know, Lisa," JoJo replied, "I read it before you got here!"

"You are a piece of work, JoJo," Lisa joked, "you got any more surprises for me today, my mammogram results maybe?"

Just then JoJo became very serious. "I found something else on the captain's desk," she said, "something that was sitting there for a week."

With that she displayed a large manila envelope addressed to "Port St. Lucie Police Department."

"You won't believe what's inside this envelope, partner."

Lisa grabbed the envelope and opened it. Inside were three photos of a dead body, a man shot in the mouth.

"Is this who I think it is?" she asked.

"Yep," JoJo replied, "It's Jimmy Foster!"

"Who on earth would send this to us? What's the post mark?"

"Looks like it was mailed at the post office on Veteran's highway," JoJo replied, "and there's a note that came with the photos. I'll read it to you."

My name is John Bannister, If you are reading this note then I must be dead. I hid these photos as an insurance policy. I killed Jimmy Foster on February 3, 1995. I was hired to kill him by Sidney Schwartz.

"It's signed by John Bannister and dated February 11, 1995," Lisa said.

"Holy shit!" JoJo replied, "the old man did it!"

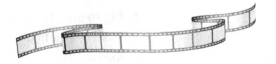

CHAPTER 28

"What ya got in the bag, Jo?' Lisa asked, as they approached the front door of the Gatlin Nursing Home.

"I baked some chocolate chip cookies," JoJo replied, "I remembered that Louise told us they were her father's favorites. I saved some for Rick too!"

"Nice touch, partner. Rick'll love them, but I don't think it's gonna make a difference here," Lisa said, as she pressed the buzzer to request entry, "the director says Sidney's pretty far gone."

The two detectives entered the nursing home and were greeted by a pleasant looking woman who appeared to be in her sixties. The woman thrust out her hand to each of them.

"I'm Brenda Gatlin," the woman said, "we spoke on the phone yesterday. Welcome to the Gatlin Home."

"Yes, that was me," Lisa said, "I couldn't help but notice that your name is the same as the home. I assume that's not a coincidence."

"No coincidence," Brenda smiled, "my parents built this home in 1988, and I've been in charge for the past ten years."

"Thanks for arranging for us to meet Mr. Schwartz," JoJo said, "I brought him some chocolate chip cookies."

"Oh, he'll love that!" Brenda said, "but, as I told you on the phone, you probably won't get anything useful from Sidney."

"You never know until you try," JoJo offered.

Brenda led the detectives to the dining room. Several residents were sitting at tables having lunch. Brenda pointed to a particular table where a white haired man was sitting with two women. "That's Sidney over there."

"And the two women?" Lisa asked.

"Oh, that's Doris and Abby," Brenda replied with a smile, "they're also residents here. They both believe that they're married to Sidney."

"Both of them?" JoJo asked .

"I know it sounds strange," Brenda responded, "but that's the world we live in here at the Gatlin Home."

"Wow!" JoJo whispered.

"Doris and Abby are wonderful ladies, and they both care deeply for Sidney. They look after him and make sure he has everything he wants. They really spoil him."

"Can we talk to Sidney now?" Lisa asked.

"Just give me a minute to move the ladies away," Brenda said, "they might get upset if they see him talking to two younger attractive women."

Brenda spoke briefly to Doris and Abby and they quickly followed her away from the dining room. As she walked away Brenda gestured to Lisa and JoJo that it was now safe to talk with Mr. Schwartz.

"Hello Mr. Schwartz," Lisa said as she sat across the table from Sidney, "my name is Lisa and this is my friend JoJo. We came to visit you today."

"How nice," Sidney replied with a smile, "I like pretty ladies."

"Mr. Schwartz," JoJo said, as she handed him the bag, "I baked you some chocolate chip cookies."

Sidney opened the bag, removed one cookie and took a bite. "Delicious," he said with a smile, "my favorite."

"Louise told us how much you like them," Lisa said.

"Who?"

"Louise, your daughter," Lisa replied. She quickly realized that Sidney had no recollection of his daughter. How sad, she thought, I hope this never happens to me and my dad.

Just then JoJo walked around the table and sat right next to Sidney. She took his hand in hers and stroked his arm. "Sidney," she said in a soft, soothing voice, "Lisa and I came to visit you today because we were hoping you could help us with something."

Sidney perked up. "Help you?" he said, "sure I can help you."

"That's wonderful, Sidney," JoJo continued to stroke his arm as she talked. "We were wondering how much you can remember from a long, long time ago."

"Who me?" Sidney replied, "I can remember everything!"

"That's wonderful, Sidney," JoJo said, "I want to take you back a long time. Do you remember your house?"

"My house? I liked the pool."

"That's great, Sidney. I liked the pool too," JoJo continued stroking, "do you remember any people in the pool?"

Sidney sat silently for several seconds.

"Sidney?"

"Vivian," he said quietly, "I remember Vivian."

"Was Vivian your wife?"

"Vivian was my friend."

"Anybody else you can remember in the pool, Sidney?"

Again he paused. "Albert."

"Albert?" JoJo asked, "was he your friend too?"

"He was my dog!"

"Sidney," JoJo said as she leaned close to him, "do you remember Jimmy?"

"Jimmy?"

"Yes, Jimmy. Do you remember Jimmy?"

"I do!"

Lisa was stunned to see that JoJo was getting through to Sidney.

"Tell me what you remember about Jimmy, Sidney," JoJo asked .

"Jimmy?"

"Yes, Jimmy, what do you remember about Jimmy."

"Jimmy?"

"Yes Jimmy!"

"Jimmy was my cat," Sidney said as he stared into JoJo's eyes,"nice cat, but he died."

"Jim died? How did Jimmy die, Sidney?"

"Somebody killed him."

"Do you remember who killed him, Sidney?" JoJo asked softly. She sensed that she was getting close to something meaningful.

Sidney paused for about minute. JoJo waited for him to speak.

"I don't know who killed Jimmy," he said, "Jimmy ran away."

"Jimmy ran away?"

"Jimmy ran away. I hated Jimmy when he ran away."

Just then Sidney began to cry. A nurse who had been monitoring the conversation quickly came over and comforted him. "I think he's had enough," she said.

JoJo reached over the nurse and kissed Sidney on the forehead. "Goodbye Sidney," she said, "it was nice talking with you today."

Sidney looked up at her as he continued to cry.

As the two detectives entered their car for the drive back to Port St. Lucie Lisa said, "JoJo, you were amazing in there! For a minute I thought we had a breakthrough with Sidney."

"I didn't tell you this," JoJo replied, "but Sidney reminds me of my dad. He died two years ago after battling Alzheimer's for five years."

"I'm so sorry, Jo," Lisa said. She was reminded of how lucky she was to have her father still healthy and lucid at eighty.

"In the end he didn't remember me either," JoJo said, as she wiped a tear from her eye.

"Hey Jo," Lisa said, "my dad is coming over Sunday to watch the Dolphins game with Rick. Why don't you bring Stuart and Billy over and we can order a couple of pizzas?"

"Sounds great, what time?"

"The game starts at one, so any time before that."

"Super! We'll be there. I think Stuart and Rick will hit it off great, and I'm dying to meet your dad."

CHAPTER 29

Lisa was excited to show her father a copy of the photos and letter they had received in the office last week.

"Dad," Lisa said "this letter says Sidney Schwartz hired a guy named John Bannister to kill Jimmy Foster."

Ernie Goodman examined the letter and photos. "You think this is legit?" he asked.

"At this point there's no reason not to believe it, sir," JoJo said.

"Please, call me Ernie."

"Okay, Ernie."

Ernie thought for a moment. "Let me ask you this," he said, "doesn't it strike you as a strange coincidence that this package comes to you right after you discover Jimmy Foster's body?"

"I think you're right, Dad," Lisa said, "it is strange."

"I'm gonna have the lab check everything to see if it's real," JoJo added. "I'm sure they can help us."

"You said you got some background on Sidney Schwartz, Dad."

"I called a couple of my old friends from Miami Vice," Ernie said.

"Miami Vice?" JoJo's husband, Stuart interjected, "you mean there really is such a thing?"

"Oh yeah," Ernie replied.

"Geez, I thought it was just an old TV show."

"Who was it the that wore the white suit?" Rick asked.

"Don Johnson!" Stuart proclaimed proudly. "He was Crocket."

"Well, I never met Don Johnson or Crocket," Ernie countered, "but there really is a vice squad in Miami. So I called a buddy of mine who's retired and he did some research for me on mister Sidney Schwartz."

"Research?" JoJo asked, "does he have a record?"

"It's very old," Ernie replied, "but yes, he definitely has a record. Sidney Schwartz grew up in the poor section of Miami in the thirties and forties. By the time he was a teenager he was working for a guy named Meyer Lansky."

"The Meyer Lansky?" Rick asked.

"The one and only Meyer Lansky, the head of the Jewish mafia."

"He's the guy that was the model for the Hyman Roth character in Godfather 2," Rick said, "great movie!"

"Better even than the original Godfather," Stuart added, "cause it brought in the De Niro version of Vito Corleone, the young version."

"Both great movies," Rick replied.

"But number 3 was a dud!" Stuart shouted.

"Stunk to high heaven!" Rick added as the two men congratulated each other for having such good taste in movies.

These two are gonna become fast friends, Lisa thought.

"So, what else did you learn about Sidney Schwartz, Dad?"

"He used to travel to Havana with Lansky. Lansky owned the Flamingo there and he made a fortune until he lost it all later in life."

"What did Sidney do for Lansky?" JoJo asked.

"He was mostly just an errand boy," Ernie replied, "nothing serious. He got arrested a few times for illegal gambling, but he never did jail time."

"So, was he really a lawyer?" Lisa asked.

"Oh, yes," Ernie replied, "he earned enough money working for Lansky to pay his way through law school. Eventually he opened a series of law offices in south Florida."

"All legit, Dad?" Lisa asked.

"As far as they know he was a straight shooter," Ernie responded, "shrewd and tough, but honest."

"What kind of law did he practice?" JoJo asked.

"Personal injury. He worked both sides of the fence, sometimes representing plaintiffs and sometimes defendants. Medical claims were his specialty. He made a fortune."

"Did Miami Vice have anything on John Bannister?"

"Sorry, Lisa, I only asked about Sidney Schwartz."

"Sidney's got Alzheimer's now, Ernie," JoJo said, "we visited him today but we couldn't get anything out of him."

"So, what else do you know about the case?" Ernie asked.

Lisa could see how energized her father was to be helping. His sharp mind was such a contrast to the man they had met at the Gatlin Nursing Home.

"We know that Jimmy was a heavy gambler," JoJo answered, "most likely a big loser."

"Looks like he borrowed a lot of money from a loan shark named Mr. Black," Lisa added, "and we haven't found out who that is yet.

"Mr. Black?" Ernie shouted, "are you serious?"

"Yeah, Dad, why?"

"Schwartz is a German name, and it's also a Yiddish word," Ernie said with a grin, "any idea what it means?"

"What?"

"It means black, that's what Schwartz means, black!"

"So, you think Sidney Schwartz could have been Mr. Black, Dad?"

"I'm just saying!"

JoJo paused for a moment. "But that doesn't make sense," she said, "does it?"

"Why not, Jo?" Lisa asked.

"First of all," JoJo began, "Ernie, you said Schwartz was a shrewd business man, right?"

Ernie nodded in agreement.

"So why would a shrewd businessman, if he was an anonymous money man who even threatened to kill people," JoJo paused. "Why would he use a name like Mr. Black, if his real name was Schwartz? He could have picked any name. I mean, why not Mr. Green, or Mr. White?"

"Or Colonel Mustard!" Rick yelled from the family room.

"In the library with the candlestick!" Stuart added, as both men chuckled and high-fived each other again.

"And here's another thing, Dad," Lisa added, "why would Sidney Schwartz lend his son-in-law money to gamble away and then have him killed?"

"It just doesn't add up," JoJo continued. "I seriously doubt if Mr. Black and Sidney Schwartz are the same man."

"I'll tell you one thing, though," Lisa said.

"What's that, honey?" Ernie asked.

"We need to find out who Mr. Black is, but we're never gonna find that out from talking to Sidney Schwartz."

Just then the doorbell rang.

"The pizza's here!" Rick yelled, "Will you get it, Lisa? The Dolphins are in the red zone."

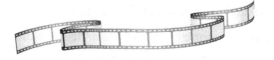

CHAPTER 30

Lisa was waiting at her desk when JoJo arrived.

"I got here before you today, partner," she said with a grin, "that's a shocker."

"Sorry to burst your bubble, partner, but I've been down in the forensics lab for a while."

"Oh, really? What's going on down there?"

"I brought them the envelope with the photos and the letter from John Bannister."

"And?"

"I asked them to tell us if the photos were real or photoshopped, and if the letter was actually written in 1995 by John Bannister."

"If anyone can figure that out, it's them."

"They're also gonna check for prints and DNA. Steve Waters said he can get me answers in a week or so."

133

"Speaking of DNA, any word on that DNA sample you got from Cary Garnet?"

"Still waiting on the lab, Lisa."

"Okay, thanks."

Lisa got up from behind her desk and began walking towards the restroom. She was stopped in her tracks by her partner.

"So, what's the deal, Lisa?" JoJo asked, with her hands on her hips.

"Deal? What deal?" Lisa responded with a bewildered look on her face.

"Are you gonna go for that interview with the FBI or not?" JoJo said.

"Actually, I am, JoJo," Lisa whispered, "The captain set it up for me next week, but I don't want anybody in the squad to know."

"Okay, mum's the word, partner," JoJo whispered, "mum's the word."

"Thanks, Jo," Lisa said. "I put a call in to John Bannister's widow. She agreed to meet with us this morning."

"Great, where is she?"

"She still lives in Port St. Lucie, in Sandpiper Bay, just off Westmoreland Boulevard. She's expecting us at ten so we should head out now."

"I can't wait to meet her."

After a short drive, Lisa and JoJo arrived at the home of the late John Bannister. They were invited in to the modest home by John's widow, Janet Bannister, a very small and frail woman who appeared to be in her seventies.

"Mrs. Bannister," Lisa began, "I'm Lisa March, and this is my partner Joanne Worthington. First let me say how much we appreciate you talking to us today."

"It's my pleasure," Janet replied, "My late husband was a detective like you are. He would have enjoyed meeting you both."

Mrs. Bannister excused herself for a minute and then returned with a tray of oatmeal cookies and a pot of tea.

"Can I offer you tea?" She asked as she poured three cups. "These were my husband's favorite cookies."

"How did your husband die, Mrs. Bannister?" JoJo asked, as she sipped her tea.

"Cancer, pancreatic cancer. He was diagnosed in August of 2015. He was hoping to make it until Thanksgiving but he didn't."

Mrs. Bannister grabbed a tissue and wiped tears from her eyes.

"Mrs. Bannister," Lisa began.

"Please, call me Janet."

"Thank you, Janet. We were wondering if you knew anything specific about the work your husband did?"

"Very little, I'm afraid. Like I said, he was a detective, a private detective, that's about all I knew. He never talked about the details of what he did, and that was fine with me."

"Did you know that he worked for a lawyer named Sidney Schwartz?"

"Sidney? Of course! He was John's main client."

"Did you know Mr. Schwartz?"

"I never met him, but he was very good to John and our family."

"How so?"

"When my son Johnny got sick the first time we had a ton of medical bills and our insurance didn't cover them all. Sidney Schwartz paid them for us. He was a very kind man."

"Janet," JoJo said, "did you ever hear John mention a man named Jimmy Foster?

"Yes, that was one of the few times John ever talked about what he did."

"What did he tell you?"

"It was a long time ago, but I remember that John followed Jimmy around because he was cheating on his wife. He said that Jimmy was Sidney Schwartz's son-in-law."

"Janet," Lisa said in a soft tone, "this is very important. Jimmy Foster disappeared in 1995. Did your husband ever talk to you about that?"

Janet paused and thought for a moment before she replied. "I remember that John was gone for a long time after that."

"Gone?"

"He said he was searching for Jimmy Foster, but he never found the guy. He told me he was gonna keep looking for Jimmy Foster no matter how long it took."

"Do you remember anything else about that time?"

"I just remember that John was very upset about the whole thing. I had never seen him that upset about anything like that."

"Did you ask him why he was so upset."

"I did, but he said he didn't want to talk about it."

"Mrs. Bannister, Janet," JoJo said calmly, "did your husband own a gun?"

"He did. He had a license and everything."

"Do you know what happened to that gun?"

"Of course I do."

Janet stood up and walked into the bedroom. She returned a moment later holding a wooden case. "It's right here," she said.

"Oh," JoJo said, "would you mind if we take it with us back to the station?"

"Sure," Janet replied as she handed the box to Lisa, "did John do something wrong?"

"Mrs. Bannister," Lisa replied, "last month the body of Jimmy Foster was found at a construction site here in Port St. Lucie. It appears that he was shot to death back in 1995. Our job is to find out how that happened."

"Oh my," Janet said, "do you think my John had something to do with it?"

Lisa retrieved her cell phone from her purse, opened it, and showed Mrs. Bannister a copy of the letter.

"Janet," she said calmly, "we received this letter in the mail along with photos of Jimmy Foster's dead body.

Janet Bannister took the phone and looked at the letter. "Oh my!"

"Janet," JoJo asked, "have you ever seen this letter before?"

"No, this is the first time I've seen the letter."

"The letter says that your husband was keeping the photos as an insurance policy," Lisa said, "does that mean anything to you?"

"Yes it does."

Lisa was surprised to hear that response from Janet Bannister.

"It does? Why?"

Janet Banister took a deep breath. "After Jimmy Foster disappeared, my husband was asked by Sidney Schwartz to try and find him. He was away for several days and, when he returned, he showed me an envelope. He said it was his insurance policy."

"Insurance policy?' JoJo asked. "What was that?"

"I asked John what he meant by that and what was in the envelope, and he said I should just trust him. I thought maybe he bought a life insurance policy for us."

"But it turns out that the letter and photos were his insurance," Lisa said.

"He told me the envelope was going into a safe deposit box, and he gave me a key." Janet continued. "He told me, after he died, I should put a stamp on the envelope and mail it. He told me I should never open the envelope, just mail it."

"So you mailed it after he died?" Lisa asked.

"No," Janet replied, "By the time John died in 2015 I had forgotten all about it!"

"But why mail it now?" JoJo asked.

"The bank called and said that the safe deposit box was being closed for lack of payment. I guess John had paid it off for several years but now it was going to be opened up and everything removed unless I paid for it again."

"So you went to the bank to empty the box?"

"I opened the safe deposit box and found the letter. I was surprised to see that it was addressed to the police."

"But you never looked inside the envelope?" JoJo asked.

"I remembered that my husband asked me not to open it, so I honored his wishes. I just took it to the post office."

"As you can see the letter was signed by your husband," JoJo continued, "and we were hoping you could help us verify that it really is his signature."

Janet looked at the letter. "It looks like John's signature. Why wouldn't it be his?"

"Mrs. Bannister," Lisa said softly, "If this letter is real then it means that your husband created a signed confession that implicates him and Mr. Schwartz in the murder of Jimmy Foster."

Janet left the room for a couple of minutes and returned with a birthday card.

"Every year on my birthday John would give me card," she said softly, "and he would always write a beautiful note to me. I saved the last one he sent me just before he died."

Janet handed the card to Lisa. "Maybe you can use this to verify that the signature is real."

"Thank you, Mrs. Bannister," Lisa replied, "I know this hasn't been easy for you."

"I just can't believe that my husband was a murderer," Janet sobbed, "he was a good man!"

As they entered their car, preparing for the ride back to police headquarters, JoJo opened the gun case that Janet Bannister had given them.

"Sure enough," she said,"it's a Glock 17, the exact same kind of gun that Stephanie told us killed Jimmy Foster!"

"But just think about it, Jo," Lisa said. "Bannister was a detective. If you used your gun to kill somebody, would you leave it in your house?"

"I guess I'd ditch it the first chance I got!"

CHAPTER 31

Lisa was nervous, more so than she had been in a long time. As she waited in the lobby she was happy to see the familiar face of Agent Bob Elliott,

"Welcome," Bob said, as he shook Lisa's hand, "I'm really glad you came today."

"Thanks, Bob," Lisa replied, "I'm looking forward to this interview."

Bob sat down next to Lisa and spoke in a whisper. "Look, they already know everything about you and they like what they see," he said, "otherwise you wouldn't be here."

"That's nice," Lisa said, "I wouldn't expect any less from the FBI."

"You're gonna be interviewed by Donna Thompson. She's the Special Agent in Charge of this office."

"Okay."

"She's exactly what you'd expect her to be, a no nonsense, get right to the point, kind of person."

"That's good to know."

"She's a tough interviewer," Elliott continued, "at least she was for me. She might try to throw you off a little to see how good you are under pressure."

"Thanks, I'll be looking for that."

"I remember when I was interviewed," Elliott said. "Donna asked me if I had any special skills so I told her that I had a photographic memory, and she decided to test me."

"How did she test you?"

"She gave me the list of the FBI's ten most wanted," Elliott replied, "and she asked me to memorize all ten faces and the information on each one of them."

"How long did it take you to memorize all that?"

"Just a couple of minutes. When Donna quizzed me she was blown away by how much I remembered!"

"Do you still remember it?"

"Oh yeah. It's stored in my brain somewhere. I really do have a photographic memory," he answered.

"Wow, when did you first learn that you had this gift?"

"My father always said the brain is like a muscle," Elliott replied, "the more you exercise it, the stronger it gets."

"That makes sense," Lisa said.

"When I was seven years old my father gave me a dollar bill and told me try and memorize the serial number on it."

"That's pretty good," Lisa said.

"Every dollar bill has a unique serial number with ten numbers and letters," Elliott continued, "eventually, he had me memorize ten serial numbers at one time."

"So, you memorized a hundred random letters and numbers?"

"I did. And when I got them all right he let me spend the ten bucks on anything I wanted!"

"Nice touch," Lisa said, "so what did you buy with the money?"

"I don't remember!"

They both laughed. Lisa felt the beginning of a bond between the two of them that she hoped would result in a strong partnership at the FBI. But first, of course, she had to get through the interview with Donna Thompson.

"Best advice I can give you," Elliott said, "is just be yourself!"

"That's what I do best!" Lisa smiled.

Five minutes later she was seated in the office of Special Agent Donna Thompson. Lisa was surprised to see that Agent Thompson was about the same age and the same size as her. She was expecting a much bigger and older woman.

Special Agent Thompson was seated in a large chair behind a huge desk. Lisa was seated in a very small chair on the other side of the desk. The intimidation begins, Lisa thought.

"Glad to meet you, Detective March," Thompson began. "I've heard a lot of good things about you."

"Thank you."

"Now, I want you tell me the bad things!"

Lisa cleared her throat. "Excuse me?"

"Look," Special Agent Thompson said sternly, "I spoke to your captain down in Port St. Lucie. He tells me you walk on water. Now I wanna hear the stuff he didn't tell me."

Lisa gritted her teeth. "So you want me to tell you what's wrong with me?"

"That's right."

Lisa was taken aback by the question. She paused for a moment and carefully crafted the answer in her mind. Then she spoke boldly and firmly.

"Okay, so here's my answer, Special Agent Thompson. I have no doubt that you are a top notch FBI agent, and I'm totally confident that you know everything there is to know about me, good and bad."

Lisa could feel her confidence growing as she continued. "So, Special Agent Thompson, if you expect me to sit here and pour my heart out to you about everything that's wrong with me then I'm not the right person for this job! But, I thank you for your time."

Lisa stood up and began to leave.

"So when can you start?" Thompson said with a big grin.

"Huh?"

Donna Thompson stood up and smiled. "Did Bob Elliott tell you I was the big bad wolf?"

"Not in those exact words," Lisa replied with a sheepish grin of her own.

"Look, we know what a great detective you are, and we want you to become a part of our team."

"So, why ask me that question?"

"I heard you had a backbone, Lisa," Thompson said, "and I just wanted to see it for myself."

"I guess I didn't disappoint you then."

"No, you didn't," Thompson replied, "you showed me exactly what I wanted to see."

"Thank you." Lisa said.

Special Agent Thompson rose from her large chair and walked around her desk to sit in a small chair next to Lisa.

"We could use you here yesterday, so when can you start?" she asked.

"Wait a minute," Lisa replied, "you may be convinced, but I'm not."

"Okay, I get that" Thompson responded, "what questions do you have for me?"

Lisa asked a series of questions that were important to her, who she might be teamed with, what additional training she would receive, how much travel would be involved.

When Lisa's questions turned to issues about salary, benefits, and relocation expenses Agent Thompson called the home office in DC.

Forty minutes later, after all of her questions had been answered to her satisfaction, Lisa thrust her hand toward Special Agent Thompson.

"I'm in!"

"Lisa March, you're gonna make a great FBI agent! So tell me, when you can start."

"I've got one open case on my desk and I want to close it before I make a move."

"Okay, so what are we talking about?

"Let me get through the holidays, close the case, and I should be able to start by the end of January."

"Okay, Agent March, welcome aboard. You'll be getting a call from Human Resources in the DC headquarters to handle all the paperwork."

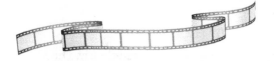

CHAPTER 32

As Lisa entered the house, Rick was waiting for her with a glass of Chardonnay.

"I can't believe it," he said, "I'm gonna be sleeping with an FBI agent tonight!"

"Was this one for your fantasies, Ricky?" Lisa joked, as she hugged her husband.

"No, but it is now!"

Lisa sipped her wine. "We've got a lot to do to make this move, Rick. Are you sure you're alright with this?"

"This is a hell of a time to ask me that, Lisa." Rick replied, "you already accepted the job, didn't you?"

"I can always change my mind, Rick," Lisa said quietly, "you always say that's a woman's prerogative."

"Honey, nobody's changing anything," Rick said, "I called Katey Mauer and she's coming over on Saturday to help us get the house ready to sell. She's the top realtor in this community.

"Thanks, babe. You're the best!"

"No, you are!" Rick joked, "Okay, it's probably me. I'm the best! Did you call your dad?"

"Oh no, not yet, but I'll do it now."

"He's gonna be so proud, Lisa. What cop wouldn't want his kid to join the FBI?"

Just then Lisa's cell phone buzzed. She saw that it was her partner calling.

"Hey JoJo, what's up?"

"What's up?" JoJo responded incredulously, "how can you ask me a question like that, Lisa?"

"I got the job!"

"I knew you would, Lisa, but I have to call you to find this out?"

"My God, JoJo, you sound just like my mother!"

"So when are you leaving me?"

"I wanna us to close the Jimmy Foster case before I leave, Jo. I told them I'd start at the end of January."

"Speaking of the Jimmy Foster case, Lisa, I just got the DNA results on Cary Garnet."

"And?"

"Are you sitting down?"

"No, but tell me anyway."

"Cary Garnet and Jeffrey Schwartz are father and son!"

"You knew that Cary was the father, didn't you, Jo?"

"So, you wanna hear my theory of the crime again?"

"I got a feeling I'm gonna hear it whether I want to or not, partner!"

"Okay, here goes."

JoJo paused and took a deep breath. "Cary Garnet was having an affair with Jimmy Foster's wife, Louise. Jimmy was embezzling money from the company and gambling it away."

"Okay."

"Jimmy owed money to this Mr. Black, and so Black threatened to kill Jeffrey, who is not Jimmy's kid, but Cary's kid. You with me?"

"Of course I'm with you, Jo. It isn't that complicated."

"So Cary kills Jimmy, takes the rest of the company's money and uses it to pay off Mr. Black."

"Uh huh."

"Then he marries Louise Schwartz and lives happily ever after with her and their son, Jeffrey. Case closed!"

"That's a wonderful theory, Jo, but there's only one problem."

"I know, the letter from John Bannister confessing that he killed Jimmy, and Sidney Schwartz paid him to do it, but I have a theory on that too."

"I'll take a rain check on that theory, Jo. But for sure we need to talk to Cary Garnet again."

"And Louise too. I'll see you tomorrow, partner, and congratulations again, I'm really proud of you."

As Lisa ended the call she turned to her husband and said, "you know, Rick, if the FBI knew how wrong I was in my first impression of JoJo Worthington they might have doubted if I had good enough judgment to be an agent."

"So, you changed your mind about JoJo," Rick replied with a smile, "it's a woman's prerogative!"

CHAPTER 33

DECEMBER 26, 2018, 10:00 AM
PORT ST. LUCIE POLICE DEPARTMENT
INTERVIEW ROOM 1

Lisa and JoJo were waiting for Cary Garnet to join them. They sat side by side on one side of the table, expecting Cary to occupy the chair opposite them. JoJo was dressed in a lavender dress with matching hat and handbag.

"I see you dressed up for Cary Garnet today, partner," Lisa said with a grin, as she examined JoJo's outfit.

"Oh, this old thing?" JoJo replied with a feigned look of surprise. "It was hanging in my closet, so I decided to wear it today, that's all!"

"We have to stay focused today, partner," Lisa said with a smile.

"I know," JoJo replied, "It's hard not to keep staring at this man. I don't think I've ever seen a better looking man in my life!"

"Lisa," JoJo whispered, "why is it that men get better looking when they get older, and women, we just get…"

"Older!" Lisa finished her partner's thought.

"Let's get it together, partner," Lisa said, "it was only a couple of days ago when you had a theory that he's a murderer! Don't forget that, Jo!"

"I really don't know anything for sure now, partner," JoJo replied, "that confession from John Bannister might be the end of this case."

"We'll see about that!" Lisa said.

Just then Cary Garnet walked into the room and sat down at the table opposite the two women. He was dressed in shorts, a tee shirt, and tennis shoes.

"Good morning, Mr. Garnet," Lisa began.

"Cary still works just fine for me," he replied, "sorry I'm so under dressed. I've got a Pickleball game I need to go to after this."

"Okay then, thank you for meeting us here today, Cary," Lisa continued, trying not to stare, "we have a very important matter that we need to speak to you about."

"Really?" he replied, "I can't imagine what that could be."

"First we need to tell you that all conversations in this room are recorded. Do you understand that, Cary?"

"Yes, I do, okay. What questions do you have for me today?"

"Cary," JoJo said, "when the skeleton was first discovered the lab was able to take a DNA sample."

"Of course," Cary responded.

"And later, when we met with Jeffrey Schwartz, he gave us a DNA sample."

Cary Garnet sat up straight in his chair. "So?"

"So," JoJo said, "the DNA sample from Jimmy Foster was not a relative match to Jeffrey Schwartz."

"Which means," Lisa continued, "that Jeffrey is not Jimmy's biological son."

"So, what does this have to do with me?" Cary asked defiantly.

"I think you know the answer to that question, Cary," JoJo replied.

"Yesterday we received the results of your DNA test," JoJo said, "and it shows that Jeffrey is actually your son."

"Wait a minute!" Cary shouted nervously, "how did you get my DNA? You never asked me for a sample!"

JoJo reached into a bag and removed the coffee cup that Cary had been drinking from in the coffee shop when they first met. She held it up for Cary to see.

"So, you took my DNA without my permission!" Cary yelled, "I'll be speaking to my lawyer about that!"

"I'm sure your lawyer will tell you that there was nothing illegal about us picking up the coffee cup that you voluntary left behind," JoJo responded.

"I'm guessing that you've known that Jeffrey was your son for a long time, Cary." Lisa said, "am I right about that?"

Cary paused for a moment to collect his thoughts. His anger subsided as he began to speak.

"Look," he said calmly, "I'm sure you know by now that Jimmy was not a good husband to Louise. He cheated on her left and right, and he was hardly ever home with her."

"So she turned to you?"

"I was her shoulder to cry on, okay," he replied, "I knew Jimmy better than anyone, so Louise always confided in me."

"So, when did the crying on the shoulder stop, and the sleeping together start?" Lisa asked, as she casually sipped her coffee.

"About four years into their marriage," Cary replied, "Louise wanted a baby and Jimmy just wasn't around enough to do his part. He knew the one thing Louise wanted more than anything was to be a mother, but he didn't care!"

"So you stepped in?"

"I guess you could say that," Cary replied.

"So why didn't Louise divorce Jimmy and marry you after she found out she was pregnant with your baby?"

"By the time things got bad enough for Louise to seriously consider divorcing Jimmy, she just couldn't go through with it," Cary replied, "her father had just given Jimmy two million dollars to buy the land in Port St. Lucie, and Louise didn't want to hurt her father by leaving Jimmy then."

JoJo leaned across the table, very close to Cary. "Cary, you told us that Mr. Black threatened to kill Jeffrey if Jimmy didn't pay his debts off, remember that?"

"Yes, he did threaten to kill Jeffrey."

"So," Lisa continued, "do you expect us to believe that you heard that and you did nothing to protect your son?"

"What could I do?"

"How about you find a way to pay off the debt," Lisa said firmly, "like taking the money from the Dreamland account."

"Jimmy was the only one who could take that money," Cary exclaimed, "he wouldn't let me get anywhere near it."

"What about your accountant, Lou Laber?" JoJo said. "You could have gotten access to the money through him."

"I didn't need to steal that money," Cary said, "Jimmy took it and paid off Mr. Black."

"And you know this, how?" JoJo asked.

"Cause he told me he was gonna do it, and after he died we never heard from Mr. Black again."

"So, Cary," Lisa said firmly, "are you telling us that you knew Jimmy was dead all along?"

"That's not what I said!"

"Cary, you said 'after Jimmy died', you didn't say 'after Jimmy disappeared', why is that?" Lisa asked. She could see that Cary was getting flustered, and that was a good thing, she thought.

"Look, I always thought Jimmy ran off, but after you told me last week that you found his body, I knew he didn't."

"But, Cary," JoJo said, "If you knew Jimmy had paid off Mr. Black, why would there be any reason for him to be killed?"

Cary sat for a moment, once again carefully choosing the words he would use.

"Okay," he whispered, "Let me tell you what actually happened to Jimmy."

"We're all ears," Lisa said.

"Sidney Schwartz hated Jimmy. He never wanted Louise to marry him. But he tolerated it because he could never say no to his daughter."

"We get that."

"Sidney had a private detective named Bannister that he hired to follow Jimmy around," Cary continued, "and when Sidney learned that Jimmy was cheating on Louise and gambling away all the Dreamland money he was furious."

"Okay, he was furious," JoJo said, "so what did he do about it."

"It all came to a head when Mr. Black threatened Jeffrey's life. There was no way Sidney was gonna let that happen to his grandson.

"So, what did he do?"

"Sidney paid off the debt," Cary said, "I think it was around eight million."

"And then what?"

Cary took a deep breath. "And then Sidney told Bannister to kill Jimmy!"

JoJo paused for a minute to absorb what Cary Garnet had just said.

"So then, what happened to the rest of the Dreamland money?" she asked.

"I heard that Sidney told the accountant, Lou Laber, to take it all out, keep a million for himself, and give the rest back to Sidney."

"And Laber did that?"

"You don't say no to Sidney Schwartz," Cary replied, "and you don't turn down a million bucks either!"

"Cary," Lisa said, "last week we received an envelope that contained photos of Jimmy Foster's dead body."

"Oh?"

"Yes," JoJo added, "and it also contained a letter from John Bannister, confessing to the fact that he murdered Jimmy Foster, and he was paid to do it by Sidney Schwartz."

"Exactly what I said," Cary replied, with a look of satisfaction.

"Yes it is, Cary," Lisa said, "but there was something else in the letter. Bannister said that it was his 'insurance policy'. Does that make any sense to you?"

Once again Cary sat for a minute and pondered his response.

"The only thing I can think of," Cary said, "is that Bannister was afraid Sidney might give him up, so he had the photos as his way of protecting against that."

"That's possible," JoJo replied, "but the only person those photos give up is Bannister himself. There's no evidence that Sidney hired him to kill Jimmy, just his say so."

"And now we have your say so, too," Lisa added, "but that doesn't constitute evidence."

"That's true, I suppose" Cary responded, "I guess that means that Bannister wasn't the sharpest knife in the drawer, and writing that letter really didn't protect him at all."

At that point Lisa stood up and shook Cary Garnet's hand. "Thank you, Cary," she said, "you've been a big help to us."

As she watched Cary walk out the door, Lisa turned to JoJo, "Partner, I think there's a lot more to this story than meets the eye!"

"My sentiments exactly!" JoJo replied.

CHAPTER 34

JoJo was sitting at her desk when she received a call from Bill Waters in the crime lab. As soon as she hung up the phone she walked over to Lisa's desk.

"The lab wants us right away, Lisa," she said, "Waters says he's got a bombshell for us!"

"A bombshell?" Lisa replied, as she stood up to leave, "let's go!"

Within five minutes they were downstairs in the crime lab where they were met by Steve Waters. Steve was fifty years old, a twenty-five year veteran of the department. He had passed up many promotional opportunities because he loved doing forensic and other lab work. Steve often told Lisa that there was nothing more satisfying to him than to see a criminal get convicted because of his work.

"You got a bombshell for us, Steve?" JoJo asked.

"Well, first of all, the photos are real." Waters said.

"No photoshop?" Lisa asked.

"No photoshop," he replied, "these photos were taken by a 1989 Nikon F-401 model camera and they were developed on Kodak paper. We know that the paper was produced between 1972 and 1992, when Kodak changed their watermark. The developing was done by hand in a dark room."

"Okay, so what about the letter?" JoJo asked.

"The letter is a different story, though," Waters replied.

"It's not real?"

We were able to track the make and model number of the printer that was used to print this document," Waters replied, "it was built long after 1995, so there's no way that letter could be legitimate."

"Wait!" Lisa exclaimed, "would you repeat that please?"

"I said the letter is a fake, Lisa!"

"Wow," JoJo said, "that really is a bombshell!"

"Can you give us the exact model number of the printer?"

"It's a Hewlett Packard Laser Jet 3500. It's a big printer that takes up a lot of space, and you usually find them in offices."

"So," Lisa asked, "you wouldn't normally find one of these connected to a home PC."

"Not unless the person had a lot of room," Waters replied, "It's really a monster!"

"So the bottom line is that there's no way John Bannister could have signed this letter because it was printed long after he died, right?" Lisa said.

"That's correct," Waters replied.

"How about the envelope?" JoJo asked, "Were you able to get any prints or DNA off of it?"

"Nothing helpful, I'm afraid," Waters said, "this envelope was handled by a lot of people!"

"How about the signature?" JoJo asked, "that has to be a fake."

"This is very interesting," Waters replied, "I asked Marissa Stevens to compare the signature to the handwriting in the note written on the card the wife gave you, and she said the signature was definitely written by the same hand as the note."

JoJo pondered for a moment. "So that means whoever wrote the signature on the letter also wrote the love note," she said, "and since we know that it couldn't have been John Bannister who signed the letter, that means the love note is also a fake!"

"You got it, JoJo," Bill Waters replied. "I bet if you can find a real sample of John Bannister's handwriting it won't match the card or the letter!"

"And I have a pretty good idea who wrote the card and signed the letter," JoJo said.

"Thanks, Steve," Lisa said, "you've given us a lot to think about!"

"Just one more thing,Steve," Lisa said, "what did you find out about the gun?"

"It's a Glock 17, Lisa," Steve replied, "you know that's a very popular gun. Over ten million are out there. So I'm afraid there's nothing we can do to connect this particular Glock 17 to the crime unless we had one of the bullets."

"Pretty sure we won't find that after all these years," JoJo said.

"And we don't even know where the crime was committed!" Lisa added.

As they left the lab Lisa said to her partner, "No question who our next interview will be."

"I'll make that happen," JoJo replied, "you call tell the captain and let him know we need an arrest warrant, fast!"

CHAPTER 35

DECEMBER 30, 2018, 2:00 PM
PORT ST. LUCIE POLICE DEPARTMENT

Janet Bannister entered the room looking more frail than the last time she had been interviewed. She appeared to be in pain as she slowly walked over and took a seat across the table from Lisa and JoJo.

"Janet," Lisa began, "it's good to see you again."

"It's good to see you too," Janet responded.

"Thank you for agreeing to meet us here, Janet," Lisa continued, "we just have a few more questions to ask you."

"My son dropped me off here," Janet said, "I don't drive any more so I'll need to call him when I'm ready to be picked up."

"That's fine, Janet," JoJo said, "we'll be happy to make arrangements for you."

"Janet," Lisa said, "we always record interviews in this room, and we wanted you to know that."

"Sure, that's fine."

"We really appreciated the love note your husband wrote to you, Janet," Lisa said with a warm smile, "we both said we wish our husbands could be so thoughtful."

Janet returned Lisa's smile. "Yes, my John was a wonderful man," she said, "that's why it's such a shock for me to learn that he killed a man!"

"I can certainly understand why you might feel that way, Janet." JoJo replied, "now, we want to go over the details of that envelope again, if you don't mind."

"Sure."

"Can you tell us again where you found the envelope?"

"It was in a safe deposit box at St. Lucie Bank. John had told me about it a long time ago but I just remembered it when the box was closed by the bank for lack of payment."

"And that was when, Janet?"

"That was a couple of weeks ago, the same day I mailed it."

"And you never opened the envelope," Lisa said, "is that right?

"Yes that's right. I honored my husband's wish and I never opened it."

"Mrs. Bannister,"JoJo said quietly, "If I were to tell you that I called St. Lucie Bank and they have no record of a safe deposit box in your husband's name, how would you respond to that?"

Janet Bannister hunched her back. She thought for a full minute and then responded. "You know, maybe I have the wrong bank," she said, "let me go back home and double check on that and get back to you."

"Janet," Lisa added, "we also have evidence that your husband's signature was forged on the note, and that the letter was printed just before you mailed it to the police."

Janet stood up and shouted "That's it, I want a lawyer. This interview is over."

As Janet Bannister walked toward the door she was met by a uniformed police officer who placed her in handcuffs.

"Janet Bannister," Lisa said calmly and slowly, "you are under arrest for forgery and obstruction of justice. You have a right to remain silent. Anything you say can and will be used against your in a court of law. You have the right to speak to an attorney. If you cannot afford an attorney one will be appointed for you. Do you understand these rights, Mrs. Bannister?"

"Yes," Mrs. Bannister said softly.

As Janet was led away, Lisa said, "I'm pretty sure we can nail her for obstruction but that still doesn't tell us who killed Jimmy Foster."

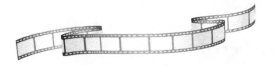

CHAPTER 36

DECEMBER 31, 2018, 10:00 PM

THE HOME OF LISA AND RICK MARCH

"Happy Brazilian New Year!" Ernie Goodman shouted.

Lisa hugged her father. "Happy Brazilian New Year to you too, Dad."

Ernie raised his champagne glass. "And here's to my daughter, Lisa," he said, "the newest and prettiest agent in the FBI."

Lisa clinked glasses with her husband and parents. "Thanks, Dad," she said, "and thanks to you, Mom, and of course to my wonderful husband. Without you guys this would never have happened."

"You know your father is crazy, don't you dear," Gloria whispered to her daughter as they hugged.

"No, Mom. I think he's brilliant!" Lisa objected, "It really is 2019 now in eastern Brazil."

"So, why stay up till midnight when you can celebrate with the Brazilians at ten?" Rick added, defending his father-in-law, "it seems perfectly logical to me!"

"Rick got the guest room all ready for you guys, we want you to spend the night here."

"Thanks, honey," Gloria replied, "I'm afraid to let your father drive in the dark, especially on a night where all the drunks and crazies are on the road."

"I don't think the drunks are out there at ten o'clock, Gloria," Rick grinned, "but you're always welcome here."

"So, whenever you guys are ready to call it a night, just head on up," Lisa added

"Your father had his nap today," Gloria replied, "because he wanted to talk to you about this skull case you're working on."

"Sure, Dad, what can I tell you?"

"Its what I can tell you, Lisa!"

"Good news I hope, Dad!"

"I found out who Mr. Black is," Ernie replied proudly, "I suppose that's good news for you, isn't it?"

"Absolutely! But how?"

"My friend from Miami Vice came through again," Ernie replied, "he was very familiar with Mr. Black."

"So, what's his real name? Don't keep me in suspense. Is it Sidney Schwartz?"

"Nope, not Sidney Schwartz, Lisa," Ernie said, "but it's an old friend of Schwartz."

"Name, Dad, I need a name!"

"Mr. Black's real name is Murray Rosenberg. He was also a disciple of Mayer Lansky. Apparently Rosenberg was in a little deeper with Lansky than Schwartz was."

"A little deeper?" Lisa asked.

"Let's just say he did things that most of us would never even think of doing, dear."

"You mean like killing people?"

"No, according to the vice guys Murray never did that, but he was involved in all the other bad stuff, money laundering, drugs, you name it."

"Was he a loan shark too?"

"That wasn't his primary source of income. He only made loans to friends."

"Friends?" Lisa chuckled, "who threatens to kill their friends' children, Dad?"

"Alright, so maybe they weren't his best friends!" Ernie laughed.

"Is he still alive?"

"Yep, still alive. He's ninety-one and he lives in an assisted living facility in Miami Beach."

"Oh geez," Lisa said, "does he have Alzheimer's like Sidney Schwartz?"

"Apparently not," Ernie replied, "he's in a wheelchair but they say his mind is as sharp as ever."

"Is he still mixed up with the mob?" Rick asked.

"No, as far as anybody knows he left the business ten years ago."

"I suppose he made enough money to retire."

"I guess so, honey, they say the place he lives is the most exclusive and expensive assisted living facility in Florida, and he built it."

"There's a lot of fancy assisted living places in South Florida," Rick added, "so if his is the best one, that's really saying something."

Lisa grabbed her cellphone and called her partner.

"Happy New Year, Jo. Rest up tomorrow cause we're gonna go visit Mr. Black on Wednesday!"

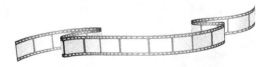

CHAPTER 37

JANUARY 2, 2019, 11:00 AM

HARRY ROSENBERG ASSISTED LIVING HOME

MIAMI BEACH, FLORIDA

Lisa and JoJo sat in the lobby of the lavish building for ten minutes until the elevator door opened and a white haired old man in an electric wheel chair emerged. He was accompanied by an attractive young woman wearing a nurse's uniform. "Take a break, sweetheart," he said, and she quickly walked away.

The man rolled his wheel chair up toward the sofa where the two detectives sat. Immediately they both stood up to greet him.

"Sit down, please," he said with a big smile on his face, "I'm not part of the royal family, not yet anyway!"

"Hello, Mr. Rosenberg," Lisa began.

"Please! Mr. Rosenberg was my father. Call me Murray!"

"Okay, Murray," Lisa continued, "I'm Lisa March and this is my partner, Joanne Worthington."

"Partner?" Rosenberg interrupted, "what are you two like, how do they say it, domestic partners? Not that there's anything wrong with that, you see. I say live and let live, you know what I mean?"

JoJo chuckled. "No, Murray, Lisa and I are detectives in the Port St. Lucie police department, so we work together."

"Port St. Lucie?" Rosenberg said, "That's way up north. You got any Jews up there?"

"A few," Lisa replied with a grin, "in fact, I'm Jewish myself!"

"Well then, you belong in Miami, a cute little Jewish girl like you. There's a lot of rich widowers down here that would scoop you up in a New York minute!"

"I don't think my husband would like that, Murray."

"Alright, then," Rosenberg replied, "to what do I owe the honor of this visit?"

"Mr. Rosenberg."

"Murray, please!"

"Murray, we're investigating the murder of Jimmy Foster."

"Murder?" Rosenberg interjected, "I thought that kid ran off with a ton of cash!"

"Actually he didn't," JoJo responded, "about six weeks ago his skeleton was found in a construction site in Port St. Lucie."

"Turns out he was murdered," Lisa added, "shot in the mouth."

"Ouch! I bet that hurt," Rosenberg smiled.

"So you know who Jimmy Foster was?" Lisa asked.

"Of course I knew Jimmy. Money lending wasn't something I did, my business was waste management. But I lent Jimmy money because I liked the kid, and he was desperate. Poor bastard blew it all at the gambling tables, I heard. He kept asking for more, but didn't have the money to pay me back, so I had to cut him off. He was a real piece of work, that kid."

"How much money did he owe you?" JoJo asked.

"Let's see if I can remember," Rosenberg said, "I think it was around eight million."

"So, did you ever get paid back?" Lisa asked.

"Oh yes, his father-in-law paid me."

"Sidney Schwartz?"

"Yes, that's him. He and I go way back. I heard he's in bad shape these days, Alzheimer."

"Murray," JoJo said, "can you think of anyone who would want to kill Jimmy Foster?"

"I suppose all the people that he screwed out of their money."

"But it definitely wasn't anyone you know, right?" Lisa asked.

Just then Rosenberg's expression changed. "Honey," he replied, with a stern look of derision, "I'm not sure what you're driving at with that question. I ran an honest business. My main business was trash collection. I wasn't a gangster and I would never ask anybody to kill anyone."

"No sir, I didn't mean…"

"And, I can assure you that if I had killed Jimmy Foster, you would never have found his body!" Rosenberg let out a loud laugh.

"Can I ask you another question, Murray?" JoJo said.

"Sure, sweetheart, anything."

"Why Mr. Black? Why that name?"

Murray chuckled. "Listen, honey," he said with a smile, "I was in a tough business, waste management, and when you're in a tough business sometimes you need to let people know that you mean business, you know what I mean, sweetheart?"

"Uh huh"

"So what name sounds tougher to you?" Murray continued, "Murray Rosenberg or Mr. Black?"

"I see," Jo Jo replied.

"Okay, thank you so much Mr. Rosenberg," Lisa added as she stood up from the sofa.

"Murray!"

"Of course, Murray."

"So, you like this place, girls?"

"It looks beautiful," Lisa replied, as she looked around.

"I built it thirty years ago," Rosenberg said proudly, "I bought two buildings side by side here on Collins Avenue. Jimmy Foster was my realtor, that's how I first met him. So I bought the two buildings, tore them both down, and built this place. I named it after my father, Harry Rosenberg. He was a great man. Now I live here myself. Go figure!"

"It's like a palace!" JoJo said.

"So, you girls wanna come up and see my apartment?" Rosenberg said with a grin, "Maybe you could arrest me and give me some discipline. I've been a bad boy!"

"Maybe some other time, Murray," Lisa replied. "Maybe some other time."

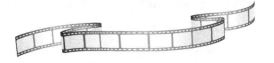

CHAPTER 38

JANUARY 3, 2019, 9:00 AM

PORT ST. LUCIE POLICE HEADQUARTERS

"Okay detectives," Captain Davis said, "your partnership has been cut short by the FBI."

"And I was just getting her broken in!" JoJo laughed.

"I'll be bringing in a new detective next week to join you," Davis said, "his name is William Sales."

"Sales?" Lisa asked, "you mean Sales as in Chief Sales?"

"Yup, it's the chief's son."

"And we got him," JoJo said with a grin, "lucky us!"

"Hey, Worthington," Captain Davis chided, "if we can put up with all those crazy clothes and hats you wear we can tolerate having the chief's kid here too."

"Ouch!" JoJo replied with a grin.

"Seriously, though," the captain said, "I talked to his precinct captain, JoJo. He's got nothing but good things to say about William. The kid earned his promotion to detective just like each one of us did, and everyone else in this department. So let's give him the same respect we would give any new member of the team, okay?"

"Sure, Captain, no problem," JoJo said.

"I'm gonna let him ride shotgun with you guys until Lisa leaves. After that I'll decide to whether to keep him with Worthington or make some other arrangements."

"We'll break him in just right, Captain, I promise," Lisa said.

"Good," Captain Davis said, "so, where are you on the skeleton case?"

Lisa spoke first. "I think we're getting close, Captain. We arrested a woman named Janet Bannister on obstruction of justice charges. She's the one who sent us the phony letter that claims her husband killed Jimmy Foster."

"So it wasn't him?" Davis asked.

"It might be him, Captain," Lisa replied, "we're working on it."

"We're hoping to get the truth out of Mrs. Bannister," JoJo said, "she's facing felony charges so she might just be ready to make a deal."

Just then Lisa's cell phone buzzed. She looked at it and said,"that's Steve Velazquez from the state's attorney's office. He was meeting with Mrs. Bannister and her lawyer this morning."

"Alright," Davis said, "go take the call, but keep me up to speed on what's going on. And, Detective Sales will be here at nine tomorrow."

"Aye aye, Captain," Lisa replied with a salute.

In a few minutes Lisa and JoJo were in the office of assistant states attorney Steve Velasquez. Steve was fifty years old, short and stout, a veteran prosecutor who was known as a fun loving joker. Not a stellar courtroom performer, Steve built his reputation as a great negotiator of plea deals. He was exactly the man they needed to meet with Janet Bannister, Lisa thought.

"I met with Mrs. Bannister and her attorney a few minutes ago," Steve began, "I told them she was looking at a felony conviction and at least five years."

"She's too old for that," Lisa said.

"That's exactly what she said," Steve replied, "so I offered her a plea deal for a misdemeanor with no jail time."

"And what do we get in return?" JoJo asked.

"We get the shooter," Steve replied calmly.

"The shooter?" JoJo shouted

"Yep, the shooter."

"So who's the shooter?" Lisa asked, "was it her husband?"

"Nope, keep guessing," Steve said with a smile.

"Then it must have been Cary Garnet," JoJo said, "he's the guy I pegged for this."

"Wrong again," Steve joked, "one final wrong guess and the game is over ladies, you lose the grand prize!"

"Okay, Velazquez," Lisa demanded, "cut the crap!"

"I have no idea!" Steve said with a big grin.

"Asshole!" Lisa and JoJo shouted in unison.

"I don't know who the hell he is, I figured you two would find him after Mrs. Bannister shows you his photo."

"She has the guy's picture?" Lisa asked.

"That's what she claims," Steve replied, "and her lawyer is ready to hand it over to us."

"So, we need to talk to Janet Bannister again!" JoJo said.

"It's all arranged, "Steve replied, "we're gonna meet with her and her attorney at one o'clock this afternoon."

"Good," Lisa said, "we've got a lot of questions to ask her."

"And I'll be there too, with the plea agreement for her to sign." Steve added, "but the deal only gets signed on my end if you guys are satisfied with what she tells you."

"Got it," JoJo said.

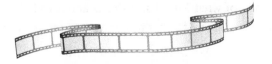

CHAPTER 39

Lisa, JoJo and Steve Velasquez sat on one side of the interview table as Janet Bannister was escorted into the room with her lawyer, Jerry Mason.

Jerry was a young lawyer only a few years out of law school, but he had already built a reputation as a formidable defense attorney. He was the son a very wealthy man who owned several auto dealerships on the Treasure Coast, and, like his famous father, he sported a small mustache and exuded confidence. Steve immediately recognized Jerry and, after introductions all around, the interview began.

"Mrs. Bannister," Steve began, "as you know we are recording this interview. For the record please state your full name and address."

Janet looked at Jerry Mason and, after a nod of approval, she began. "My name is Janet Marconi Bannister, and I live at 2121 Sandpiper Way in Port St. Lucie, Florida."

"Thank you Mrs. Bannister," Steve continued, "as part of the pending plea agreement you have agreed to answer questions from detectives

March and Worthington truthfully and completely. Do you understand that, Mrs. Bannister?"

Once again Janet Bannister glanced at her lawyer and, after a definitive nod, she replied, "Yes I do."

"Mrs. Bannister," Lisa said, "please tell us everything you know about the murder of Jimmy Foster."

"Before we begin," Jerry interrupted, "it's important to state for the record that much of what Mrs. Bannister is about to tell you is her best recollection of what was told to her by her husband over twenty years ago."

"Yes, we know that, Mr. Mason," Steve replied.

"And again, for the record," Jerry said, "Mrs. Bannister is seventy-one years old and her memory is obviously not as sharp as it once was."

"So, where are you going with this counselor?" Steve asked .

"I just want the record to note that my client is willing to answer your questions fully and accurately to the best of her ability and memory," Jerry replied.

"So noted, Mr. Mason," Steve said with a derisive smirk, "now is she finally ready to talk to us?"

Janet took a moment to collect her thoughts.

"My husband, John Bannister was employed by Sidney Schwartz," she began, "and one of the things he often did for Mr. Schwartz was to follow Jimmy Foster and take photos of the things Jimmy was doing."

"On the night of February 3, 1995 my husband observed Jimmy Foster leave the Breakers Hotel around eleven pm. Jimmy got into his car and began to drive away."

"My husband began to follow Jimmy's car when he noticed a man in the back seat holding a gun to Jimmy's head."

"John followed the car until it stopped at a building on Federal Highway in Port St. Lucie. My husband used his camera and telescopic lens to take photos of the man forcing Jimmy into the building at gunpoint."

"About thirty minutes later my husband heard a single gunshot. And then, shortly after that, the man ran out of the building and drove away in Jimmy's car."

"Right after that my husband entered the building and observed Jimmy's body. There was no doubt that Jimmy was dead, so my husband took photos of the body and then left the building."

"Then, what happened after that?" Lisa asked.

"A few days after the incident my husband came home. I don't know where he was during that time, I didn't ask him."

"But when he came home he showed me all the photos and I asked him what he was going to do with them. He said he heard that all of the money in Jimmy's account was stolen and transferred to a foreign bank account. He figured that the guy in the photo had forced Jimmy to make the transfer from a computer before he shot him."

"Did your husband give you any specifics about this building?" JoJo asked, "the address or the name on the building? Anything like that?"

"I don't think so," Janet replied, "if he did, I can't remember."

"So, what did your husband do with the photos?" Lisa asked.

"I asked my husband what his options were and he told me he had three choices. One, he could take the photos to the police. Two, he could take them to Sidney Schwartz. Or three, he could use them for our benefit."

"Your benefit?" JoJo asked.

"We had a lot of debts hanging over our heads," Janet replied, "One of our sons had serious medical problems and he could never get a job, and our daughter was going through a nasty divorce so she had legal bills to pay. John's only client was Sidney Schwartz and he knew that job could be terminated at any time. Once Jimmy was dead, John wasn't sure if Schwartz would keep paying him. Turns out he was right!"

"Schwartz fired your husband?" Lisa asked.

"Following Jimmy around was pretty much all John was doing for Sidney Schwartz," Janet said, "so once he was gone my husband was out of a job. We lived on the money we got from the photos he took."

"So, what did your husband do with the photos?" Lisa asked, "how did you get money from them?"

"It took him a few weeks to find out who the man in the photo was, but he finally did."

"Did he explain how he was able to do that?"

"He said he went back to the same building the next night as soon as it got dark. He waited there for a long time but then he saw a car pull up and two people removed the body and put it in the trunk of a car. He got the license plate and found that it was a rental car. He traced it and found who rented it."

"So he knew who the shooter was?" Lisa said.

"Yes, but he would never tell me," Janet replied, "He said he wanted to protect me, and the less I knew the safer I was. But I do have the photos he took of the guy."

"You said there were two people at the building the second night?" JoJo asked.

"Yes, he said it looked like the second person was a woman."

"Did he get photos of the woman?"

"He said he was about to take photos but they saw him so he jumped into his car and drove away."

"So, what did he do next?" Lisa asked.

"My husband contacted the guy and sent him a copy of all the photos. He told the guy that he would keep the photos hidden as long as the guy hired John and paid him ten thousand a month."

"And the man agreed to this?" Lisa asked.

"He never missed a payment," Janet replied, "even after John died the payments kept coming."

"Let me ask you," JoJo said, "as far as you know did your husband ever tell anyone else about what he had witnessed that night?"

"No, not that I know of."

"Mrs. Bannister," Lisa said, "the envelope we received in the mail only had photos of the dead body. You mentioned that your husband also took pictures of the man who shot Jimmy Foster."

Janet 's lawyer opened his briefcase and handed an envelope to Lisa. "I think you'll find everything you're looking for in here."

Lisa quickly opened the envelope and looked at the photos. "Okay," she said, "these will be helpful to us."

"There's also a complete set of negatives in there," Janet's attorney added, "and these negatives are date stamped to prove the exact day and time they were taken."

"Where were these photos kept all these years. Mrs. Bannister?" JoJo asked.

"John kept a set of photos and the negatives hidden in our house in fireproof packaging," Janet replied, "and after each of my kids moved to their own place he gave them a set to keep in their houses."

"Your kids never asked about them?" Lisa asked.

"The photos he gave them were sealed and they were told it was our will and life insurance policy," Janet said, "neither of my children ever asked about them so I'm sure they never opened the package."

"Do you have any guess as to who this person is who sends you the money?" JoJo asked.

"No, I'm sorry but I still don't know that. I was just happy to receive the money."

"How does the money come to you each month?"

"The money comes by electronic transfer on the fifth of every month. That's all I know about it."

"Okay," Lisa replied, "so tell us about what prompted you to forge your husband's signature and send those photos to us."

"Right after the word got out that the police found Jimmy Foster's body a package was delivered by a courier to my house. The package contained the letter that I sent to your police department."

"The letter that had your husband confessing to killing Jimmy Foster," JoJo offered.

"Yes, that's the letter that was sent to me. There was also a note attached to it telling me that if I wanted to keep receiving my money each month I had to sign John's signature on it and send it with photos of Jimmy Foster's dead body."

"And what about the birthday card you gave us, was that really a card from your husband?"

"It was, but it didn't have the writing on it. He never signed his cards. After you called and said you wanted to speak to me I figured you'd be asking about the signature," Janet replied, "I found one of his cards and wrote the note so it would match the signature I used on the letter."

"And you realize that this letter labeled your late husband as a murderer," JoJo said.

"Of course I did!" Janet shot back, "but since John had passed away, and I needed the money, I did it. I have no other income other than Social Security and I can't live on that. I didn't think it was such a bad thing I did."

"And the Glock 17?" JoJo asked, "was that really John's gun?"

"Yes, that was really his gun."

"Did you happen to save the envelope that the letter came in?"

"No, I threw it away."

Lisa and JoJo exited the interview room, leaving Steve Velasquez to finish up the paperwork with Janet Bannister and her lawyer, Jerry Mason.

As soon as she was out of the room Lisa said. "The guy in these photos is no dummy, Jo."

"How's that, Lisa?"

"That letter implicates two men in Jimmy Foster's murder, one of them is dead."

"And the other can't remember anything!" JoJo added.

Lisa grabbed her cellphone and called Bob Elliott at the FBI.

"Hello, Agent March!" Bob said with glee, emphasizing the word agent.

"Hey Bob, I need your help again," Lisa replied, "another missing person!"

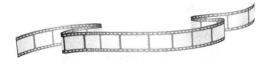

CHAPTER 40

JANUARY 4, 2019, 11:00 AM

THE HOME OF LOUIS LABER

PLANTATION, FLORIDA

"Good morning, Mr. Laber," Lisa began, "thanks for letting us visit you today."

"You want to talk about Dreamland, right?" Laber asked. He looked even older than his seventy-five years, Lisa thought, a lot older than my dad.

"Mr. Laber," JoJo said, "we're investigating the death of Jimmy Foster and we're hoping you can give us some background information."

"I didn't kill him," Laber replied, "although, to be honest, there were many times when I wanted to!"

"Why was that?" JoJo said.

"Look," Laber replied, "by now you must know all about what a jerk Jimmy Foster was. The only thing he cared about was himself!"

"Did Jimmy do anything to harm you, Mr. Laber?"

"He ruined my career, that's all!" Laber shouted.

"And how did he do that?" Lisa asked.

"I'm an honest man," Laber said, "and I always did everything in my power to make sure that my clients were honest too. But with Jimmy it was just impossible."

"Why was that?" Lisa asked.

"Because Jimmy wouldn't listen to me," Laber said, "he treated me like a lap dog rather than the professional accountant that I was. He was that way with everybody, even his best friend, Cary Garnet!"

"Mr. Laber," JoJo whispered, "were you aware that Jimmy was taking money from the Dreamland project and gambling with it?"

"At first, no," Laber replied, "in the early stages Jimmy would take money from the loan account and use it for legitimate expenses, but then he started losing at the casino and he took money to cover his losses."

"And you knew about this?" Lisa asked.

"I told Jimmy that the bank would demand proof of how their loan money was spent, and he basically told me to mind my own business."

"So, what happened next?" JoJo asked.

"After he went through all twelve million of the loan money he asked me to get him access to the escrow fund. That's the deposit money we collected from the buyers."

"And how much was that?" Lisa asked.

"That was eighteen million dollars, but I told Jimmy that money had to be used for construction of the houses, nothing else."

"But he took it anyway?" Lisa asked.

"I can't prove he took it, but after he disappeared all the escrow money was gone. I'm convinced Jimmy took it to pay off his gambling debts."

"Mr. Laber," Lisa said calmly, "I want you to think long and hard before you answer this question. Did you have anything to do with he disappearance of the Dreamland escrow account money?"

"No!" Laber replied in at the blink of an eye, "I never touched that money!"

"You didn't take some for yourself and give some to Sidney Schwartz?"

"Absolutely not!" Laber yelled, "I am an honest man, not a thief!"

"Okay, Mr. Laber," JoJo asked in a quiet tone, "now that you know Jimmy's dead, is there anyone else you can think of who might have killed him and taken that money?"

"All I can say is that it wasn't me!" Laber replied forcefully. "I was accused of stealing the money, even though there wasn't a shred of evidence to back up that claim. It was all over the news that I was under suspicion."

"I suppose it was hard to find clients after that,"JoJo said.

"It ruined me," Laber replied, "I had a good practice going, but just about every client fired me. I had to take a job selling shoes, for God sakes, and I'm still working!"

"I'm sorry for you," JoJo said.

"I only wish Jimmy's body had been found a long time ago," Laber said quietly, "then I would have been able to live in peace all these years."

As the detectives walked away from Laber's house, Lisa said, "I believe this guy."

"Me too, Lisa, " JoJo replied, "but that means the story Cary Garnet told us about Laber taking the money wasn't true."

"Cary said he heard that Laber took the money," Lisa said, "I wonder who told him that?"

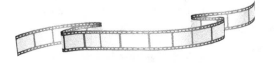

CHAPTER 41

Jimmy Foster pulled his Lamborghini into the parking lot of a warehouse on Federal Highway in Port St. Lucie.

"Get out!" the gunman whispered forcefully to Jimmy as his car stopped in the rear of the building, "and don't even think about running."

"What do you want from me?" Jimmy said in a panic, "I have money. I can pay you!"

"Inside!" The gunman said.

The two men walked into the building, Jimmy first, followed by the gunman.

Waiting for them inside the building was an attractive young woman.

"What the fuck!" Jimmy yelled when he saw the woman, "what's going on?"

The woman walked toward Jimmy and pointed to a chair. "Sit down!" she said.

The gunman held the gun very close to Jimmy's head.

"Just tell me what you want, and I'll do it!" Jimmy pleaded, "I just don't want any trouble!"

The woman pointed to the desktop computer on the table in front of Jimmy.

"We've got the bank website, Jimmy," she said, "so all we need now is for you to enter your password."

"But I don't know the password," Jimmy said in a panic, "only the accountant has that, I swear!"

"Okay then, Jimmy, I guess we'll have to kill you and then go find your accountant," the woman said calmly, "shoot him!"

The gunman raised his weapon and pointed it at Jimmy's head.

"Wait!" Jimmy screamed, "don't shoot!"

"Did you just remember the password, Jimmy?"

"The accountant told it to me once," Jimmy said, "I'm not sure if I can remember it."

"I'll tell you what, Jimmy," the woman said with a grin, "I want you to remember that password like your life depends on it, okay?"

Jimmy reached for the keyboard and entered the nine digit password given to him by his account. Instantly the account opened.

"Get up!" The woman shouted as she took over the seat in front of the computer. She entered several numbers and, in an instant, the loan account was visible.

"Where's the money from the loan account, Jimmy?" she said firmly.

"It's gone." Jimmy whispered, "I'm sorry!"

"You gambled it all away, Jimmy," the woman said calmly, "and now you're gonna lose everything."

The woman methodically hit several keys on the keyboard and all of the money was transferred out of Dreamland's escrow account.

"Please," Jimmy pleaded, "I'll be a dead man if you do this!" Jimmy pleaded.

"It couldn't happen to a more deserving guy, Jimmy!"

The woman unplugged the computer and turned to the gunman. "Finish up!" she said, "and then get the hell out of here."

She walked toward the side door, stepped into her car, and sped away.

Minutes later John Bannister entered the building from the rear door.

CHAPTER 42

"My boss wasn't too thrilled with the idea of me coming here today, Bob."

"He needs to start weaning himself from you, Lisa," Bob Elliott replied, "He just needs to accept the fact that his best detective is joining the FBI."

"He's happy for me, Bob, really he is," Lisa said, "don't get me wrong. It's just that…"

"It's just that he agreed to give you up at the end of January and this is only the 8th, I get that."

"Well, at least I'm here working on my last case for his department, and the faster we close this case the faster you get me!"

"I love a challenge, Lisa! Did you bring the photos?"

Lisa opened a brief case and removed a large envelope. "They're all in here, and so are the negatives. Most of them are pretty dark. It was night time and he shot them from pretty far away."

Elliott took the folder from Lisa and led her out the door toward the lab.

"I'm gonna introduce you to a guy named Gus Haney" he said, "this guy is an absolute genius when it comes to this kind of stuff."

In a few minutes Lisa was standing beside Agent Gus Haney, who was seated at his computer. She handed him the photos taken by John Bannister that showed a man forcing Jimmy Foster into the building.

"They're very dark, "Lisa said, "and they were taken from far away."

"Gus Haney laughed, "that's okay, Agent March," he said, "I think I can make them real pretty for you!"

Haney placed the first photo in the scanner next to his computer. With the touch of his mouse and a few keystrokes things began to change. In less than thirty seconds the photo became clear and the darkness turned to daylight.

"How does he do that?" Lisa whispered to Bob Elliott.

"Like I said, he's a genius!"

"I'm glad he's on our side," Lisa joked.

"Hey," Elliott replied, "don't think the bad guys can't do this too!"

After clearing up three more photos, Agent Haney said "I think we've got enough now for facial recognition."

"Remember, these photos are twenty-four years old, Gus," Elliott said.

"I can see that," Gus Haney replied, "they're date stamped for February 3, 1995."

With a few more mouse movements the photo began to change. Right before their eyes the gunman was aging by twenty years.

"Now that's like something out of a sci-fi movie!" Lisa exclaimed.

"All in a days work," Haney responded, "now we find out who he is!"

"How does that work?" Lisa asked.

"We've got over four hundred million faces in our data base," Haney replied, "if we can't find this guy, nobody can!"

"Except maybe Facebook!" Elliott joked.

"Facebook?" Haney shot back, "amateurs!"

"How did you get four hundred million faces?" Lisa asked.

"First, we have every person who applies for a US Passport," Haney replied, "and then you can add in the people who have drivers licenses in a lot of states, and mug shots taken of criminals too."

With those words Haney started the facial recognition scan. "This might take a while," he said.

"Do me a favor," Lisa asked, "can you bring up the photos of the outside of the building again?"

A few keystrokes and Lisa's request was granted.

"What are you looking for, Agent March?"

"It's okay to call me Lisa," she said with a smile, "unless that's forbidden in the FBI."

"No, it's perfectly fine, Lisa," Agent Haney replied, "and you can call me Gus. My real name is Albert, but I was a junior so they always called me by my middle name."

"So, Gus" Lisa continued, "I'm hoping we can go back and look inside that building, but first we have to find it."

"Not much chance you'll find anything useful twenty-four years after the murder took place, Lisa," Bob Elliott chimed in.

"You're probably right, Bob," Lisa responded quickly, "but I think it's worth a look. Maybe we can see some telltale markings that will help us find the building. We think it's on Federal Highway in Port St. Lucie."

Gus Haynes worked his mouse around several times, stopping to highlight and enlarge certain sections of the photos.

"Look!" He shouted, "there's a number."

"It's the number five," Lisa said, "any chance we can see the other numbers ahead of it?'"

Gus tried for several minutes before he gave up. "I'm afraid that's the best I can do for you on that, Lisa," he said.

Lisa grabbed her cellphone and called JoJo.

"How's it going Jo?"

"Great Lisa. I'm here with our new teammate, William Sales. I know you're gonna love him. Right now we're working on the Jimmy Foster case. What's up with you and your new FBI friends? Did you forget about us already?"

"Very funny, JoJo," Lisa replied with a grin, "actually, we're very close to finding out who the shooter was."

"Really? That's great!"

"I can't wait to tell you all about this place, Jo. It's truly amazing! And I've got a lead on where the shooting took place."

"You mean the warehouse in Port St. Lucie? What ya got, Lisa?"

"Well, we know it's on Federal Highway."

"Yep."

"Our amazing tech guy was able to pull up the last digit on the street number. It's five, but that's the only number visible in the photos Bannister took."

"Thanks, Lisa, that'll really help. Now we know what side of the street to look on and it really narrows down the number of buildings."

"I thought so too, Jo."

"William and I will go an expedition today to see what we can find."

Just as Lisa was about to end the call she heard Gus Haney shout, "we got him!"

"We got the shooter," he repeated, "his name is Adam McNeely!"

"Who the hell is that?" Lisa shouted, "he's completely off our radar screen."

"Well then," Bob Elliott replied, as he sat down in front of his computer, "I guess we'd better find out who Mr. Adam McNeely really is."

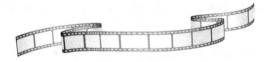

CHAPTER 43

JANUARY 8, 2019, 2:00 PM

FEDERAL HIGHWAY

"I really love your outfit, JoJo," William Sales said, as the two detectives drove north on Federal Highway, searching for the Jimmy Foster murder scene.

"Why thank you, William." JoJo replied with a smile, "I'm not used to getting compliments from my colleagues. Usually they just roll their eyes when I walk into the office."

"Well, I'm a big believer in individuality. People need to be themselves."

"So, tell me about yourself, William."

"First thing is, I prefer to be called Will, not William, and definitely not Willie!" A big smile came next.

"Okay then, Will, tell me about yourself."

Will thought for a moment and then began. "Well, as you surely know, my dad is the chief of police."

"I know that, Will, but I'm interested in learning about Will Sales, not Chief Sales!"

"That's fair, JoJo, but you must realize that a big part of who I am was shaped by the fact that I come from a long line of police officers. My grandpa, my dad, and two of my uncles were all police officers. There was never a time in my life that I didn't want to be just like all of them."

"Why was that, do you think?"

"JoJo, I'm only twenty-seven, but in my lifetime I've seen a lot of black men get disrespected. Maybe some deserved it, but a lot of them didn't. I grew up in a family of black men who commanded respect, and they got it. That always meant a lot to me."

"Good for you, Will, I'm happy to be working with you, for however long this lasts."

"Me too, JoJo."

"I think we'd better start looking for the building."

Will reviewed the enhanced photos that had been sent from Melbourne and studied them carefully. "We know the address ends in five, so it will definitely be on the east side of the highway."

"Can you see anything in the photos that would help us identify the exact building?"

"No, not yet, except that…"

"Except what?"

"This one photo shows a wide angle view of the front parking lot, and it's very unusual."

"Unusual, what do you mean?"

"Pull over for a minute and let me show you."

JoJo stopped the car in a strip shopping center and looked at the photo Will was showing her.

"See," Will said, "most parking lots are rectangular in shape, but this one is more like pie shaped."

"I see," JoJo replied, "that is unusual."

"I'm not sure if it still looks like that today, but at least it's a good landmark for us."

Five minutes later Will saw what he believed to be the building. "I think we just passed it," he said.

JoJo guided the car through a U-turn and then pulled into the odd shaped parking lot. Sure enough, on the building was the number 11375.

"This must be it!" JoJo said with excitement.

She grabbed her cellphone and called back to the office.

"Captain," she said, "I think we found the Jimmy Foster murder scene. Can you ask someone to pull up the ownership history back to 1995 on 11375 Federal Highway in Port St. Lucie? Thanks!"

"Thats was so nice, JoJo," Will said, "so the captain's gonna get right on it?"

"No, Will, that was his voicemail. He probably won't listen to it until we get back and then he'll tell me to do the research myself!"

The both enjoyed a good laugh as they exited the car and walked toward the building, which appeared to be empty. They approached the door and JoJo tried to open it.

"It's locked," she said.

"I'll go try the other doors," Will said, as he walked around the back of the building. No sooner had he reached the rear door than it opened for him. JoJo was standing in the doorway.

"How'd you get in? Will asked.

"It's a miracle!" Lisa replied, with a wry smile.

"I believe it's actually called breaking and entering!" Will said with a chuckle, as he joined JoJo inside the building.

"I don't know if this place has ever been occupied in the past twenty-four years," JoJo said.

"No power," Will said, as he turned the useless light switch on and off several times.

"Good thing we brought flash lights,"JoJo replied.

For the next twenty minutes the two detectives stood at the doorway and looked around the empty building. The floor was covered in dust, and the lone remaining chair and desk appeared to have almost rotted away completely."

"We're not gonna find anything this way, partner," JoJo said. "Let's go back to the station, get a warrant, and send the forensics team down here to check this place out."

"It'd be awesome if they found traces of Jimmy Foster's blood in here, or the killer's DNA."

"And maybe even a shell casing or two."

As they drove back to Port St. Luce Will turned toward JoJo. "You know you called me partner in there," he said.

"No I didn't." JoJo mused.

"Yes you did. You said 'we're not gonna find anything this way, partner.' You said partner!"

"Really?"

"Yes, really, you said…."

"I'm teasing you, Will," JoJo said with a smile, "I know what I said, and I meant it!"

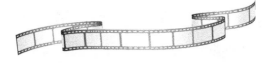

CHAPTER 44

Agent Bob Elliott looked up from his computer.

"Lisa," he said, "the last known address we have on Adam McNeely is in Bonita Springs, Florida."

"Any criminal record?" Lisa asked.

"This guy is squeaky clean," Elliott replied, "nothing but a couple of speeding tickets."

"What does he do for a living?"

"McNeely owns twelve self storage facilities throughout the area. Apparently he does very well. His tax return for 2017 showed a gross income of over two million dollars. His house is valued at over five million, he drives a BMW 700 series, she drives an Audi SUV, and they belong to a swank country club.

"Not what we were expecting, huh?" Lisa said.

"The guy built twelve self storage facilities between 1996 and 2001, at a cost of over nine million, and he has no mortgage on any of them," Elliott said, "that money came from somewhere."

"And maybe that somewhere was the Dreamland escrow account!" Lisa replied.

"McNeely started investing in Bitcoin in 2009 when the price of a coin was about ten cents," Elliott continued, "and now the coins are worth about $4,000 each!"

"Wow! How much of this Bitcoin does he have?"

"Are you ready for this, Lisa?"

"Let me have it, Bob."

"The McNeelys are worth about sixty million today!"

"Smart guy, so, what else do we know about McNeely?" Lisa asked.

Once again Elliott checked his computer screen. "McNeely married Barbara Winters in 1996. They've got two daughters, seventeen and fifteen, who both attend an exclusive private prep school in Naples."

"You think maybe the facial recognition program got it wrong, Bob?"

"Anything's possible Lisa, but I've never seen Gus Haney make a mistake before."

"How about a doppelgänger?"

"A what?" Elliott asked.

"Doppelganger!" Lisa repeated, "it's someone who looks exactly like you. I read somewhere that everyone in the world has a doppelgänger."

"Do you?"

"Actually, it's pretty funny," Lisa replied, "I was investigating a murder in Port St. Lucie last year and the victim was an avid Pickleball player. So, after we closed the case, I decided to take up the game myself, and that's when I met her."

"You met your doppelgänger?"

"I was invited to play at a private club in St. Lucie West and, when I walked in, people kept saying 'hi Jodi' to me. I didn't think anything about it until someone invited me to play a game."

"That blew your cover?" Elliott asked with a grin.

"Apparently this Jodi was a really good player and she could hit the ball super hard."

"And you?"

"I was just a beginner. I could barely hit the ball over the net. So, everyone started asking 'are you alright Jodi?'. And then all of a sudden, in walks the real Jodi!"

"Did she look like you?"

"I swear, Bob, we could have been identical twins separated at birth. We looked at each other and it was like a scene from that movie The Parent Trap. She was exactly my height…"

"You mean Munchkin level height!" Elliott said with a grin.

"Ouch!" Lisa said with a grin, "fun sized is what I prefer!"

"So be it!" Elliott replied.

"Anyway," Lisa continued, "Jodi looked exactly like me. Her hair was just like mine, and, believe it or not, we were wearing almost the same clothes! It was like I was looking in a mirror!"

"Now, tell me you were born the same day!"

"I didn't ask her what her birthday was, but that night I called my mother and asked her if she gave a baby up for adoption. She told me I was nuts!"

"So, did you keep in touch with this Jodi?"

"Sadly, no," Lisa replied, "we said we should get together but we never did. That was the one and only time I ever saw her. I should call her though, and maybe I will."

"Well," Bob Elliott said, "I never met my doppelgänger, and I hope I never do."

"Okay, but I'm just saying that we could have the wrong guy, that's all."

"So let's go meet him and find out, Lisa!"

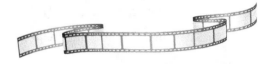

CHAPTER 45

"How's school going?" JoJo said as she, her husband Stuart, and their son Billy sat at the dinner table."

"Not bad, Mom," Billy replied, "we start the tennis season next week and the coach says I can play warm-ups!"

"Did you ever play Pickleball, Billy?"

"No, it's dumb!" Billy said, shaking his head and rolling his eyes.

"Dumb?"

"It's like a tiny tennis game, Mom," Billy replied, "Brian's mom plays all the time."

"I don't know," Stuart jumped in, "a lot of my friends are playing Pickleball and they say it's a great game!"

"That's cause they're old, Dad!" Billy smiled.

Stuart Worthington was fifty-three years old, a little paunchy, and a full ten years older than his wife. They had met in 1998 when Stuart came to

Port St. Lucie on a business trip. At the time JoJo Dimitrius was a rookie cop who stopped Stuart for speeding on Port St. Lucie Blvd.

Stuart knew then that he was guilty, and he would normally have simply paid the fine, but he was so smitten with this beautiful blonde police officer that he chose to go to court, simply hoping to meet her again.

They married eighteen months later.

"What's up with the skeleton case, Jo?" Stuart asked.

"I saw what we think is the actual crime scene today."

"You're kidding!" Stuart replied, "The crime was over twenty years ago!"

"I traced the building's usage over the past twenty-four years. Believe it or not it's been empty. Actually it's been empty for even longer than that!"

"So, somebody has been paying taxes on a building for years and years and then letting it sit empty?"

"That's right, and I even got the owner's name, are you ready for this? Dreamland Estates Limited, the company owned by Jimmy Foster!"

"That makes sense," Stuart said, "big developers often buy or rent warehouse space to store supplies until they need them. This allows them to buy in large quantities and get a big discount from the supplier."

"Listen to you!" JoJo said seductively, "you're as smart as you are cute!"

"But, what I don't understand," Stuart continued, "is how Jimmy Foster could pay the taxes on the building if he's been dead all this time."

"Somebody paid them, but we don't know who it was."

"So, what else you got, babe?"

"Believe it or not the FBI id'd the shooter today, Stu."

"Oh yeah, who is he?"

"Some guy we never heard of," JoJo replied as she looked down at her cell phone, "His name is Adam McNeely."

"So, what's his connection to the dead guy?"

"I looked for that all afternoon, Stu, but I just couldn't put the two of them together."

"Didn't you tell me there was a woman involved too?"

"We heard that from the wife of the guy who took the photos of McNeely, but he didn't get a shot of the woman so we have no idea who she was."

"Well, I have no doubt you'll figure it all out, sweetheart."

"I know we will."

"By the way, Jo, Rick March called me. He wanted to know if Billy and I would like to watch the playoff games this Saturday at his house."

"Sounds great!" JoJo replied, "Billy will love it, and I'll bring some food."

"He didn't mention you, honey," Stuart laughed, "but I guess you can come too if you really want to!"

"That's okay, dear," JoJo said with a smile, "maybe Lisa and I will go shopping. I really need a new outfit!"

"Of course you do, honey," Stu chuckled, "but it's just too bad our closet is totally filled up."

"I know it is," JoJo replied, "I guess we can either move your stuff out or get a bigger house!"

"How about you give away some of the clothes that have been taking up space in your closet for years, Jo?" Stu said, as he feigned concern, "you've got some really old stuff you're keeping around."

Just then JoJo walked over to her husband and lovingly placed her arms around him.

"Honey," she said with a wry smile, "There's nothing in my closet older than you and I'm still keeping you around!"

Stuart turned and kissed his wife.

"Ugh!" Billy yelled, "get a room you two!"

As soon as the tender moment with her husband subsided, JoJo grabbed her cellphone and called Lisa.

"I've got another bombshell for you, partner!"

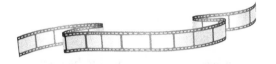

CHAPTER 46

JANUARY 9 , 2019, 9:00 AM
THE HOME OF LISA AND RICK MARCH
PORT ST. LUCIE, FLORIDA

"Thanks for picking me up, Bob," Lisa said as she sat down inside the car of Agent Elliott.

"Hey," Elliott replied, "you drove all the way up to Melbourne and back yesterday. This was the least I could do."

"So we're going to Bonita Springs?" Lisa asked rhetorically.

"I've got McNeelys' address," Elliott said, "it's in the high rent district for sure. And I've got warrants to search his house and all of his storage offices, and we're going after his bank accounts, too. And then I have a warrant to arrest him if we think he's our shooter."

"You're a good man, Bob!"

"Lee County has a team of officers ready to help us, all I gotta do is call."

"You know," Lisa replied, "yesterday when you told me all about what a successful family man McNeely is, I was almost expecting to find out that he was also a deacon in his church and that he ran a homeless shelter!"

Elliott laughed. "Not quite, Lisa," he offered, "but they do support a lot of charities. Seems like the McNeelys are pillars of the community."

"You know, that's what they found out about some of those serial killers," Lisa mused, "choir boy by day, serial killer by night!"

"So, what's your partner in Port St. Lucie working on, Lisa?"

"Oh, she called me last night. They found the building where the murder took place, and you'll never guess who owned it."

"Not me!" Elliott laughed.

"Jimmy Foster!"

"Really? So Foster was killed in a building he owned. I wonder what happened to it after he died."

"Apparently nothing." Lisa said, "We think the place has remained empty for twenty-four years."

"But why do that?" Elliott asked, "why not get rid of the place?"

"The only thing I can think of is that whoever killed Jimmy didn't want a new owner finding anything that might incriminate him."

"So he just let it sit empty for all those years and paid all the taxes on it?"

"JoJo says the taxes were only a couple of thousand each year, and whoever paid the tax bills paid them from a Swiss bank account."

"Do you really think there's any evidence left in that warehouse?" Elliot asked

"JoJo's got forensics checking out the crime scene," Lisa continued, "She says it looks like it hasn't been touched in twenty-four years."

"Well then, maybe they can find something beneath all the dust that must have accumulated."

"She and her new partner are driving down to Ft. Lauderdale today to meet with Cary Garnet and see what he knows about all this."

As they continued on the three hour drive to Bonita Springs, Lisa took the opportunity to learn more about the man who might be her future partner.

"You always seem like a man of mystery to me, Bob."

"How's that?"

"Well, it's like, I feel like I know you, but I don't know anything about you."

"So, what do you want to know?"

"Okay, what do you tell people when they say they don't know anything about you?"

"I say, 'what do you want to know'?"

Lisa chuckled, "I can see this is gonna be like pulling teeth."

"Yours, I hope, not mine," Bob Elliott replied.

"Okay, then," Lisa said, lets' go….. born?

"Yes, definitely yes."

"Where?"

"Michigan."

"Married?"

"Divorced."

"Kids?"

"Two."

"Whew! This is tough." Lisa said, "I think I'll leave it at that for now."

"Good."

Just then Lisa's cell phone buzzed. It was JoJo. Lisa answered and placed the call on speaker.

"Hey Jo, I'm here with Agent Elliott of the FBI, and you're on speaker, okay?"

"Hi Agent Elliott!" JoJo shouted into the phone.

"He says you can call him Bob, JoJo, so what's up?"

"Will and I are on our way down to Ft. Lauderdale to meet with Cary Garnet."

"Good, be sure to let us know how that turns out."

"Will do," JoJo replied, "and forensics is over at the crime scene in the warehouse on Federal Highway. They said it could take two or three days to finish up."

"Good, I'll be anxious to hear if they find anything," Lisa said.

"I've been playing the Kevin Bacon game with Adam McNeely, Lisa."

"What game?"

"The Kevin Bacon, Lisa, don't tell me you never heard of that."

"Okay I won't tell you, Jo, but what the hell is it?"

"Its called six degrees of separation. The theory is that every actor that's ever appeared in a movie can be traced back to Kevin Bacon in six steps or less."

"JoJo," Lisa replied with a grimace, "I don't know what in the world you're talking about."

"Alright, never mind, Google it sometime. What I'm doing is trying to make a connection between Adam McNeely and Jimmy Foster. What person did McNeely know who knew someone else who knew someone else..."

"I get it, Jo, I get it. So, did you do it yet?"

"No luck yet, Lisa, but I'm still trying. I did find out that McNeely lived in West Palm Beach from 1992 through 1995."

"Okay, Jo, keep me posted."

As Lisa ended the call she turned to Bob Elliott. "You know, JoJo's a great detective, but sometimes I just can't figure out how her mind works."

"You mean that thing she was talking about?" Elliott replied, "the Kevin Bacon game?"

"You know about that?

"Sure! I thought everybody did!" Elliott laughed.

CHAPTER 47

JoJo and Will sat quietly in the outer office until Cary Garnet signaled for them to enter his private space. He was as handsome as ever, JoJo thought.

"Joanne, right?" Cary said, as he reached his hand out to JoJo.

"That's correct," JoJo replied, "and this is my partner, Will Sales."

As Cary and Will shook hands Cary said, "what happened to the partner you had at the last time we met? Her name was Lisa, right?"

"Detective March is transitioning to a position with the FBI," JoJo replied, "I'll send her your regards."

"This is quite a nice place you have here, Mr. Garnet," Will said, as he looked out the window to the waterway below.

"It's just about the best location on Las Olas," Cary responded proudly, "we were lucky to get into this building. They say all the movers and shakers in Ft. Lauderdale work here!"

"I love the view of the boats!" JoJo added.

"So, what can I help you with today, detectives?" Cary said with a smile.

"As I said on the phone," JoJo answered, "we wanted to bring you up to date on the progress of our investigation into the death of Jimmy Foster.

"That's good, my wife and I have been wondering how it's going, and of course, Jeffrey is really anxious about it."

"Can I ask you a question first, Cary?" JoJo said, "does Jeffrey know who his biological father is?"

"He does now," Cary replied, "we had a long talk about it after you confronted me with the DNA results."

"I certainly hope it wasn't too big a blow to him," JoJo said.

"Actually, he was relieved," Cary replied, "Jeff said he always suspected that I was his biological father but he didn't want to upset his mother so he never said anything about it. He was young when Jimmy disappeared so he considered me to be his dad anyway."

"Mr. Garnet," Will began, "our investigation leads us to believe that someone from inside the Dreamland organization was involved in killing Mr. Foster."

"Wow!" Cary said, "that's a shocker! And just how did you come to that conclusion?"

"John Bannister," Will replied. "the private detective hired by Sidney Schwartz…"

"Of course, I remember Bannister," Cary replied, "I always thought he might have had something to do with Jimmy's disappearance."

"Well," JoJo said, "he does, but probably not the way you think he does."

"I'm not following this," Cary said. For the first time since the conversation began his smile was gone.

"Mr. Garnet, we've uncovered a series of photographs that Mr. Bannister took," Will said, "we think these photos identify the man who shot Mr. Foster."

"We believe his name is Adam McNeely," JoJo added, "does that name mean anything to you, Cary?"

"McNeely," Cary pondered for a moment, "no it doesn't. I'm afraid I can't help you there."

"Okay, but we think Mr. McNeely was somehow connected to someone in the Dreamland organization," Will said.

"What makes you think that?"

"Well, first of all," JoJo replied, "Jimmy was murdered in a warehouse that was owned by the Dreamland company."

"The one on Federal Highway?"

"On Federal Highway, yes," Will responded.

"Jimmy didn't own that warehouse," Cary said, "he just leased it."

"No sir," JoJo replied, "we have tax records that show the property was owned by Dreamland limited."

"And it sat empty all this time while somebody was paying the taxes every year," Will added.

"Wow, that's all news to me," Cary said. "Jimmy told me he wanted to buy the building, but I thought I had convinced him just to lease it."

"Mr. Garnet," Will continued, "we also believe that the killer was able to log into Jimmy's bank account and transfer all of the money to a foreign bank."

"Damn!"

"So," JoJo continued, "that's why we believe that the killer had to be working with someone inside the Dreamland organization."

"I always though it was Lou Laber," Cary replied

"The last time we spoke you told us that you heard Lou Laber stole the money," JoJo responded, "how did you know that?"

"I don't know it, really," Cary said, "it was just a guess on my part because Laber was the only one other than Jimmy who had access to the money."

"So, you have no evidence that Laber took the money, right?"

"That's true."

"Do you have a list of all the Dreamland employees?" Will asked.

Cary rolled his chair to a file cabinet in his office. He opened two drawers and closed them before he settled on the third drawer. From that file drawer Cary removed a manila folder.

"Let me show you something," he said, as he opened the manila folder.

"This was a group photo taken of the Dreamland team. It was taken the same night Jimmy disappeared."

"This will be very helpful, Cary," JoJo said, "can we have this copy?"

"Yes, sure, I have several copies so you can certainly take this one."

Will examined the photo. "By any chance do you also have a list of the names of the people in this photo?" he asked.

Cary reached into the folder again and removed a list of names.

"This was the list of each sales associate and how much their commission check was," he said. "You know, at first I was certain one of them had killed Jimmy."

"Why was that?" JoJo asked.

"When I handed out those commission checks we knew there was no money in the loan account to cover them."

"They were all worthless checks?" Will said.

"I told Jimmy that it was wrong to give these people bad checks," Cary said, "but he told me he was gonna make sure the money was in the account by Monday morning when the people went to cash them."

"How much are we talking about, Cary?" JoJo asked.

"Just over a million total."

"Did he say where the money would come from by Monday morning?"

"No, but I assumed he was going to the casino hoping to win the money," Cary replied, "Jimmy always thought he was one winning streak away from success!"

"So, I guess there were forty angry people on Monday when the checks bounced!" JoJo said.

"That's the weird thing," Cary replied, "I didn't get one call from a sales associate, not one!"

"So their commission checks didn't bounce?" Will asked.

"I guess not. I'm sure I would have heard if they bounced. I got so many calls from angry buyers that eventually I had to turn my phone off."

"So, Jimmy must have put the money in the loan account to cover the checks," Will said.

"I guess he did!"

"Can you make a copy of the list for us please, Cary?" JoJo asked.

Once again Cary rolled his chair, this time he stopped at a large printer. He opened the lid and placed the list under it. In two seconds a copy came out.

"Cary," JoJo said as she looked at the list, "do you have any idea which of these people would know about the warehouse and the escrow account?"

Cary sat quietly for one minute.

"I really can't think of anybody."

"Okay, then, did any of them make a special effort to get close to Jimmy?"

Cary looked carefully at the group photo.

"This one," he said. "The one on the far right, front row."

"Why her?" Will asked.

"Because she slept with Jimmy at the hotel a week before he disappeared," Cary replied, "she was our top seller, and Jimmy really liked her."

"So, they spent the night together?"

"Yes, I remember that night."

"She was the top seller, you said?"

"Yes she was. A very smart young lady."

"Do you remember her name, Cary?" JoJo asked.

Cary looked at the list of sales associates. "Yes," he said, "here she is, Becca Raymond. You see, she got the highest commission check."

"Thank you very much, Cary," JoJo said, as she got up to leave, "you've been a big help to us."

"I hope you find out who did this!" Cary said with a stern look.

"Oh, don't worry," Will replied, "we will!"

A few minutes later JoJo and Will were back in their car about to embark on the ninety minute drive to Port St. Lucie.

"I'm gonna start checking up on this Becca Raymond as soon as we get back to the office," JoJo said.

"Did you notice the model number of the printer in Garnet's office?" Will asked.

"No," JoJo replied, "but I'm guessing you did."

"It's a Hewlett Packard Laser Jet 3500."

"No!"

"Yes, just like the one used to print that letter for Mrs. Bannister to sign."

"That's too much of a coincidence, Will."

"I need you to get us a warrant right away, JoJo. We need to look at the cache in that printer."

"The cash? Why would there be cash in the printer.?"

Will chuckled. "It's cache, c-a-c-h-e, not cash like money."

"So, what is cache?"

"It's the printer's non-volatile internal memory. Everything that gets sent to the printer is saved in its cache until it gets cleared out," Will explained. "We might just find that letter sitting there in the printer's cache!"

"How do you know so much about this stuff, Will?"

"My dad bought me my first computer when I was eight. Ever since then I've been hooked. I guess you could call me a computer junkie."

"Or a computer nerd, right?"

"I prefer junkie, Jo!"

"Okay then, let's go have lunch in one of these fancy Las Olas restaurants. I'll call for a warrant and hopefully they can text it to me while we're eating."

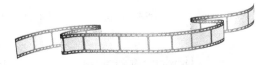

CHAPTER 48

JANUARY 9, 2019, 12:45 PM
BONITA SPRINGS, FLORIDA

As Lisa and Agent Bob Elliott approached Bonita Springs, Elliott was on a speaker phone with Captain Dan Barker of the Lee County Sheriff's office.

"We're close to Bonita Springs, now, Dan," Elliott said. "My GPS says we're fifteen minutes from the McNeely house."

"I've got twelve deputies waiting for you, Bob," Captain Barker said, "that's the most I can spare."

"Twelve is perfect, " Elliott replied, "I texted you a list of addresses and also of list of things to search for."

"Okay Bob, I've alerted the Collier County Sheriff that we'll be issuing two of the search warrants in Naples. He's sending a couple of his people to help us, but my team will be in charge."

"Thanks, Dan," Elliott said, "I owe you one, partner."

"No problem, Bob, I'll wait for your call before I turn them loose."

As soon as Agent Elliott ended the call Lisa fired a series of questions.

"How good are these deputies, Bob?"

"I've known Dan Barker for ten years, Lisa," Elliott replied, "He wouldn't send us anyone who wasn't experienced at handling search warrants."

"That's good," Lisa continued, "twelve gives us one for each storage site. You and I can handle the house."

"Once we tell McNeely that we have the search warrants we have to start the searches right away, before he has time to hide or destroy any evidence." Elliott said.

Just then Lisa received a call from JoJo. She spoke briefly and ended the call.

"JoJo says they found a Hewlett Packard Laser Jet 3500 printer in Cary Garnet's office in Ft. Lauderdale."

"That's great!"

"They checked something called the cache, c-a-c-h-e."

"I know what cache is, Lisa," Bob Elliott laughed.

"They were looking for any evidence that Cary sent that letter to Janet Bannister," Lisa replied, "but the cache was erased two weeks ago."

"How convenient!"

"We need to make sure that we check the cache if we find one of those printers anywhere today."

"Absolutely!" Elliott replied.

"Good, what else are we looking for?"

"I told them to search for weapons, of course, although I can't imagine they would be dumb enough to keep the murder weapon for twenty-four years. And then we want them to search for any documents, emails, or messages that would link McNeely to anyone from the Dreamland group, or to John Bannister, Janet Bannister, Sidney Schwartz, or even that Mr. Black character."

"JoJo just texted me a list of Dreamland sales people."

"Okay, text it to me and I'll forward it to the Captain when we get there. He'll make a copy for each of the deputies."

"Done. How about financial transactions, Bob?"

"They're gonna be looking for any trail, paper or electronic, that would connect McNeely with any foreign bank accounts, payments of the tax bill on the warehouse in Port St. Lucie, or payments to the Bannisters. And finally, I asked them to look for information about when each storage facility was purchased and where the money came from to buy it."

"That's a pretty comprehensive search plan, Bob."

"Oh, and one more thing," Elliott replied, "I asked them to look for copies of the photos that Bannister took."

As their car approached the entrance to Bonita Country Club Estates Lisa was impressed by the huge fountains that greeted each car as it entered. Elliott stopped the car at the guard house and showed both badges to the guard on duty. He directed them to the home of Adam McNeely and his wife, Barbara.

"Wow!" Lisa said as they pulled up beside the McNeelys' Mansion. "We've got some big houses in Port St. Lucie, but nothing like this!"

"This is basically Naples, Lisa," Bob Elliott replied. "It's a whole different world over here."

Agent Elliott rang the doorbell and, in a few seconds, the large solid wood door was open.

"Hi, I'm Barbara," the woman said. "You must be from the FBI. Come in please."

Barbara McNeely was a small, very attractive brunette with a big smile. She appeared to be in her late forties.

Lisa and Bob entered the house and sat in the living room.

"Adam just sent me a text," Barbara said, "He just finished his round of golf and he's on his way home. Sorry to make you wait for him."

"No problem," Lisa said, "we're actually a few minutes early."

"You must be hungry," Barbara said, "let me get you a little something."

Just then two teenage girls walked into the house. "Mom, I'm starving!" The older one yelled. She stopped in her tracks when she notice Lisa and Bob. "Oh, I'm sorry!" she said.

Lisa laughed. "No need to apologize," she said, "I raised a teenager too."

"I'm Becca," the older sister said, "and this is my sister, Emily."

"Pleased to meet you girls. I'm Lisa, and this is Bob."

The girls headed for the kitchen just as Adam McNeely entered the house. He was a tall man, tanned and toned, like a man who enjoyed his wealth and privilege. He immediately thrust out his hand to the two agents,

"How can I help you folks today?" Adam said with a warm smile.

Lisa began. "Thanks for meeting us today, Mr. McNeely."

"Adam, please."

"Okay, Adam," she continued, "we are investigating a murder that took place over twenty years ago in Port St. Lucie."

"That's on the East coast isn't it?" Adam replied.

"Yes," Elliott responded, "It's fifty miles north of West Palm Beach."

"On February 3, 1995 a man named Jimmy Foster was shot to death inside an empty warehouse on Federal Highway in Port St. Lucie."

"Jimmy Foster?" Adam pondered for a moment. "Never heard of him."

"Well, Adam, it seems we have a problem with that," Elliott said, "you see, we have an eye witness who saw you march Jimmy Foster into the building at gunpoint and then heard a gunshot. Then he saw you drive away in Jimmy's car."

Adam McNeely grinned. "You're kidding, right?" he said, still smiling. "This is some kind of joke, isn't it? I bet Paul Abernathy put you guys up to this, that son of a bitch!"

Bob Elliott was stoic, with not even a hint of a smile on his face.

"Come on guys, really?" Adam pleaded, "you don't really think I killed a man twenty years ago, do you? This has to be a joke. I never even heard of this guy!"

"Where did you live in 1995, Mr. McNeely?"

"West Palm Beach."

Just then Barbara McNeely came back from the kitchen with a pitcher of iced tea and a plate of cookies.

"Not now Barbara, please!" Adam said, with a look that told her she needed to leave the room, which she did.

"Seriously, I am not, nor have I have ever been, the kind of person who could kill someone. I've never even owned a gun, for God's sake!"

Adam was sounding pretty convincing, Lisa thought. He's either a great actor or we've got the wrong man.

Agent Elliott was not convinced.

"Adam, do you have any foreign bank accounts? We're gonna need those account numbers."

McNeely paused for a few seconds. "Ah, yes I do, but what has that got to do with this?"

"Actually," Elliott replied, removing the search warrants from his briefcase, "we have warrants to review all of your bank accounts and to search your entire house and each of the offices of your twelve self storage facilities."

"What?" McNeely shouted, "this is outrageous! I'm a law abiding citizen and you think you can just come in here and tear apart my home, my bank accounts, and my businesses?'"

"I'm sorry for the inconvenience, sir," Lisa replied, "but these warrants were signed by a judge. We'll try to disturb your life as little as possible, but the searches will be completed."

"I'm gonna call my lawyer!"

"Feel free to do so, Mr. McNeely," Elliott replied coldly, "a group of deputies from the Lee County Sheriff's department will be conducting the searches. They will identify themselves before they begin."

"I will ask you and your family to vacate this house for the next several hours," Lisa added, "and we'll contact you when it's okay to return."

"And please do not try to speak to your employees at the self storage facilities until after the search is completed."

Bob Elliott called Captain Barker and the searches began.

As they watched the McNeely family vacate their home in disbelief, Lisa wasn't sure. They seem like such nice people, she thought, I hope we've got the wrong guy.

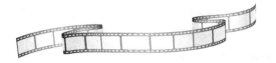

CHAPTER 49

"Dan Barker says this is the best steakhouse in Fort Myers," Bob Elliott said, "by the way how's your room, Lisa?"

"A room is a room, Bob," Lisa replied. She was sitting opposite him in a booth near the front of the restaurant.

"Captain Davis refuses to sit near the front of a restaurant," Lisa said, "he likes to be in the back, up against the wall. He says it's safer that way."

"Yeah," Elliot replied, "we've got a few agents like that, too. They're afraid someone's gonna sneak up behind them."

"Obviously, you're not."

"I think they've all seen too many cop shows on TV!"

"So, this is a steak house?" Lisa asked

"You a steak eater?" Elliot replied.

"Not my favorite, Bob, to be honest."

"You're not one of those vegan people are you, Lisa?"

"No," Lisa chuckled, "just not a fan of red meat. I'll order the salmon."

"Well, that was five hours of my life I'll never get back!" Bob said with a grin.

"Nothing to show for it," Lisa replied, "but let's hope one of the deputies found something at a storage site. The captain is bringing them all together in his office at eight tomorrow to show us what they found."

"I guess, when you think about it," Elliot said, "McNeely would have to be real dumb to keep anything incriminating in his house, especially when he's got an endless supply of storage space to hide stuff."

"The key to solving this case could rest in the McNeelys' foreign bank account," Elliot said. "Once we tap into that I think we'll learn a lot about the McNeelys."

Just then a couple walked into the restaurant, passed by the table where Lisa and Bob were sitting, and proceeded to the back of the restaurant, where they sat at the bar.

"I did get one thing that might help us, though," Lisa said, "I found a wedding photo of Adam and Barbara McNeely. I want Gus Haney to compare that photo to the one that was taken the night of the murder."

"Huh?"

"I said I found a wedding photo," Lisa said, "You obviously weren't listening."

"Sorry, Lisa," Elliott replied, "I was watching the man who just walked in."

"You know him?"

"Lisa," Bob whispered, "I think that guy is Ralph Stanley Hartong."

"Hartong? Who's that?"

"I think he's the Ralph Hartong that's on the FBI's ten most wanted list!"

"What did he do?"

"Hartong robbed a bank in El Paso in 2016," Bob replied, "and he killed two people in the process."

"How'd he get away, Bob?"

"That I don't know."

"And you're sure that's him?"

"I'm ninety percent sure, Lisa."

Bob grabbed his cellphone and called Dan Barker.

"Sorry to bother you again, Dan, but I'm at Adams Steakhouse on Griffin Parkway. I think I'm sitting close to a fugitive. I need backup right away."

"We're on our way, Bob."

"And Dan, come in heavy!"

Bob and Lisa sat at their table waiting for the sheriff to arrive. Two minutes later they watched as the bartender handed a bag of takeout food to the man. The man examined the contents of the bag, then he and woman got up and walked toward the front door of the restaurant.

Bob reached for his gun. As the couple reached the door Lisa yelled "excuse me!"

The couple stopped short of the exit and the man said, "did you want something?"

"I think you left something at the bar!" Lisa replied.

The woman stood by the door as the man walked back toward the bar. He spoke to the bartender, looked around, and walked back toward the door. On his way past he gave a menacing look to Lisa.

Lisa grabbed her gun and waited two seconds for the signal from Bob. They walked quickly toward the door and followed the couple outside.

"Ralph Hartong," agent Elliott yelled, his gun drawn and pointed, "you're under arrest. Get on the ground now!"

The man looked behind him at Lisa and Bob. He turned and began to flee, running right into the arms of two deputies who had just arrived on the scene. Lisa cuffed the woman and took her to one of the awaiting cars.

A minute later Captain Barker arrived at the scene. He read both their rights and carted them off to the Lee County jail for booking.

"That was great work in there, agent March!" Elliott said.

"You amaze me, Bob!" Lisa replied.

As they walked back into the restaurant several diners and waiters stood and applauded them. They both smiled sheepishly, acknowledged the crowd, and sat back at their table.

"I'm starving!" Lisa said with a grin.

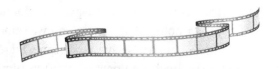

CHAPTER 50

JANUARY 11, 2019, 9:00 AM

PORT ST. LUCIE POLICE HEADQUARTERS

"Welcome back, stranger," Captain Davis said. "what's the latest on the skull case?"

Lisa leaned back in her chair. She was happy to be back home and back, at least for a while, working with JoJo Worthington and William Sales.

"Did forensics find anything at the crime scene, Jo?" she asked.

"They found traces of blood underneath all the dust," JoJo replied, "and they sent a sample to our DNA lab to see if it matches Jimmy Foster's DNA."

"My guess is that it'll be a match," Will said, "and that'll confirm that this was the murder scene."

"Which makes those Bannister photos truly valid," JoJo added.

"Anything else?" Lisa asked.

"They also found a casing from a Glock 17."

"Bannister's wife gave us his gun," Lisa said, "I remember it was a Glock 17!"

"That's good evidence but you know they can't trace a shell casing to a particular gun," Captain Davis offered, "only a bullet can be traced."

"Yeah," JoJo replied, "but it sure is a coincidence that the gun Bannister owned and the gun that apparently killed Jimmy Foster are the same brand and caliber."

"How did you make out on the West Coast the past two days, Lisa?" the captain asked.

"We completely struck out with our suspect in Bonita Springs," Lisa said, "over seventy man-hours of searching and we came up empty handed. Nothing that links Adam McNeely to the crime. I'll tell you, this was a nice family and I was actually hoping it wouldn't be him!"

"Were you able to link McNeely to the Dreamland money in any way?" Will asked.

"Good question," Lisa replied, "the FBI experts found McNeely's foreign bank account. It's in the Cayman Islands and they're reviewing it now. They've already discovered that the McNeelys got the money to build all of their self storage facilities from that account."

"That sounds pretty suspicious to me," JoJo said.

"Me too, Jo. It was nine million bucks, but there's no way to prove that was the Dreamland money."

"True," JoJo replied, "but it also gives the McNeelys a lot of explaining to do!"

"We're still looking at that account to learn about all the transactions the McNeelys used it for."

"I always thought it was impossible to get information about Cayman bank accounts," JoJo said.

"That's what I always thought too, Jo," Lisa replied, "I guess it isn't easy, but we did it last year on the Pickleball murder case."

"Hey, I heard you guys had a little excitement in a restaurant the other night!" Captain Davis said.

"I guess you could say so," Lisa replied, "we captured someone on the FBI's ten most wanted list."

"You did that, Lisa?" JoJo asked with excitement.

"Bob Elliott is amazing," Lisa responded, "he picked the guy out from memory and it turned out we was absolutely right!"

"You've got a commendation coming from the Chief, Lisa," Captain Davis said with a smile.

"Wait till my dad learns that I'm replacing you," Will grinned. "Talk about some big shoes to fill!"

"Size five and a half, Will," Lisa joked, "not so big."

"We're all proud of you Lisa," JoJo said, "and we're all gonna miss you."

"And believe me," Lisa replied softly, "I'll miss you all too!"

"Okay," Captain Davis said, "let's put this love fest on hold and get back to the case. This is starting to sound like the last scene in the Wizard of Oz!"

"Did they find any Hewlett Packard Laser Jet 3500 printers over there?" Will asked.

"Not a one, Will."

"And nothing that can help us link this guy to Jimmy Foster?" JoJo asked.

"You know those tee shirts that say, 'my parents went to Disney and all I got was this tee shirt'?" Lisa asked with a grin.

"I actually got one of those!" Will grinned.

"Well," Lisa said, as she showed the wedding photo to her colleagues, "you could say 'my partner went to Bonita Springs and all I got was this crummy wedding photo'!"

"Why'd you walk away with that, Lisa?" Captain Davis asked.

"I took two photos, actually," Lisa replied, "and agent Elliott took one of them back to his lab in Melbourne. We want to see if McNeely really matches the photo from the night of the murder. This photo show him much closer to the age he was when Jimmy was killed."

JoJo took the wedding photo and examined it carefully.

"I'll be darned!" she exclaimed.

"What is it, Jo?" Lisa asked.

"Is this Adam McNeely's wife?" she asked.

"Yes," Lisa replied, "her name is Barbara."

"What was her name before she married McNeely?"

Lisa checked her notes. "Winters," she said, "Barbara Winters."

"What do we know about her?"

"Nothing really," Lisa asked, "why?"

JoJo reached into her folder and removed the group photo that Cary Garnet had given her. She looked back and forth between the wedding photo and the group photo several times before she finally spoke,

"Take a look at the woman on the far right, front row," she said.

Lisa examined both photos for a moment.

"You think?" she said.

"This is Becca Raymond," JoJo said, pointing to the group photo, "Cary Garnet gave us her name."

"Garnet told us that she was their best sales associate," Will added, "and he also told us that she spent a night in a hotel room with Jimmy Foster."

"Look at the two women," JoJo said, "one's a brunette and one's a blonde, but I'm guessing that Becca Raymond and Barbara Winters are the same person!"

Lisa looked at the photos. "If that's true then we're back to Adam McNeely being the shooter."

"We've got a lot more work to do, folks!" Captain Davis said.

As the three detectives exited Captain Davis' office, Lisa called Agent Elliott in Melbourne.

"Bob, did you get a chance to show that wedding picture to Gus Haney?"

"Not yet," Elliott replied, "he's on another project but he promised me he'll get to it this afternoon."

"Okay, listen, I've got a group photo that was taken the night Foster disappeared," Lisa said, "it shows all of the Dreamland sales people."

"Uh huh."

"Bob, we think one of these sales people is Barbara McNeely."

"Holy shit," Bob exclaimed, "really?"

"We need Gus and his magical computer to confirm it," Lisa said, "can I scan the photo and send it to you?"

"Do it now, Lisa. I'll get Gus working on it this afternoon when he does the wedding photo."

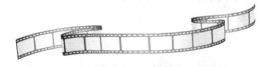

CHAPTER 51

JANUARY 11, 2019, 7:00 PM
THE HOME OF LISA AND RICK MARCH

"This is great pie," Ernie Goodman said.

"Lemon meringue was always your favorite, Dad!" Lisa replied with a warm smile.

"He's pre type 2 diabetes, Lisa," Gloria Goodman said knowingly, "I hope you made it sugar free."

"Light sugar, Mom," Lisa replied as she winked at her father, "very light sugar!"

"So, what's the latest on the Jimmy Foster case, Lise?" Ernie asked.

"We think we know the shooter, Dad," Lisa replied, "and possibly the person who set the whole thing up."

"Great!" Ernie said with a grin, "any chance you can get me my money back?"

"I wish, Dad. Right now I'm not sure we even have enough evidence to arrest them!"

"Lise," Ernie said, "have you have heard of something called Occam's Razor?"

"Occam's Razor?" Lisa replied, "Never heard of it."

"Apparently, hundreds of years ago, there was this philosopher named Occam, and he said that whenever there are several possible solutions to a problem then the simplest one is most often the correct one."

"Thanks, Dad. I'll keep that in mind."

"So, what's the working theory?"

"A woman named Becca Raymond is selling houses at Jimmy Foster's Dreamland Estates."

"Okay."

"She and Jimmy spend a night together, and while he's sleeping, she sneaks into his briefcase and gets the information for his two accounts. All she needs to steal the money is the password."

"Two accounts?"

"One was for the money the bank loaned Jimmy. That's the money he gambled away."

"How much?"

"Twelve million!"

"Ouch!"

"The second account had the eighteen million collected from buyers like you and Mom."

"They told us that money would be in escrow," Ernie said.

"It was," Lisa replied, "but we think Becca and her boyfriend, a guy named McNeely, abducted Jimmy at gunpoint and forced him to give them the password so they could steal all the money out of the escrow account."

"And then they killed Foster?" Ernie asked.

"We think they killed Jimmy and buried his body, so it looked like he ran away with the money."

"Sounds like a good plan to me!" Ernie said.

Just then Lisa's cellphone buzzed.

"Got some good news for me, Bob?" she said.

"Oh, I've got more than that, partner!" Bob replied. He paused for a moment.

"Are you gonna make me beg?" Lisa pleaded.

"Okay," Bob replied, "here goes. Number one, the man in the wedding photo and the man in the Bannister photo from the crime scene are one in the same."

"For sure?"

"One hundred percent sure, Lisa. McNeely is our man!"

"Okay, what's number two?"

"Number two, the woman in the wedding photo and the woman in the group photo you sent me are the same person!"

"One hundred percent again?"

"A hundred percent!"

"So that means Barbara McNeely was Becca Raymond."

"Wait, there's more!" Bob said.

"I'm all ears, partner!"

"Rebecca Lee Raymond was born on February 17, 1972 in North Lauderdale, Florida. She graduated from North Lauderdale High School in 1990. Then she studied at Lynn University from September,1990 through May, 1994. She received a degree in business and marketing."

"Anything on Barbara Winters?"

"Barbara Jane Winters was born on June 3, 1971 in North Hollywood Florida."

"A coincidence?" Lisa asked, "I don't think so!"

"Here's where it gets very interesting," Bob continued, "Barbara Winters drowned in a swimming pool accident in August, 1977 at the age of six."

"Wow!"

"Are you ready for the best part?"

"Hit me!"

"In May of 1995 Barbara Jane Winters applied for a passport. We brought the photo up on our screen and, presto change-o, the old Rebecca Raymond is new Barbara Winters!"

"Then Barbara Winters marries Adam McNeely." Lisa said.

"Yep. They tied the knot on July 22, 1999."

"So then, what happened to Rebecca Raymond?"

"She vanished, Lisa, completely off the radar screen."

"No travel?"

"No travel, no credit cards, no banks, no nothing!"

"Wow, Bob," Lisa said, "I think we've definitely got enough to charge the McNeelys with identity theft, fraud and embezzlement, if nothing else. Remember, we've got proof that they built all twelve self storage facilities with nine million dollars cash, and that money came from their Cayman bank account."

"No doubt we could nail them for fraud and embezzlement, but murder is another story. I think you should talk to your local prosecutors and see what they think."

"Hey thanks, Bob. You're wonderful!"

"Believe it or not, Lisa, there's more!" Bob said.

"More, what more?" Lisa asked.

"We were able to look at the two accounts," Bob said, "the loan account and the escrow account. We were able to see that the entire eighteen million was taken out of the escrow account on February 3, 1995."

"Just as we thought," Lisa repaid.

"Here's the interesting part," Bob continued, "exactly one million, forty-six thousand dollars was transferred from the escrow account to the loan account."

"So that covered all of the commission checks for the sales people!" Lisa said, "any idea who did it?"

"That could have been Jimmy Foster's doing, we really don't know," Elliott replied, "but we do know that, after that transfer, the rest of the escrow money was deposited into the McNeelys' Cayman Bank account."

"Anything else for me, Bob?"

"We're certain now that Bannister was blackmailing the McNeelys."

"Really? How do we know that?"

"We found a convoluted transfer trail every month that took ten thousand dollars from the McNeelys' Cayman account and sent it to a Cayman based corporation called RLR Limited."

"RLR, as in Rebecca Lee Raymond?" Lisa said.

"Never thought of that, Lisa!"

"You see, Bob, we make a good team!"

"RLR Limited was a shell corporation that sent the ten thousand each month to another company called Sandpiper," Elliot continued, "and guess who's the sole proprietor of the Sandpiper Company?

"John Bannister?"

"Close, but it's actually Janet Bannister."

"I don't know how to thank you, Bob," Lisa said, "You are truly amazing!"

"Do me a favor, Lisa."

"What's that, Bob?"

"Close this case and get your ass up here. We need you!"

Lisa smiled as she ended the call.

"Dad, have I got a story for you!"

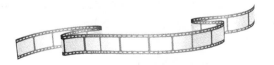

CHAPTER 52

Megan Harris was a five year veteran of the state's attorneys office. Having worked with her on previous cases, Lisa had all the confidence in the world that Megan would be a good working partner on this case.

For fifteen minutes Megan listened as Lisa methodically presented all of the evidence she and JoJo had collected to date.

"So, that's what we've got so far, Megan," Lisa concluded, "JoJo, do you have anything more to add?"

"Just a couple of things," JoJo said, "the letter that was sent to us that supposedly was a confession from John Bannister turned out to be fake. We know that now."

"And we know that it was printed on a Hewlett Packard Laser Jet 3500," Will added.

"And we found that exact model printer in the real estate office of Cary Garnet and Jeffrey Schwartz."

"From what you told me, it sounds like Cary Garnet had a very good motive to kill Jimmy Foster," Megan commented, "it looks like he lived happily ever after with both the wife and the kid."

"I agree," Lisa replied, "but he has a solid alibi. The police verified it back in '95. Cary was with Jimmy's wife and her father all weekend, and we having nothing to prove that he ever had contact with the McNeelys."

"Okay," Megan said, "here's what I think. We can bring in the McNeelys and book them for embezzlement. I'm confident we can get an indictment on that count. We can't go for identity theft because the statute of limitations has run out."

"What about murder?" JoJo asked.

"Not without more evidence, I'm afraid."

"What about the things John Bannister saw and heard that night and the next night when they moved the body?" Will asked.

"Bannister is dead," Megan replied, "so that makes it all hearsay. No judge would ever admit that as evidence in a trial."

"We do have the photos of McNeely forcing Jimmy into the warehouse, though," JoJo said, "can you add kidnapping to the charges?"

Megan looked at the photos carefully. She showed them to Lisa, JoJo, and Will.

"What do you see?" she asked.

"I see Adam McNeely forcing Jimmy Foster to go into the warehouse." JoJo said.

"Forcing?" Megan asked, "how do you know that? Do you see a gun?"

"Actually, no," Will replied, 'it just looks like two guys walking into the building."

"Bingo!" Megan said, "you'd never get a kidnapping conviction based on these photos."

"But the gunshot was heard later..." Lisa said.

"By who?" Megan snapped back, "by Bannister? The dead guy?"

"The forensics team found traces of Jimmy Foster's blood in the warehouse."

"That proves only one thing," Megan said, "at one time, and we don't know when, Jimmy Foster was in a building, owned by him, and he bled a little. It doesn't prove murder and it certainly doesn't prove who did it. You guys know better than that!"

"What about the Glock 17 shell casing?" Lisa asked, "what does that buy us?"

"Nothing," Megan replied, "not unless we can put that same gun in the hands of McNeely."

"This is frustrating," Lisa said, "it's been two months since Jimmy Foster's body was found. We're pretty certain we know who killed him and we're grasping at straws to prove it."

"Evidence is the only thing that matters, folks!" Megan replied. "We've got solid evidence to charge the McNeelys at least with embezzlement."

"We know that the wife worked for Foster and that she took on a new identity after Foster disappeared. Even though it's too late to charge her on that count I'm gonna surprise her with the fact that we know all about it."

"We can put the husband in the warehouse with Jimmy Foster the night he disappeared and the escrow money was transferred to a Cayman Bank account. We can show that the McNeelys got the seed money for their storage business from a Cayman Bank account and we can prove they were paying ten thousand a month to the Bannisters from that same account. I doubt that they have a good explanation for any of this."

"So, I guess you're saying…" JoJo began.

"I'm saying bring me the McNeelys with an embezzlement charge, and I'll offer them a plea deal on that charge only. Hopefully we can get them to make the buyers whole for what they lost."

"And maybe you can get them to come clean about the death of Jimmy Foster." Lisa said.

As the trio walked out of the office Lisa remembered, once again, why she had so much respect for Megan Harris. She grabbed her cellphone and called Bob Elliott in Melbourne.

"Hi Bob. We just met with the prosecutor. Can you get me the phone number for Captain Barker in the Lee County Sheriff's office?"

"Sure, Lisa, what's up?"

"We're gonna arrest Adam and Barbara McNeely, and I need his help to arrange to get them over here to Port St. Lucie."

"Great news, Lisa," Bob replied, "what's the charge?"

"Embezzlement, for now."

"Okay, I'll call Dan Barker and take care of it for you."

"Thanks a million, Bob!"

"Hey Lisa," Bob said, "did you happen to catch the name of the McNeelys' oldest daughter?"

"No," Lisa replied with a grin, "but I bet you did. So, what was her name?"

"Becca!"

"No!"

"Yes, Lisa, it was Becca."

"Another one of those coincidences, Bob?"

"I don't think so, Lisa."

As Lisa ended the call she said, "Bob Elliott is a detective living in a world we can only dream of, Jo. He sees and remembers things that go right over my head."

"Don't sell yourself short, partner," JoJo replied, "you do the same thing to me sometimes!"

"Bob's gonna have the McNeelys brought here for us, and he'll get the arrest warrant, too."

"He really wants to wrap this case up quickly," JoJo said, "doesn't he?"

"He says they need me in Melbourne," Lisa replied, "I'll start there on the first of the month as promised, but I'm not giving up on this case until we nail the people that killed Jimmy Foster!"

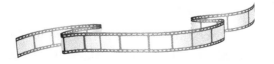

CHAPTER 53

JANUARY 25, 2019, 9:00 AM

PORT ST LUCIE POLICE DEPARTMENT

INTERVIEW ROOM 1

Lisa and Megan watched as Barbara and Adam McNeely were escorted into the room, along with their attorney, JD Treem. JoJo and Will sat in the outer room, watching the interview through a one way mirror window.

After introductions Megan Harris spoke first.

"Good morning Mr. Treem," she said with a smile, "it's nice to see you again!"

JD Treem returned Megan's smile. "The pleasure is all mine!" He replied.

JD Treem was well known throughout South Florida as the premier criminal defense attorney. Whenever a wealthy person was charged in a high profile case, JD Treem was the man they chose. JD was a grizzled veteran of forty years whose reputation was that he would do anything to win a case, regardless of whether it was ethical or not.

JD was a small man, no more than five foot-four, with a large crop of curly white hair. His signature dress was a suit with suspenders and a big

bow tie. Over the course of his career JD had defended wealthy social-
ites, politicians, TV stars, and even a United States Congressman. Any
prosecutor who faced JD Treem in court would have to work harder and
smarter than they ever had before, and most of them failed to live up to
the task.

Megan Harris wasn't the least bit intimidated by JD Treem, however.
She had faced off against Treem in the high profile Pickleball murder trial
last year, and she was more than confident she could do it again if this case
went to trial.

Based on her previous conversations with Treem about this case,
however, she was pretty certain that a trial would not be necessary.

"Mr. and Mrs. McNeely," Megan began, "You need to understand that
you are under arrest for the embezzlement of eighteen million dollars
from the bank account of Dreamland Limited in February of 1995. You
have been read your Miranda rights and you are here today with your
attorney. This interview will be recorded for future reference.

"We're very confident at this point that we have enough evidence to
convict you both and to have you sentenced to up to twenty years in
prison. We also believe that we have sufficient evidence to put you both
on trial for the kidnapping and murder of Jimmy Foster."

"Mr. Treem," Megan continued, "I assume that you have conferred
with your clients and that they fully understand the discussions you and I
have had over the last few days."

"Yes, they are fully aware," Treem replied, "and they have agreed to
plead guilty to the embezzlement charge against them and to repay eighteen million dollars plus an additional eighteen million dollars in interest
charges."

"Now, under the terms of the plea agreement," Megan responded,
"your clients will each receive prison sentences of five years, which will be
suspended if they cooperate fully with our investigation into the death of
Mr. Jimmy Foster. This agreement also requires truthful responses to all
of our questions."

"My clients have accepted this agreement, and will cooperate fully."
Treem replied.

"What did they just say?" Will asked in the observation room.

"It sounds like they agreed to plead guilty, Will."

"So, Mr. and Mrs. McNeely, do you both understand and accept the terms of this agreement?" Megan asked.

Both heads nodded.

"I'm sorry," Megan said, "I need you to affirm with the word yes."

"Yes," the McNeely couple said in unison.

"Go ahead and ask your questions, Ms. Harris." Treem said, "I can assure you that my clients will fully cooperate, as per our agreement."

"Okay." Megan said, as she opened her briefcase. She removed the group photo of the Dreamland sale associates and handed it to Barbara McNeely.

"Mrs. McNeely, do you recognize the woman on the far right in the front row?"

Barbara McNeely looked flustered when she saw the photo. After a brief pause she said, "Hmm, I can't say that I do."

"Well then, let me help you. Your birth name was Barbara Jean Winters, is that correct?"

"Yes, that is correct."

"And you were born on June 3, 1971 in North Lauderdale, Florida, yes?"

"Yes."

Megan reached into her briefcase and revealed a document from the FBI.

"It seems that Barbara Jean Winters from North Lauderdale, Florida drowned in a pool in 1977. That wasn't you now, was it Mrs. McNeely?

"No."

Another document came out of the briefcase. "And then in 1995 this same person, now alive, received this passport."

Barbara McNeely studied the passport.

"I'm sure you know who that is, don't you Mrs. McNeely?

"Yes, that's me," Barbara said stoically.

"Have you heard the name Rebecca Lee Raymond, Mrs. McNeely?"

At this point JD Treem jumped in.

"Don't answer that!" he yelled to his client, "what in the hell does any of this have to do with your murder case, Ms. Harris?"

"I think your clients both know the answer to that question, Mr. Treem," Megan said with a smirk, "I suggest you ask them."

"I would like a moment to confer with my clients" Treem said.

"Sure thing," Megan replied calmly, "we'll be in the room next door. Please have the guard come and get us when you're ready."

"I want another room to talk with my clients," Treem demanded, "One that's not bugged!"

Treem and the McNeelys were escorted to a private office as Megan and Lisa moved to the observation room to meet with JoJo and Will.

"It looks like they never told Treem who Barbara McNeely really was," JoJo said.

"That doesn't make them guilty of embezzlement or murder, though," Lisa said.

"No," Megan responded, "I just wanted to throw JD off his game by opening with that."

"So what's next?" Will asked.

"They might just clam up and refuse to talk," Megan replied, "but if they want this deal they have to talk. So we'll see what happens."

"You offered them a suspended sentence?" JoJo asked

"What we really want is the killer," Megan replied, "and, by getting them to pay back the money they stole, plus interest, we can return it to the people who were swindled out of their deposits."

"My dad will be happy about that!" Lisa said, "how did you get them to pay thirty-six million dollars?"

"They offered eighteen," Megan replied, "I wanted them to double it so I demanded they pay fifty million. We settled on thirty-six."

"Remind me to take you with me the next time I buy a car, Megan!" JoJo joked. "But, with a suspended sentence, it seems like the McNeelys are getting off easy here."

"Paying back all that money lets the McNeelys off the hook, for now," Megan replied, "but they'll both be convicted felons forever."

"And let's not forget, they also might be murderers!" Lisa added.

"That's the big prize," Megan added, "and if these two killed Foster they'll be charged and convicted, I can promise you that. This deal is only for the embezzlement charge."

"If those two can afford to pay back thirty-six million they must be loaded!" Will said.

"They're smart business people," Megan replied, "there's no doubt about that."

"According to the FBI they're worth over sixty million." Lisa added, "that's serious money, right Jo?"

"So, it looks like they're willing to give up more than half of it to stay out of prison," JoJo replied.

Several minutes later the signal came from Treem for Lisa and Megan to return to the interview room.

"I want you to know," Treem began, "that I advised my clients not to answer any more questions, however they insisted that they want to fully cooperate and answer your questions."

Back in the observation room JoJo spoke. "That sounds like a load of crap to me!"

"I also want to make sure," Treem continued, "that anything related to the change of my client's name is included in the plea deal."

"That's fine, Mr. Treem," Megan replied, "So, Mrs. McNeely, I will ask you again if you recognize the woman in this group photograph?"

"Yes, that's me," she replied in a whisper.

"Okay, thank you Mrs. McNeely," Megan continued, "as Rebecca Raymond, actually I think they called you Becca, is that correct?"

"Yes, it was Becca."

"Thank you. Now, as Becca Raymond, you were a sales associate for the Dreamland project owned by Jimmy Foster? Is that correct?"

"Yes, that's correct."

"And, at the time of your employment at Dreamland were you in a relationship with your current husband, Adam McNeely?"

"Yes, we were dating back then."

"And, on one occasion, did you spend a night in a hotel room with Mr. Jimmy Foster?"

Barbara McNeely looked at her husband. He nodded and she responded. "Yes, that's true."

"And, during that encounter, did you open Mr. Foster's briefcase and examine his financial documents, including his bank accounts?"

"Yes, I did."

"And, on the evening of February 3, 1995, did you meet Mr. Foster and Mr. McNeely at an empty warehouse in Port St. Lucie?"

"Yes, I did."

"And, on that occasion, did you force Mr. Foster to give you the passwords to his bank accounts?"

Once again Barbara looked at Mr. Treem. He nodded.

"Yes."

"And, did you then transfer money from the Dreamland escrow account into a Cayman Bank account in your name or your husband's name?"

"Yes, the account was in both of our names."

Megan shifted in her chair. "So, let me ask you this, Mrs. McNeely. There a was also a transfer of just over one million dollars made from the escrow account into the loan account. Did you make that deposit?"

For the first time since the interview began, Barbara McNeely became animated. "Look," she replied, "those sales associates worked very hard to sell houses for Jimmy Foster, and he gave them all commission checks that were worthless!"

"How did you know that, Mrs. McNeely?" Megan asked.

"When I was leaving the dinner that night, Jimmy asked me to spend the night with him," Barbara explained, "I said no, but as I was walking away I heard Cary Garnet say that there was no money in the account to cover the checks."

"So you put the money in the loan account to cover those checks?"

"I did, yes," Barbara said, "it was the least I could do for the sales team. Jimmy was gonna screw them out what was rightfully theirs."

"So, you moved the money to cover the commission checks."

"Originally, that was all I was gonna do, but then I saw that eighteen million sitting there and I just knew Jimmy was gonna blow all of it, so I decided to take it before he did!"

"You took it, Mrs. McNeely," Megan said, "and you could have returned it to the buyers. But instead you chose to keep it all for yourself, didn't you?"

Barbara pondered for a moment. "I guess that's true."

"So, just for the record," Megan said, "you transferred all of the money out of the escrow account, a little over one million of which went to the loan account to pay the sales commissions, and the rest went to a Cayman Bank account for your benefit. Is that correct Mrs. McNeely?"

"Yes, that's correct."

"Let's get back to the night of February 3, 1995, Mrs. McNeely," Megan said, "when you left the warehouse that night, was Jimmy Foster dead or alive?"

"He was alive. I swear he was alive!"

"And, Mr. McNeely remained in the warehouse with him when you left?"

Barbara looked at her husband. "Yes, he did."

"One final question, Mrs. McNeely. Do you know who killed Jimmy Foster."

"No!"

"Mrs. McNeely," Megan said, as she moved her face closer to Barbara, "I want you to think very carefully before you answer this question. Your plea agreement rests completely on the truthfulness of your answer. I will ask it one more time. Do you know who killed Jimmy Foster?"

"No, I do not know who killed Jimmy Foster," Barbara replied, "I have a suspicion but I don't know for certain who killed Jimmy."

"And your suspicion, who would that be?"

Barbara paused for a moment. She looked at JD Treem, and then she looked at her husband.

"I think he was killed by John Bannister."

"And what makes you say that?"

"Because I saw Bannister sneaking around the warehouse when I left."

"How did you know it was John Bannister?"

"I knew Bannister because I had met him before."

"When and how did you meet Bannister?"

"The night I spent at the hotel with Jimmy, Bannister was there. I guess he was spying on Jimmy."

"Did you speak to him that night?"

"Not that night, but the next morning, as I was leaving, he was there again. He took a picture of me leaving Jimmy's hotel room. So I asked him what he was doing and he said he was working for a divorce lawyer and he was documenting all of Jimmy's extra marital affairs."

"So, then you saw Bannister again outside the warehouse on February 3, 1995?"

"Yes, he was taking pictures again."

"So what makes you think he killed Jimmy?"

"Because Jimmy was alive when we left him, and he was dead after that, and Bannister was the only other person around, that's why!"

"Mrs. McNeely, why would you leave Jimmy Foster alive after you had just stolen all of his money?" Megan asked, "he was an eye witness to what you did!"

"Because we aren't murders, that's why!" Barbara said forcefully, "look, everybody knew Jimmy was a liar, a cheater, and a big time gambler. He stole the loan money and he would have taken the escrow money if we hadn't gotten to it first. Nobody was gonna believe that he didn't steal the escrow money too!"

Then Megan turned her attention to Adam McNeely. "Mr. McNeely, did you force Jimmy Foster at gunpoint to drive with you to the warehouse from the Breakers Hotel?"

"No, I've never owned a gun in my life."

"So then, how did you get Jimmy to drive you to the warehouse?"

McNeely thought for a moment and then spoke. "I told him Becca was waiting for him," Adam said, "so he was happy to go."

"So you're saying that Jimmy went to the warehouse voluntarily?"

"Yes, that's what I'm saying."

"Okay, Mr. McNeely," Megan responded, "so when you got to the warehouse how were you able to get Jimmy to give up the passwords you needed to transfer the money from his account?"

Adam paused, looked at JD Treem, and then replied. "We told Mr. Foster that we had his son, and if he didn't cooperate he would never see the son alive again."

"Was this true?"

"No, but he believed it."

"So tell me Mr. McNeely, why would a smart man like Jimmy Foster believe such a claim without demanding proof?"

"We had a photo of his son."

"Where did you get the photo?"

"It was in Jimmy's briefcase the night Barbara spent with him."

"So you showed Jimmy this photo and he believed you had his son?"

"He did."

"And so, based on that, and that alone, he gave you the passwords, correct?"

Before Adam could respond JD Treem spoke up. "I'd like another break to confer with my client."

Back in the observation room," JoJo said, "I think the guy is lying and his lawyer knows it."

"The plea deal depends on them telling the truth," Will replied.

Three minutes later, Treem and his clients were back in the room.

"Once again I need to clarify the terms of this plea agreement," Treem said.

"I think the terms are pretty clear, Mr. Treem."

"Look," Treem sad sternly, "my clients did not kill Jimmy Foster. That's the truth. So before we go any further with this interview I want to make sure that the plea deal and suspended sentence includes any activities that may have taken place regarding the transfer of assets from his bank account."

"That's my understanding, Mr. Treem," Megan replied, "but if we find out that either of your clients killed Foster there is no immunity from that. Do you understand?"

"That's fine," Treem said, "now, Mr. McNeely would like to amend his answers to your previous line of questioning. Go ahead, Adam."

Adam McNeely took a deep breath.

"I had a gun," he said, "but it wasn't even loaded. I just used it to scare Jimmy."

"So you were waiting for him with the gun when he entered his car at the Breakers?"

"The unloaded gun." JD Treem intervened. "This was not a kidnapping."

"Oh, it most certainly was a kidnapping, Mr. Treem," Megan shot back, "but don't worry, we're not gonna charge your clients for that if they cooperate fully and tell the truth."

Back in the observation room Will asked, "I wonder why they're arguing about whether it was considered kidnapping or not?"

"Kidnapping could be a separate charge from embezzlement," JoJo replied, "and I believe there's no statute of limitations on that."

"So the lawyer wanted to make sure that any kidnapping charge would be included in the suspended sentence deal," Will said, "remind me, if I ever need a lawyer, to call this guy!"

"We'd all better hope we never need the services of JD Treem!" JoJo replied with a grin.

Back in the interview room Megan continued with her questions.

"Then you used the gun to threaten Jimmy so he would give up the passwords, correct?" Megan said.

"Yes, that's correct," McNeely replied.

"And what did you do with Mr. Foster after you stole the money?"

"Barbara left the warehouse and drove away in a rental car," Adam replied, "and I stayed behind for a few minutes."

"What did you do then?"

"I took Jimmy's phone away from him and took his car keys. Then I showed him the photo of his son, and I told him if he accused us of this we would kill the boy. He swore he wouldn't say a word about us."

"Then you left?"

"I grabbed the computer off the desk and drove away in Jimmy's car."

"So, where did you leave Jimmy's car?"

"I met Barbara in the long term parking lot, and that's where we left Jimmy's car."

"Okay then, Mr. and Mrs. McNeely," Megan said, "let me recap what you've told me. You readily admit that you embezzled all of the money from the Dreamland escrow account, except for a small amount that you placed into the loan account to cover the commission checks."

"But they did not kill Jimmy Foster," Treem proclaimed, "he was alive when they left him that night."

"So noted," Megan replied, "I have a few more questions for your clients."

"Okay."

"Mr. and Mrs. McNeely, shortly after Jimmy Foster's body was found the police received copies of photos that John Bannister apparently took of Jimmy's dead body inside the warehouse."

"So you have your killer!" Treem said, "and Barbara was right."

"Actually, Mr. Treem," Megan replied, "We later also received the photos of Mr. McNeely leading Mr. Foster into the warehouse that night."

"So what?" Treem replied, "my clients have admitted to that."

"Mrs. Bannister claims that her husband was blackmailing someone with those photos and that she was receiving a substantial payment each month to keep them silent."

"Mr. McNeely, is this you in the photo?"

Megan handed the photo to Adam. He glanced at it briefly. "Yes, that's me."

"Is this the first time you've ever seen this photo, Mr. McNeely?"

McNeely paused for a moment, looked at his attorney, and answered. "No, it's not."

"We know that, Mr. McNeely," Megan replied, "and we also know that you have been paying Janet Bannister ten thousand dollars a month through your Cayman bank account for twenty-four years. That's also true isn't it, Adam?"

"Yes, it's true," Adam replied meekly.

"So let me ask you this, Mr. McNeely," Megan said, "why would you agree to pay Janet Bannister every month if you didn't kill Jimmy Foster?"

At this point JD Treem spoke. "Look, Ms. Harris, paying blackmail money to someone is not a crime. The Bannisters are the ones who were committing a crime by blackmailing my clients."

"I get that, Mr. Treem," Megan replied calmly, "but paying a blackmailer is also as close to an admission of guilt as you can get."

"Yes, it is," Treem shot back, "and my clients have admitted to the crime of embezzlement. They're not murderers, Bannister was!"

"Okay, somebody has been paying the taxes on the empty warehouse for all these years from a Swiss bank account," Megan added, "was that you, Mr. McNeely?"

"No, that wasn't me!" McNeely pleaded, "I don't have a Swiss bank account, I swear!"

"We'll see about that, Mr. McNeely," Megan replied calmly, "now you're both free to go. Mr. Treem and I will work out the final details of your plea agreement."

CHAPTER 54

JANUARY 27, 2019, 7:00 PM

SAILORS RETREAT RESTAURANT

STUART, FLORIDA

It had been seven months since Lisa and Rick last had dinner with Megan Harris and her then fiancé, Ed Borden. A lot had happened since the last time the couples dined together. The Pickleball murder case had closed and Megan and Ed had been married in a small ceremony in her hometown of Columbia, Maryland.

"It's great to see you guys again," Lisa said, as Megan and Ed walked in to join them at their table. The newlyweds made a beautiful couple, both tall, mid thirties, sandy blond hair. They look like a real life Ken and Barbie, Lisa thought. This evening they were dressed in matching floral blue and gold outfits. Ed's shirt was the same pattern as Megan's dress.

"I see you guys are still dressing alike" Lisa laughed, "how cute!"

"What can I say," Megan replied, "Eddie buys shirts to match my dresses."

"I still tell people we're twins!" Ed said with a grin, "they love it!"

"Oh my," Lisa said, "here comes JoJo. Wait till she sees you guys!"

Just then JoJo and her husband, Stuart walked up to the table. JoJo was wearing a cranberry and gold dress, gold hat, gold boots, and she was carrying a gold stagecoach shaped handbag. Stu was wearing a solid cranberry sweater to match his wife.

"Oh my God!" Lisa laughed, "you too!"

Megan and Ed stood to introduce themselves to Stuart. No sooner did they stand than JoJo notice their matching outfits.

"I love it, you guys! You look fantastic!"

"I'm so glad we all got a chance to do this," Megan said, as she sat back down in her chair.

"Stu," Lisa said, "Megan has been working with JoJo and me on the Jimmy Foster case."

"We're hoping to put somebody away for killing Jimmy," Megan added.

"We just haven't quite figured out who that is yet!" JoJo mused.

"Oh, I'm sorry," Stu said with a grin, "I thought you guys had zeroed in on Colonel Mustard!

"In the dining room!" Rick added.

"With the lead pipe!" all three husbands shouted in unison.

"You guys are a hoot," Lisa said with dripping sarcasm, "I'm so happy that you're able to amuse each other so well!"

"Seriously, though," Ed said,"isn't this a fantastic restaurant?"

"It certainly is," Rick replied, "I love the view of the boats, and right here in Stuart."

"Hey, did you guys know that my hubby was named after this town?" JoJo said with a grin.

"Really?" Megan asked, "why did your mother choose Stuart, Stuart?" She laughed at the phrasing of her own question.

"My parents used to ride their bikes around here and my mom just liked the name Stuart, so she gave it to me," Stuart explained.

"And it's a good thing the town changed its name to Stuart," JoJo added, "it used to be called Potsdam!"

"I kind of like that name!" Stuart chuckled, "Potsdam Worthington."

"Sounds like an English Duke!" Ed said with a grin, "Sir Potsdam Worthington, Viscount of Essex. I can hear the trumpets playing!"

"And for short they would've called you Potsie!" Rick added.

"What happy days those would have been!" Stuart said with a belly laugh.

The server came and took their drink orders, and, as soon as he left the conversation shifted gears.

"Hey, Lisa," Ed said. "Megan tells me you're gonna become an FBI agent. Congratulations!"

"Thanks Ed," Lisa replied, "Yes, I'll be moving up to Melbourne as soon as we close this case. That's where the field office is located."

"So, Lisa," Stuart asked, "do you think you'll ever have to go under cover to solve a case?"

Lisa pondered for a few seconds. This seemed like a ridiculous question, she thought, but then again, Stu must have had a reason to ask. "I suppose that might happen," she replied, "why do you ask?"

"So, what name would you pick for yourself if you had to make one up?" Stu continued.

"To be honest, Stu, I really hadn't given it any thought."

"I heard you're supposed to take your first pet's name and the name of the street you lived on as a kid," Ed said with a grin, "mine's Fluffy Faulkner."

"No," Rick replied, "that's supposed to be your porn star name!"

"I'm not sure why my husband knows that," Lisa said with a smile, "but I like my name just the way it is, Lisa March."

"March," Stu said, "how about you pick another month for your last name?"

"Like what?" Lisa asked.

Stuart thought for a moment and replied, "how about November? That's the month I was born."

"Lisa November?" Lisa laughed, "I don't think so Stu. Maybe I could be Lisa May, but not Lisa November!"

"I know you ladies don't wanna talk shop when you're out with your dashing and charming husbands," Rick said, "but I wanted to let you know that my law firm has been in contact with all of the Dreamland buyers we can find. We're gonna represent them and get their deposits back, with interest, from the McNeelys' thirty-six million."

"One of them is my parents." Lisa added, "and I contacted the FBI to see if we could track down every buyer, even the ones Rick's firm can't reach."

"I imagine some of them may be dead after twenty-four years," Ed said, "wasn't it a senior community?"

"Fifty-five plus," JoJo replied, "so these people will be in their eighties and nineties by now."

"I suppose they have beneficiaries who would qualify to receive the money if they're no longer alive," Ed said.

"That's where it gets a little bit tricky," Rick commented, "but my firm can help them navigate those waters."

The server returned with the drinks.

"So," Stuart asked, "how close are you to nailing the killers?"

"Didn't you tell me you decided that the McNeelys killed Jimmy Foster, Lisa?" Rick asked.

"At one time we were pretty certain they were the killers," Lisa responded quickly.

"But now we're not sure if they did it." JoJo added.

"So, who's next on the list of suspects?" Stuart asked.

"I think there's a strong possibility a private detective named John Bannister was the shooter, and I believe he was paid to do it by Cary Garnet," JoJo replied.

"Cary Grant?" Stu chimed in.

"Garnet," Lisa shot back, "he was the Dreamland sales manager who fathered a child with Jimmy Foster's wife, and then ended up marrying her after Jimmy disappeared."

"Whew!" Ed said, "that sounds like an episode of Days of Our Lives!"

"Oh, are you a soap opera fan, Ed?" JoJo asked with a grin.

"No, but my mother was," Ed replied, "All My Children was her favorite. She had a party when Susan Lucci finally won an Emmy award."

"One of the reasons we think Cary Garnet is good for the murder," Lisa said, ignoring the soap opera discussion, "is that we got a letter in the mail that was supposedly a confession from John Bannister. It said he was paid to kill Jimmy Foster by Sidney Schwartz."

"Who's Sidney Schwartz?" Ed asked.

"Sidney Schwartz was Jimmy Foster's father-in-law. He's ninety-two years old now and he lives in a nursing home." JoJo replied.

"He has Alzheimer's so bad he can't remember a thing," Lisa added.

"According to the FBI, Bannister's confession letter was a fake," JoJo continued, "turns out it was printed on a Laser Jet 3500, or something like that, and it wasn't printed until long after John Bannister died."

"And we found that exact model in Cary Garnet's office in Fort Lauderdale," JoJo explained, "but the cache was dumped so we couldn't prove anything."

"I'm familiar with that model," Stuart said, "Hewlett Packard, right?"

"You know about these things, Stuart?" Megan asked.

Stuart smiled. "I run the IT Department at my company," he replied, "we're loaded with HP products."

"And I didn't even know what cache was, Stu!" JoJo laughed, "we need to communicate better, honey bunny!" She smiled and rubbed her husband's arm.

"If the cache was erased you can still find out if that printer was used to print the document you're looking for," Stu said.

"How do we do that?" Lisa asked.

"Look," Stu explained, "if that printer was used then the document had to come from a source, a desktop, laptop, or even a cellphone or iPad that was connected to the printer."

"So," JoJo replied, "we need to find out what the source was, right?"

"Of course," Stu continued, "it could be wired to the printer, or connected by wifi or bluetooth."

"And then we can check those devices to see if the document was created on one of them," Lisa added.

"Yes," Stu replied, "and most likely if the creator of the document took the time to erase the cache on the printer, they also deleted the document from the source."

"So, what can we do about that?" Lisa asked.

"Any tech savvy person can retrieve a deleted file," Stu said, "I'm sure you can find one. But if you can't, I'll be happy to do it."

"We might take you up on that, Stu," Lisa said.

"At my usual rates!" Stu joked. He looked at JoJo with a grin.

Just then JoJo's cell phone buzzed. She looked at the phone and saw that it was from University Hospital in Tallahassee. Immediately she stood up and walked away from the table.

"Excuse me please," she said as she walked away. "I have to take this call."

"I bet it's Madison, our daughter," Stu told the group, "she calls her mother every day."

Five minutes later JoJo returned to the table. She was visibly shaken.

"Maddy's in the hospital," she said, "I have to go!"

"What happened, Jo?" Stu asked.

"That bastard beat her up again!" JoJo said, gritting her teeth. "I'm going up there now!"

"Is she okay?" Stuart asked.

"They say she's not in critical condition," JoJo replied, "but she's been badly beaten. That son of a bitch. That son of a bitch!"

"I'm coming with you, Jo," Stu said, as he rose from his seat.

"No, Stu," JoJo responded quickly, "you stay here. Billy needs you at home."

"Then let me come with you, JoJo," Lisa pleaded, "you're in no condition to drive up there all by yourself this late at night."

"Look," JoJo said forcefully, "I appreciate your offers, but this is my battle and I'm the one who's gonna protect my daughter!"

With that JoJo bolted out the front door and ran to her car. When she got there she opened the glove box with her key and removed her gun. She checked to see that it was loaded.

Back in the restaurant Lisa said, "I'm worried about her, Stu. The last time she confronted that guy she almost killed him. I'm afraid of what she might do now."

"I've known JoJo for twenty-one years," Stu said, "and when my wife makes up her mind she's gonna do something, even the Pope couldn't talk her out of it."

Lisa grabbed her cellphone and called Bob Elliott.

"Hey Bob, sorry to bother you on a Saturday night."

"No problem, Lisa. I'm just sitting here watching TV with Edna."

"Edna?"

"My golden retriever."

"Oh, okay. I really need your help, Bob."

CHAPTER 55

JoJo was exhausted, but three cups of coffee, five calls to the hospital, and the adrenaline caused by fear and anger had kept her awake during the five hour drive from Port St. Lucie to Tallahassee.

She navigated her way to the parking lot of University Hospital. Because it was so late at night she was able to get a parking space close to the front door.

JoJo entered the building, where a lone security guard greeted her. "Visiting hours are long over ma'am," he said, "are you a staff member?"

JoJo reached into her bag and removed he badge. "I'm a police detective," she said, "my daughter was just admitted and I need to see her now."

"What is your daughter's name, please?"

"It's Worthington," JoJo said abruptly, "Madison Worthington. I need to see her right away!"

"The guard began to search through the records on his computer. "I don't see her ma'am," he said, "perhaps she's in a different hospital."

JoJo exploded. "For God's sakes she came in here five hours ago, and this is absolutely the right hospital. Now where is my daughter?"

JoJo walked through the metal detector, which immediately buzzed when it picked up the gun in her handbag. She continued walking toward the emergency room.

"Stop!" The security guard yelled. JoJo didn't turn to look back. She quickly followed the signs to the Emergency Room and spoke to the nurse on duty.

"My name is Joanne Worthington," she said, "my daughter Madison is in this hospital. Is she here?"

"Yes, Mrs. Worthington, we've been expecting you. Your daughter is in room seven."

As soon as JoJo reached her daughter's room she was overcome with emotion. Maddy's face was bruised and battered. Her left arm was in a cast. When she saw her mother she began to cry.

"Mom!" was all she could say through her tears.

JoJo ran over to the bed and sat down beside her daughter. She held Madison tightly and cried. No words were spoken for several minutes. It was just a mother sheltering her injured child.

For ten minutes JoJo sat with her daughter, until finally she was able to ask Madison what happened.

"It was JT again, Mom," Madison said, between the tear drops. "He had a key to my room and, when I came home after dinner he was waiting for me."

"What happened when he saw you?"

"He was in a drunken rage," Madison began, "he yelled at me and called me the c-word, then he said that I was the reason he lost his football scholarship, and I ruined his life."

"And then he hit you?" JoJo asked.

Madison began to cry again. "He wouldn't stop hitting me, Mom!" She paused to catch her breath and continued. "The only reason he finally stopped is because he heard someone coming."

JoJo then addressed the attending nurse. "What's the extent of her injuries?"

The nurse walked close to JoJo and spoke in a calm, soft voice. "She has a broken left arm, several bruises all over her body. At this point we don't think she has any internal bleeding but we're continuing to monitor her very carefully," she said, "it was a vicious and brutal attack!"

By now JoJo had reached a boiling point. She bolted out of the bed and began to leave the room. As she reached the door she was met by two uniformed police officers.

"Detective Worthington," the larger of the two men said, "my name is Officer Warren Oberon, and this is Officer Wayne Stevenson of the Tallahassee police department."

"Did you see what that monster did to my daughter?" JoJo screamed.

"Detective Worthington," Officer Oberon replied, "we were alerted by the FBI that you would be coming here tonight, and we're very concerned that you might try to take the law into your own hands."

"Did you see what he did?" JoJo cried, "that's my baby in there!"

"I completely understand how you feel, detective," the officer replied, "I have a daughter almost the same age as your daughter. If I saw my daughter injured like that I would surely want to find the monster that did it and do to him what he did to my daughter."

"But please listen to me, Mrs Worthington," he continued, "your daughter needs her mother right now. And the most important thing you can do for her is to be here, not out there hunting down a criminal."

"Is anybody going after him?" JoJo asked.

"We know his car and we have an APB out on him," Officer Oberon replied, "there's no doubt we will find him, and when we do I can assure you he will be prosecuted to the full extent of the law."

JoJo was so overwhelmed with emotion that she fell into the arms of the officer. Through her tears she whispered "thank you."

She calmly walked back to her daughter's bed, sat down next to Madison, held her daughter in her arms, and rubbed her head.

"I love you, Mom," Madison said.

"I love you too, my sweet, sweet girl!"

CHAPTER 56

JANUARY 30, 2019, 11:00 AM

INTERSTATE 95, WEST PALM BEACH, FLORIDA

This was the first time Lisa had been given the opportunity to spend time with William Sales. She was happy to meet the son of the Chief of Police. As they drove toward the Palm Beach Sheriff's office, Will spoke.

"What's the latest from JoJo, Lisa?" he asked.

"They released her daughter from the hospital and she's bringing her home today," Lisa answered, "I guess Maddie's gonna sit out this semester."

"Did they catch the guy that did it?"

"I guess you could say that, William."

"Huh? What do you mean, Lisa?" Will asked.

"JoJo told me the cops spotted him on I-85 north just outside of Atlanta," Lisa replied, "they chased him until he drove off the road and hit a tree. He was declared dead on arrival at the hospital."

"Damn!"

What followed were several minutes of silence until Lisa once again broke the ice.

"You know, your dad saved my job once, William. The mayor wanted me to go but your father stood up for me."

"It's Will," he replied with a smile, "and I have no doubt my dad did the right thing by saving you, Lisa. I hear that you're the best detective in the department, or were the best, I should say."

"You know, I'm really gonna miss this department. Lots of great memories."

"What's your fondest memory, Lisa?"

"I guess it was when I came back to work after my husband had a heart attack last year. I was on leave of absence for a month while he recovered. So when I came back everyone cheered for me and for my husband's recovery. They made me feel loved and very special that day."

"You know," Will said quietly as he drove, "my dad is known as a tough guy, but he had some great sayings. He often told me 'son, people won't always remember what you say or what you do, but they'll never forget how you made them feel.'"

"Wise words, Will. Wise words."

Just then they arrived at the Sheriff's office in West Palm Beach. They were greeted by a deputy who led them into the crime lab on the second floor. Waiting for them there was a young man who looked like a teenager.

The young man thrust out his hand to greet Lisa and Will. "I'm Rusty Pratt," he said, "I'm the technician here, welcome to my lab."

Lisa glanced around the room and saw a variety of computers and cellphones spread out along a table in front of Rusty Pratt.

"Nice to meet you, Rusty," Lisa said, "so, did they get all the devices we asked for?" Lisa asked.

"Apparently, the warrants were issued yesterday," Rusty replied, " I heard the people were not happy about giving up their devices!"

"They never are, Rusty," Lisa replied, "I wouldn't be happy either if it happened to me."

"So, what did you get?" Will asked.

Rusty opened a folder and removed a list. He read it to the detectives.

"We got three desktops from the Ft. Lauderdale office of Garnet and Schwartz Realtors. We got one desktop and one laptop from the home of Louise Schwartz, and one desktop and an iPad from the home of Jeffrey Schwartz."

"Any cellphones?" Will asked.

"Yes, "Rusty replied, "we have the cellphones of Louise and Jeffrey Schwartz and the cellphone of Cary Garnet."

"That's good," Lisa said, "I faxed a copy of the document we were looking for. Did you get it?"

"I did," Rusty replied.

"So?" Will asked, "were you able to find the document?"

"I went through every device, searching the saved files and also the deleted files," Rusty said, "but unfortunately, I wasn't able to retrieve that document from any of these devices."

"Are you sure you checked everything?" Lisa asked.

"I'm sure," Rusty replied, "I'm sorry, but that document just wasn't created on any of these devices."

"Wait a minute," Will said, "JoJo told me that Jeffrey Schwartz had a wife. I think she joked that they called themselves Jack and Jill."

"That's true," Lisa replied.

"We should get her cellphone."

"I'll call the captain and ask him to arrange it," Lisa said, "In the meantime let me take you to one of my favorite diners here in West Palm Beach."

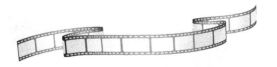

CHAPTER 57

FEBRUARY 1, 2019, 9:00 AM
FBI FIELD OFFICE
MELBOURNE, FLORIDA

Lisa was nervous on her first full day as an FBI agent. As she entered the building she was greeted by a chorus of song from the group of seven agents who were waiting for her.

"It's fun to work in the F B I," they sung in unison to the tune of the YMCA song, "it's fun to work in the F B I." Lisa laughed as she watched the group of five men and two women contort their bodies to form the letters F B I as they sang.

"It's a tradition here in Melbourne," Bob Elliott said with a grin, "these idiots did the same thing to me when I joined last year."

"Well, thank you all for that warm welcome," Lisa said with a broad smile, "I just hope that none of you ever have to go undercover as a professional singer!"

After the laughter subsided and the introductions concluded, Special Agent Donna Thompson, the Field office leader, called Lisa into her office.

"Welcome aboard, Lisa," Donna said with a handshake. "We've been looking forward to having you join the team."

"Thanks, Special Agent," Lisa replied.

Donna chuckled. "In here I'm just Donna, okay?"

"Okay!"

Donna opened her desk drawer and removed a folder. She handed it to Lisa.

"Here's all the paperwork you need to fill out in order to start getting paid. I assume you would like to be paid."

"That would be nice."

"Anything new on your move?"

"We listed the house starting today, so we're hoping for a good offer to come our way," Lisa replied, "in the meantime the commute is only a little over an hour, so I can handle it."

"I've scheduled you for orientation at the DC headquarters the week after next," Donna continued, "you'll be up there for two days so please make arrangements to go."

"Sure thing," Lisa replied.

"Oh," Donna added, "I've decided to pair you up with a partner and I'd like you to meet him now."

Lisa was apprehensive and excited to meet her new partner. She remembered her disappointment when Captain Davis had teamed her with JoJo Worthington, and she was hoping that this time she would be happy with her new partner.

On cue Bob Elliott walked into Donna's office. "Nice to meet you, partner!" he said with a smile.

"Likewise, I'm sure!" Lisa replied. She was thrilled to have a partner with whom she was already so comfortable.

"Okay, you two," Donna said, "go to work. And I'm expecting you to catch the other eight most wanted real soon!"

"We're all over it, boss!" Bob said, as he and Lisa exited the office.

"I've got something really special to show you, Lisa," Bob said, as he led her to the lab. Agent Gus Haney was waiting for them.

"Hey. Gus," Lisa said, "good to see you again."

"Let me show you guys something," Gus replied, "I was setting up a folder on this case and putting away all the photos you gave me."

"Thanks, Gus," Lisa said, "you know, because of your work with facial recognition we were able to recover all of the stolen money, plus interest!"

"That's good to hear," Gus replied, "but I've got something you might be interested in."

Gus opened the folder and removed three strips of negatives that Lisa had given him. He carefully placed them on the table in front of him.

"Take a look at this," he said as he held up the first strip, "negatives are numbered sequentially to make it easy for people to order prints. Instead of trying to describe what's in the photo you can simply ask for the prints by the negative number. So, for example, you could order five, three by five prints, of negative number nine."

Lisa examined the first negative strip. "I see the numbers," she said.

"Okay, so here's what I found," Gus continued, "the first strip of negatives has numbers one through six. The second has numbers seven through twelve."

"I see that," Lisa replied.

"Okay, Gus said, "now look at the negative numbers on this next strip."

Lisa examined the negatives. "It's sixteen through twenty-one." she said.

"So, what happened to negatives numbered thirteen, fourteen, and fifteen?" Gus asked.

"You're sure they're not here?" Lisa said.

"I triple checked, Lisa," Gus replied, "we never got those negatives!"

"I wonder what's in those photos?" Bob Elliott asked.

Lisa examined the negatives. "It looks like the first few are photos of the building," she said, "then we have the photos of McNeely walking Jimmy Foster into the building."

Bob was looking at the next strip. "Negative sixteen starts the photos of Jimmy Foster's body," he said.

"So," Lisa said, "The missing negatives were taken after they entered the building and before Jimmy died."

"My guess is that they're photos of the actual shooting taking place!" Bob said.

"Wait a minute!" Lisa said, "If these photos were taken by John Bannister, and if they are the actual shooting…"

"Then there had to be another person in the room," Bob interrupted, "and those photos should show us who shot Jimmy."

"You'll never prove anything without those negatives," Gus said, "and I bet Janet Bannister destroyed them."

"You know," Lisa replied, "Janet told us that her husband hid duplicate envelopes with these same photos in the homes of his son and his daughter."

Lisa grabbed her cellphone and called JoJo back in Port St. Lucie.

"Hey, former partner!" Lisa said, "what's new with the Foster case?"

"We keep hitting dead ends," JoJo replied, "we checked every cellphone and computer associated with the printer in Cary Garnet's office. We even checked Louise Schwartz's phone."

"Nothing?"

"Nada!" JoJo replied, "I guess we have to accept the fact that the letter didn't come from that printer. I sure wish we could find out where else those Laser Jet 3500 printers were installed around here."

"Good idea, Jo. I'll work on that."

"Thanks, Lisa. I wanna to know who created that phony letter!"

"Hey, Jo, do you remember Janet Bannister telling us that there were two other sets of photos from the warehouse the night Jimmy was killed?"

"Sure do. She said her husband hid them in their kids' houses."

"You need to get a warrant and grab those folders right away. This could be the breakthrough we've been waiting for!"

"I'm on it partner!"

"Hey Jo?' Lisa said softly, "how's Maddy doing?"

"She's feeling good, Lisa, anxious to go back to school."

"That's great news! Please send her my best."

As Lisa ended the call she turned to her new partner. "Hey, Bob, can we find out where those Laser Jet 3500 printers were installed in south Florida?

Bob laughed. "You're not asking for too much, now, are you,

Lisa?"

"Hey!" Lisa shot back, "this is the FBI. I thought we could do anything!"

Bob rolled his eyes. "Lisa, do you remember the song that goes 'the difficult, I'll do right now, the impossible will take a little while'?"

"Can't say as I do, Bob."

"Well then, we'll just have to make it happen!"

CHAPTER 58

FEBRUARY 3, 1995, 11:50 PM

FEDERAL HIGHWAY

PORT ST. LUCIE, FLORIDA

John Bannister watched as a woman exited the warehouse and drove away. He quickly grabbed a pad and pen from his pocket and wrote down the license plate number.

Bannister then waited until he saw Jimmy's car leave the parking lot, and, as it sped away, he noticed that there was nobody in the back seat this time. He was wondering if Jimmy was driving or if it was the gunman, so he decided to go inside the building and see.

After a few minutes had passed, he left his car and walked toward the building. He entered the building to be met by Jimmy Foster, sitting alone and crying.

"Jimmy," Bannister said, "what the hell happened in here?"

Jimmy looked up and spied Bannister. "What the fuck are you doing here, Bannister?" he shouted, "Did my wife's asshole father send you here to spy on me?"

"No, he didn't Jimmy," Bannister replied.

"That's bullshit!" Jimmy yelled, "that's your whole job, following me around like a fucking puppy dog! You're a worthless piece of shit, Bannister!"

Jimmy stood up and began walking toward Bannister. As he approached he was distracted by another person who entered the warehouse. She was carrying a Glock 17.

"You're right, Jimmy." Janet Bannister said, "my husband did come here to spy on you tonight."

"Then what the fuck did you come here for?"

"Like I said, Jimmy, my husband came here to spy on you tonight," Janet repeated, as she pulled the gun from her handbag, "but I came here to kill you."

Janet Bannister pointed the gun at Jimmy's face and Jimmy instinctively put his hand up in a futile effort to block the oncoming bullet. Janet fired one shot, and in an instant Jimmy was dead.

Janet waited as her husband took a series of photos of Jimmy's dead body. She walked back to her car and returned with a large blanket to wrap the body in.

Five minutes later, Janet and John Bannister loaded the body into the trunk of their car. Ten minutes after that they were at the site in Port St. Lucie where the hole had been prepared to bury Jimmy Foster forever.

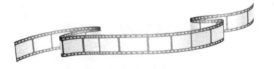

CHAPTER 59

FEBRUARY 2, 2019, 6:00 PM

THE HOME OF LISA AND RICK MARCH

Ernie Goodman bounded into the house carrying a bottle of champagne.

"The drinks are on me tonight!" Ernie shouted with a big smile.

"Ernie just got the good news, Lisa," Rick said, "He's gonna get a boatload of money from the McNeely settlement deal."

"Fifty-nine thousand eight hundred sixty-two, to be exact," Ernie said with glee, "we put up thirty and get back almost double, thanks to you, my detective daughter!"

"Oy," Gloria Goodman moaned, "Myron Greenberg says we're gonna have to pay a lot of taxes."

"Gloria," Rick explained, "you only have to pay taxes on the extra money, not on the thirty thousand that you originally invested."

"That's not what Myron says," Gloria deadpanned, "he's an accountant and I think he knows a little more about taxes than you do."

"Okay, Gloria, " Rick sighed, "suit yourself."

"Rick," Ernie said, "if Gloria wants to be miserable about somebody giving us sixty thousand bucks I say, let her!"

Just then the doorbell rang.

"Hi Lisa, it's Jo!"

Lisa rushed to the front door to let her partner in. "What's up, Jo?"

JoJo entered the house as she spoke. "Sorry to bother you at home on a Saturday night, Lisa, but I just couldn't wait to show you this."

"JoJo was carrying a manila envelope. Quickly she opened it to show Lisa what was inside.

"Did you find the negatives?" Lisa said excitedly.

"Better than that, Lisa!" JoJo exclaimed as she removed three photos to show Lisa.

Lisa looked at the three photos and shouted, "Dad, you hit the jackpot today and so did we!"

"What you got there, Lisa?' Ernie asked.

"Dad, what we have are real time photos of the killing of Jimmy Foster!"

"John Bannister left a complete set of photos at his son's house," JoJo said, "I don't think anybody ever opened this envelope."

Lisa stared at the photos for several minutes.

"Are you thinking what I'm thinking, Jo?"

"It's definitely a woman," JoJo replied," and she's twenty-four years younger than today."

"This one is from a bad angle. You can barely see her face."

"But these two are much better. Her face is clearly visible in both of them."

"Whoever took these photos wanted to make sure he had the goods on the shooter."

"I'll be damned!" Lisa replied, "This looks like Janet Bannister!"

"That's exactly what I was thinking, Lisa."

"No wonder she cut out those negatives and didn't give us these prints."

"Can you take this to Melbourne Monday and have your guy use that facial recognition program?"

"Absolutely!" Lisa replied, "I wish Gus was there right now. I'd drive these photos right up there!"

CHAPTER 60

FEBRUARY 4, 2019, 9:00 AM

FBI FIELD OFFICE

MELBOURNE, FLORIDA

Lisa bolted into the office and made a beeline for Gus Haney. Excitedly she opened the envelope and showed him the three photos of the killing of Jimmy Foster.

"I'm pretty sure I know who this is, Gus," she said, "but I need you to confirm it for me."

"Lisa," Gus said with a grin, "do you remember when we told you there are four hundred million people in our database?"

"Uh huh."

"Well then," Gus said with a laugh, "this thing would go a lot faster if you tell me who you think it is!"

Lisa chuckled. "Of course it would, Gus. It's Janet Bannister. She lives in Port St. Lucie and she's seventy-one years old."

Gus aged the photos and compared them to the most recent driver's license photo taken of Janet Bannister.

"We got a hundred percent match, Lisa," Gus said proudly, "Janet Bannister is your shooter."

Just then Bob Elliott entered the lab.

"What'd I miss?" he asked.

Lisa showed the photos to her partner. "It's Janet Bannister," she said.

"Well then, this must be our lucky day, partner." Bob replied.

"There's more good news?" Lisa joked, "I don't know if I could handle any more today."

"How about this, Lisa," Bob said, "we got a list of installations of Hewlett Packard Laser Jet 3500 printers in south Florida."

Bob handed Lisa the list.

"There's twenty-nine on that list, Lisa," Bob said, "but take a look at number eleven."

Lisa was astounded when she saw the location of the eleventh printer on the list.

"This is the public library on Morningside in Port St. Lucie," she said, "It's just around the corner from Janet Bannister's house."

"You said the new guy, Will, knows how to check the cache, right?"

In an instant Lisa was on the phone with JoJo.

CHAPTER 61

FEBRUARY 5, 2019, 3:00 PM

PORT ST. LUCIE POLICE DEPARTMENT

INTERVIEW ROOM 1

JoJo and Megan watched as Janet Bannister arrived in the interview room. She was wearing a jumpsuit provided by the jail and, once again, she was accompanied by her lawyer, Jerry Mason. JoJo recalled that the last time they had interviewed Mrs. Bannister her lawyer had been very aggressive in his approach to Steve Velasquez.

I doubt that Megan Harris will let him be so aggressive, JoJo thought.

"Mr. Mason," Megan began, "This meeting is being recorded for future use. You understand that your client has been arrested for the murder of Jimmy Foster. She has been read her rights and has chosen to speak with us, and she has chosen you to be her attorney of record. Is that correct?"

"Before we continue," Jerry said, "there are a few things I want to make clear."

"Mr. Mason," Megan replied forcefully, "I asked you a question that requires a simple yes or no response. I can assure you that you will have ample opportunity to speak on behalf of your client, but not until you answer my question. Yes or no, Mr. Mason, do you understand?"

JoJo could easily see the difference in style between Steve Velasquez and Megan Harris. She was taking control of the meeting right from the start.

"Yes," Mr. Mason replied sheepishly.

"Now, what was it you wanted to say, Mr. Mason?"

Jerry Mason sat up straight in his chair and stared at Megan Harris across the table. In a strong and confident tone he spoke. "Ms. Harris, my client is willing to plead guilty to manslaughter two and to answer all of your questions to the best of her ability."

Abruptly Megan Harris rose and began to collect the papers in front of her. She looked at Mr. Mason.

"I think we're done here," she said, "Detective Worthington, please have Mrs. Bannister returned to her cell."

JoJo followed Megan's lead and brandished her handcuffs as she walked toward Mrs. Bannister.

"Wait!" Jerry Mason yelled as Megan was about to exit the room.

"What is it, Mr. Mason?" Megan asked curtly.

"I would like a word with my client please," he said softly, "and I would ask you to put this meeting on hold until after I speak with her."

"You've got five minutes, Mr. Mason," Megan said, as she and JoJo walked out of the room.

"What was that all about?" JoJo asked.

"Her lawyer was just putting on a show for his client," Megan replied, "they do it all the time."

"Do what?"

"JoJo," Megan continued, "this guy knows full well that we will never accept a plea deal for manslaughter two."

"You offered him manslaughter one, didn't you?" JoJo responded.

"Exactly," Megan replied, "manslaughter two is when someone recklessly caused the death of another person, manslaughter one is when someone intentionally causes harm to another person which resulted in their death."

"It's been a while, but I remember that," JoJo said. "It's all about intent."

"Yes," Megan replied, "and there's little doubt when you point a gun at someone's head and fire it that you intended to kill him!"

"What's the difference in the sentence for involuntary versus voluntary manslaughter?"

"For manslaughter two she could get as little as eighteen months," Megan replied, but for manslaughter one we agreed on ten years."

"She's pretty old," JoJo said, "she'll be eighty-one when she gets out."

"Yep, that's true. And I'm pretty sure this next meeting will be different than the last one," Megan said, "now that he demonstrated how he's fighting for his client they'll come back to the deal I offered."

Just then Megan and JoJo returned to the interview room.

"Your five minutes are up, Mr. Mason," Megan said abruptly. "Are you ready to continue?"

"Yes, we are," Mason replied, "against my advice my client has decided to accept your offer and she will plead guilty to the charge of manslaughter one, in exchange for a sentence of ten years."

"That's fine, Mr. Mason," Megan said, "now I need Mrs. Bannister to affirm this."

Janet Bannister looked at her attorney. He nodded and she replied, "I accept the offer."

"Now, before this offer is finalized, Mrs. Bannister, you understand that it also requires you to answer all of our questions completely and truthfully, yes?"

Mason nodded and Janet replied, "Yes."

"Before we begin," Jerry said, "it's important to state for the record that much of what Mrs. Bannister is about to tell you is her best recollection of what was told to her by her husband over twenty years ago."

"Stop right there, Mr. Mason!" Megan said forcefully, "I don't want to hear it!"

"But…"

"But nothing, sir!" she yelled. "I saw the video of your meeting with Mr. Velasquez. You made the same speech then, Mr. Mason, and most of what your client told us was not true. As a matter of fact I would be perfectly justified in reopening the obstruction of justice charge against her and that will add another five years to her sentence."

Mason sat quietly for a moment. "Ask you questions," he said.

"JoJo?" Megan said, deferring to the detective.

"Okay, Mrs. Bannister," JoJo began, "please tell us the events that led up to your shooting Jimmy Foster."

Janet Bannister took a deep breath.

"My husband came to me in late January, 1995 and he told me that Mr. Schwartz wanted him to kill Jimmy Foster."

"That would be Sidney Schwartz?"

"Yes, Sidney Schwartz." Janet continued, "But John, my husband, said that he couldn't do it. He said he just wasn't a killer."

"Did your husband say why Schwartz wanted Jimmy Foster killed?"

"He said Mr. Schwartz hated Jimmy. Jimmy was cheating on his wife, she was Mr. Schwartz' daughter. He said Jimmy ran up big gambling debts from these mafia guys, and they were threatening to kill Mr. Schwartz' grandson if he didn't pay back the money."

"And what was Mr. Schwartz going to do for you if your husband killed Jimmy?" JoJo asked.

"John said that Mr. Schwartz promised to take care of Johnny's medical bills, that's our son, John Jr. He was very sick and the bills were sinking us. We owed over a hundred thousand dollars and Mr. Schwartz paid them all. He also promised to pay us an extra amount on top of the bills."

"How much did he agree to pay you?"

"He said he would give us a total of two hundred and fifty thousand," Janet replied, "Mr. Schwartz said if anybody asked why he paid us that much money we should say that John was still looking for Jimmy, and that's the money he was getting paid to do it."

"Mrs. Bannister," JoJo said, "you told us that your husband refused to kill Jimmy Foster, is that correct?"

"He said he couldn't do it," Janet replied, "so, I said, if he wasn't gonna do it, then I would!"

"Had you ever shot a gun before, Mrs. Bannister?"

"Oh yes, I was very familiar with guns. Long ago, when my husband got a weapon, I learned to shoot, too."

"Why was that?"

"I wanted to be capable of protecting myself in case something went wrong in John's business."

"So tell us what happened on the night of February 3, 1995."

"I went with John to the Breakers in Palm Beach. We knew that Jimmy was hosting a big event there so we parked near his Lamborghini. We waited in our car, and, not long after we arrived, we watched a man break into Jimmy's car and hide in the back seat."

"Did you know who the man was?"

"No," Janet replied, "it was dark, and we couldn't see his face. But we were hoping maybe the guy was one of the mafia henchmen, and maybe he would kill Jimmy, so we could take credit without having to do it."

"And when did Jimmy Foster come out of the Breakers?"

"It was around eleven. He got in his car and immediately we could see the guy in the back seat point a gun at Jimmy's head. They drove away and we followed them."

"So, what happened when you got to the warehouse?"

"John took a bunch of pictures and we watched the man and Jimmy go inside."

"Isn't it true that your husband eventually found out who that man was?"

"Yes, he saw a woman waiting at the warehouse in a car, so he wrote down the license plate. Then he checked the rental car company and found out that it was rented by a man named Adam McNeely."

"Mrs. Bannister," Megan asked, "have you ever heard of the Sandpiper company?"

Janet Bannister froze. "I'm not sure," she said meekly.

"Let me refresh your memory, Janet," JoJo said. "The FBI was able to look at McNeely's Cayman Bank account and we now have proof that he was paying you ten thousand a month through this Sandpiper company, wasn't he, Mrs. Bannister?"

"Yes, that's true," Janet Bannister replied softly.

"So, your husband used the photos he took of Adam McNeely to black-mail him," Megan said, "is that right?"

"Yes, that's right."

"Okay," JoJo asked, "so what happened after McNeely and Foster went into the warehouse that night?"

"We waited until after McNeely left in Jimmy's car and then we went inside. We were hoping to find Jimmy's dead body, but he was alive."

"Jimmy was there alone?"

"John went in first and talked to Jimmy for a couple of minutes. Then I opened the door and it looked to me like Jimmy was going after John, so I shot him."

"She was clearly protecting her husband," Jerry Mason added.

That's when Megan spoke up. "Mrs. Bannister, Jimmy Foster was shot in the mouth from close range, and you told us you went there to kill him. So please don't try to convince us that this was some kind of self defense deal. I'm not buying it and neither would a jury."

"Did you know your husband was taking pictures of you when you were shooting Jimmy?" JoJo asked.

"No, I didn't see him doing that."

"Why do you think he did that, Mrs. Bannister. Why did he take photos of you killing Jimmy?"

Janet paused for a moment, and her demeanor changed to anger. "I think my husband would have thrown me under the bus to save his own ass, if push came to shove."

"What makes you say that?"

"My husband was a nice guy, but he was a wimp," Janet said. There was fire in her eyes as she spoke.

"He refused to do what he needed to do to save our son, for God's sake. He wasn't a man, he was a wimp!"

"So," JoJo continued her questions, "just to be clear. You shot and killed Jimmy, then you took his body and buried it, correct?"

"Yes," Janet replied, "I did the shooting, then John and I buried the body."

"So, when did you find out that your husband had photos of you doing the shooting?" JoJo asked.

"Not until I sent the photos of Jimmy's body to you. I had never looked at the photos until then."

"So, you removed those photos and negatives, showing you with the gun, before you met with Steve Velasquez to plead guilty to obstruction."

"I did, yes."

"Now, Mrs. Bannister," JoJo said, "this is very important. You said that Sidney Schwartz asked your husband to kill Jimmy Foster. Did you ever confirm that it was Schwartz who did that?"

"Well," Janet replied, "John said he called to offer us the money we needed to pay all of our bills."

"And you're sure it was actually Sidney Schwartz who called John?"

"I had no reason to doubt my husband, I mean, why would he lie about that?"

"So, the truth is, you can't confirm that it actually was Sidney Schwartz that hired your husband to kill Jimmy," Megan said.

"Well, that's what my husband told me," Janet replied, "he said Sidney hated Jimmy Foster and wanted him gone from his family."

"Janet, how much were you paid to kill Jimmy Foster?"

"It was two hundred fifty thousand dollars."

"And how did the money come to you?"

"We had a wire transfer for one hundred and ten thousand upfront, and we used it for Johnny's medical bills. Then we got another hundred and forty thousand after the work was done."

"Okay, Mrs. Bannister, let's talk about that letter you sent to the police after we discovered Jimmy's body." JoJo said.

"I wrote that letter and signed my husband's name."

"Yes, we know that now," JoJo said, "we also know that you used the printer at the public library on Morningside Avenue."

"I did."

"In the letter you wrote that the photos were John's insurance policy. What did you mean by that?" Megan asked.

"John said we could use the photos to make sure McNeely kept paying us," Janet replied, "so that's why he called the photos his insurance policy."

"I need you to help me understand exactly why you wrote the letter, Mrs. Bannister?" JoJo asked in a quiet, calm voice.

"You see, I was afraid that, once you found the body, you might start an investigation, and eventually you would figure out that I was the one who shot Jimmy," Janet replied, "so I wrote the letter, hoping that it would put an end to the case. Since my husband was dead, I didn't feel bad about saying that he was the one who killed Jimmy Foster."

"Your husband is dead, and Sidney Schwartz has Alzheimer's," Megan replied, "so that left nobody for us to charge with Jimmy's murder for hire. That's very convenient, Mrs. Bannister."

Jerry Mason intercepted that comment. "Are there any more questions for my client?" he asked.

Megan glanced at JoJo.

"No, that's it for now," she said, "but we may have more questions later."

JoJo led Mrs. Bannister out of the interview room and back to her jail cell. After they left, Megan spoke to Jerry Mason.

"I think your client is protecting someone," she said abruptly.

"What?" Mason replied with indignation.

"Sidney Schwartz is just too easy," she said, "and if we find out your client lied to us again, all bets are off!"

"At this point, what possible motive is there for her to lie?" Mason asked.

"Mr. Mason," Megan said firmly, "your client is a very clever woman, and lying is one of the tools she uses to get what she wants in life."

"I don't have a clue as to what you're talking about, Ms. Harris!"

"Janet Bannister received over two and a half million dollars in ransom money from the McNeelys. Do you think she reported that income on her tax returns?"

Mason paused. "I really don't know."

"Well, I do know, Mr. Mason," Megan replied quickly, "and the answer is no. You'll be hearing from the I.R.S. very shortly."

Mason waked out of the room shaking his head.

Shortly after JoJo released Janet to a uniformed officer for transport to the jail, her cellphone buzzed. It was Lisa.

"What's up, Agent March?" JoJo answered.

"How'd you make out with Janet Bannister, Jo?"

"She took the plea deal and confessed to killing Jimmy."

"Did she give up the name of the person that hired her?"

"She said it was Sidney Schwartz, Lisa," JoJo replied, "but she only identified him from what her husband told her."

"Are you sitting down, Jo?"

"No," JoJo replied, "but I will if you say so!"

"I just got a phone call this morning from a woman who claims she knows who hired the Bannisters to kill Jimmy Foster," Lisa said, "it's not Sidney Schwartz and it's someone we've never even heard mentioned before!"

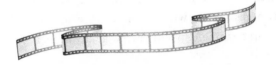

CHAPTER 62

FEBRUARY 8, 2019, 10:10 AM

PORT ST. LUCIE POLICE DEPARTMENT

INTERVIEW ROOM 2

Lisa was happy to be back in the interview room, although she assumed this would be her last time. Her first week on the job with FBI had been great, and she was starting to get comfortable with her new team and surroundings. Several potential buyers had seen her house, but, so far, no offers had been made. She was still a little anxious about the move.

She and JoJo waited impatiently as their scheduled ten o'clock interview was late.

"Maybe she's not gonna show," JoJo said, as she sipped her coffee.

"Wouldn't be the first time I was stiffed by a witness who claimed to have information but never showed," Lisa said.

Just then the interview room door opened and in walked a tall, attractive woman, who appeared to be in her fifties. She was dressed in expensive, stylish clothes that JoJo could admire.

The woman was accompanied by a gentleman, either her husband or her lawyer, Lisa thought.

After introductions were made the detectives began the interview.

"Good morning to you both," Lisa began. "This interview is being recorded for future use. Please begin by giving us your names."

The woman spoke first. "My name is Kathleen Jameson, formerly Kathleen Prentice."

"And I am Robert Wilson, Mrs. Jameson's attorney."

"Thank you," Lisa continued. "Now, Mrs. Jameson, our understanding is that you are here of your own volition, you are not charged with a crime, and that you can terminate this interview at any time. Is that your understanding as well?"

"Yes, it is," Kathy Jameson replied.

"Okay then, Mrs. Jameson. A couple of days ago you called and told me that you knew who paid for the murder of Jimmy Foster."

"That's correct, and you can call me Kathy."

"Alright, Kathy, please tell us what you know and how you know it."

Kathy Jameson took a moment to compose her thoughts.

"The man who hired Janet Bannister to kill Jimmy Foster was my husband, or should I say, my ex-husband, Roy Prentice."

"Now, Kathy," JoJo interjected, "that is a very serious accusation, I'm sure you know that. So please tell us everything you know that leads you to conclude that your ex-husband is guilty of this crime."

"Let's start from the very beginning, Kathy," Lisa added, "tell us how you first met your ex-husband."

"Roy and I met when we both lived in Nashville. I was working as a TV spokesmodel and his advertising company hired me to do a commercial."

"This was for Prentice Builders?"

"Yes. They had a new development going up in the suburbs of Nashville, and they were making a TV commercial. Roy was in it, and so was I."

"And you began dating after that?" JoJo asked.

"Yes, we dated for about six months, and then we got married."

"And that was when, what year?"

"It was 1987 when we got married, and in 1990 we moved to Florida so Roy could manage a new Prentice housing development."

"Did your husband own the company, Prentice Builders?"

"Not at first," Kathy replied. "His father, George Prentice, had started Prentice Builders back in the sixties, so he owned it. But, after he died, Roy took over."

"So, what happened after you moved to Florida?" Lisa asked.

"Well, we moved into a nice house that Roy had built for us. Everything was good, but I wasn't happy."

"Why not?"

"I missed my family and friends in Nashville," Kathy said, "Roy was working all the time, and we just weren't getting along."

"So, that's when you met Jimmy Foster?" Lisa asked.

"I met Jimmy Foster when we first moved to Boca in 1990," Kathy replied. "He was a salesman for Prentice Builders, and I thought he was very handsome and a charming man!"

That he was, Lisa thought. "Go on," she said.

"It was June of 1991 when I saw Jimmy at a restaurant. He was sitting by himself at the bar, and I was with a few friends at a table. As I walked to the restroom I passed by Jimmy, and he slipped me a note asking if I wanted to meet him for a drink after I finished with my friends."

"So you said yes?"

"It was hard to resist Jimmy Foster, and I was very lonely, and one thing led to another."

"So you and Jimmy had an affair?"

"Yes, we did. We were both married at the time, and he even had a young son. We both knew it was wrong, but we couldn't stop seeing each other."

"So, then what happened?" Lisa asked.

"My husband must have suspected I was having an affair because he hired a private detective to follow me around and take pictures."

"Did you know the name of the detective?" JoJo asked.

"Yes, it was a guy named Bannister, John Bannister."

Lisa and JoJo looked at each other. Each nodded and raised her eyebrows.

"So, what did your husband do when he found out about you and Jimmy?" Lisa asked.

"First, he went to his father and had Jimmy fired," Kathy replied, "and then he told Jimmy that if he ever came near me again, he would kill him!"

"So, your husband threatened to kill Jimmy Foster," JoJo said firmly.

"That's correct."

"How do you know he did that?" Lisa asked.

"Jimmy told me, that's how I knew."

"So," JoJo asked, "did you and Jimmy end your affair after he was threatened by your husband?"

"Yes, we stopped seeing each other for a while," Kathy replied. "We talked, but we never got together for sex."

"You say you stopped for a while?" Lisa said, "How long did that last?"

"I'd say it was about two years," Kathy responded. "But then I saw Jimmy in a TV ad for his Dreamland project. I called to congratulate him on the project, and he asked me if I would be willing to meet him for a drink."

"And so you rekindled your affair?"

"Like I said, it was hard to resist Jimmy Foster!"

"So, Kathy," Lisa asked, "what makes you believe that your husband was responsible for Jimmy's murder?"

"Okay, one time I was with Jimmy and I noticed that John Bannister was following us. He was even taking photos of us together. So, I knew he was gonna show them to my husband."

"So, what did you do about it?"

"I contacted Bannister and offered to pay him to give me the negatives and not to show the photos to my husband."

"Did he take the money?"

"I offered him a thousand dollars but he demanded ten. I told him there was no way I could get ten thousand dollars without my husband finding out about it, but he said it was either ten grand or he would go to my husband."

"Did you come up with the ten thousand?" JoJo asked.

"Jimmy gave it to me, and I paid Bannister. Then he gave me the negatives."

"So, what happened after that?" Lisa asked.

"Bannister kept after me. He said he still had copies of the photos, and I had to keep paying him to keep him from telling my husband."

"Bannister was blackmailing you," JoJo said. "So what did you do then?"

"Jimmy gave me another five thousand. I gave it to Bannister and told him that was the last time I would pay him."

"Then what happened?"

"Then Jimmy Foster disappeared!"

"And you suspect that your husband had Jimmy killed?"

"I don't suspect it," she said, "I know it!"

"And how do you know this, Kathy." JoJo asked.

"After Jimmy disappeared, and everybody was saying he ran off with the money, I filed for divorce from my husband," Kathy continued. "My lawyer demanded half of his assets and alimony of twenty thousand a month."

"I take it your husband wasn't too happy with those terms," JoJo said.

"Roy told me that if I didn't back off, he would do to me what he did to Jimmy," Kathy said, as tears filled her eyes. "He said he could make me disappear and nobody would ever find me, just like Jimmy!"

"Kathy, why didn't you go to the police back then?" Lisa asked. "Your husband threatened you and admitted to murder!"

"I was afraid of him, so I just kept quiet. I didn't want to die!"

"And the divorce?" JoJo asked, "how did that turn out?"

"Roy had some expensive lawyers, and I had to settle for alimony of eight thousand a month, that was all. I was just happy to get away from Roy Prentice and start my life over again, so I accepted it."

"And did you get away from him, Kathy?" Lisa asked

"Six months after we got divorced Roy remarried. She was a very young girl who worked for him. Her name was Emily Kotzen. Roy was forty and she was twenty-two."

"And did you remarry as well?"

"I got married to a wonderful man named Joe Jameson in 2002, and I've got three beautiful children."

"So then, why are you coming forward with this information about Roy Prentice now, twenty some years later?" Lisa asked.

Kathy paused for a moment before she spoke. "Because he did it again!" she said.

"What?" Lisa and JoJo yelled out in unison.

"Late last year Emily Prentice, Roy's second wife, disappeared," Kathy explained. "She just vanished into thin air!"

"I assume that Roy was a suspect in that disappearance," Lisa said.

For the first time Kathy's attorney, Robert Wilson, spoke. He took a notepad out from his briefcase and read from it.

"Emily Prentice was last seen alive in Boca Raton on Christmas Eve of last year. Shortly after the new year her body was found buried in a secluded area in Boynton Beach. Last week, the Palm Beach County police arrested a man named Mason Jones and charged him with the murder of Emily Prentice. As part of a plea deal, Mason identified Roy Prentice as the man who had paid him to kill Emily and bury her body. He had even taped several conversations between himself and Roy Prentice."

"Wow!" Lisa said, "That's a lot to absorb right now!"

"We've been investigating this case for almost three months trying to find out who was responsible for Jimmy Foster's death," JoJo added, "and you've just given us the name we've been looking for."

"Is there anything else you want to add at this time?" Lisa asked.

Both Kathy and her attorney said no, and JoJo handed business cards to each of them. "Thank you both for your time today, she said, "I'm sure that Megan Harris, from the state attorney's office, will want to speak with each of you in the very near future."

"In the meantime," Lisa added, "if you think of anything else that might be helpful, please give detective Worthington a call."

CHAPTER 63

FEBRUARY 11, 2019, 4:30 PM

THE OFFICE OF PROSECUTOR MEGAN HARRIS

FORT PIERCE, FLORIDA

JoJo and Lisa sat quietly as Megan Harris watched the recording of the interview with Kathy Prentice Jameson.

"I spoke to the States Attorney in Palm Beach," Megan said. "They think they have a rock solid case against Roy Prentice for the murder of his second wife, Emily Prentice."

"He's been arrested?" Lisa asked.

"He was arraigned, and he's in jail right now. The judge denied bail. And guess who his lawyer is!"

"Not JD Treem?" Lisa shouted.

"The one and only!" Megan replied with a smile.

"So, if Prentice is gonna be tried for killing his second wife, then what's your plan for the Jimmy Foster case?" JoJo asked.

"Well," Megan replied, "we obviously have a strong case against Prentice here, but I want to wait and see what happens in Palm Beach before we move forward with our case."

"Maybe they can get him to plead guilty to both killings," Lisa said.

"That's doubtful, Lisa," Megan replied. "He's professing his innocence, and it looks like the trial won't take place until some time later in the year."

"The wheels of justice turn slowly," JoJo lamented.

"That's true," Megan replied, "but the prosecutor's very confident that Roy Prentice will eventually be found guilty. Their case is stronger than ours because they have the shooter identifying Prentice. That was part of his plea deal, and he got twenty-five to life."

"We have the ex-wife's testimony in our case," JoJo said.

"The key word there is ex, JoJo," Megan replied. "Juries don't always look at exes as the most reliable witnesses, especially when they're bitter about the terms of a divorce."

"But I guess it doesn't really matter," Lisa said, "as long as Prentice gets put away for the murder of his second wife."

"And you can be sure that I'll be keeping a close watch on that case." Megan added.

"So," JoJo said, "I guess we can close the Jimmy Foster case for now."

"For now," Megan responded with a smile.

As they left Megan's office, JoJo and Lisa walked across the street to the Three Nines Bar to commiserate.

CHAPTER 64

FEBRUARY 11, 2019, 5:00 PM

THREE NINES BAR

FORT PIERCE, FLORIDA

Lisa ordered Chardonnay, JoJo had Prosecco.

"Well, partner," JoJo said, as she sipped her Prosecco, "I think this is it for us, case closed!"

"What a ride this has been, Jo."

"First, we had to figure out who the victim was," JoJo said, "and that wasn't easy!"

"If Jimmy Foster hadn't stuck his wedding ring in his pocket the night he was killed," Lisa added, "we might never have figured out it was him."

JoJo raised her glass. "To Jimmy's ring!"

"To his pocket, too!" Lisa added, as the two partners sipped their drinks.

"Then," JoJo continued, "once we knew it was Jimmy Foster we had to figure out where the murder took place."

"And we can thank your new partner Will Sales for finding the warehouse on Federal Highway," Lisa replied.

"To Will!" JoJo said, as the two glasses clinked.

"Once we knew where the murder took place," Lisa said, "we had to determine who actually killed Jimmy. And what a surprise that it was Janet Bannister, and not her husband."

"That phony confession letter really threw us off, Lisa. She tried to convince us that Sidney Schwartz paid John Bannister to kill Jimmy."

"A dead man hired by an Alzheimer patient," Lisa replied, "how very clever of her."

"Of course, the Sidney we met at the Gatlin Home was just a dear sweet man who loved your chocolate chip cookies, Jo."

JoJo raised her glass. "To Sidney," she said softly.

"You know, if Janet hadn't used that library printer we might never have figured out that it was her who wrote the letter, not her husband."

"She played the part of the clueless, sweet, old lady," JoJo added, "and, without her husband's photos and the FBI facial recognition program, we could never have proven that she was the one who pulled the trigger on Jimmy."

"Janet was a smart lady," Lisa said, "but she made a huge mistake when she didn't destroy the photos that were kept in her son's house."

"To Janet's huge mistake!" JoJo said, as the two detectives paused to drink again.

"So, then we had to find out what happened to all the money," JoJo continued. "That wasn't easy either."

"The McNeelys were very clever, Jo, but thanks to John Bannister's photos of Adam McNeely outside the warehouse the night Jimmy disappeared, we nailed him!"

"We were lucky that Cary Garnet kept that group photo of the Dreamland sales people all these years," JoJo said. "And what a break when you took that wedding photo of the McNeelys and we used both photos to figure out that Barbara McNeely was really Becca Raymond."

"The Dreamland sales person who slept with Jimmy," Lisa added.

"To Becca Raymond!" JoJo said, as they each sipped again.

"You know, John Bannister was pretty shrewd," Lisa continued. "He and Janet got paid to kill Jimmy and then they were lucky to find Adam McNeely breaking into Jimmy's car."

"So, Bannister took photos at the crime scene and used them to blackmail the McNeelys," JoJo added.

"His insurance policy!" Lisa declared.

"You know," JoJo observed, "John Bannister was a snake. He blackmailed the McNeelys, Kathy Prentice, and who knows how many others, but without him and his camera we would have been nowhere on this case."

"To John Banister's camera!" Lisa grinned, as the two partners clinked glasses, giggled, and sipped. By then it was time for a refill of each glass.

"Hey!" JoJo said, as she lifted her glass again, "We can't forget that FBI guy who recognized all the faces!"

"To Gus Haney!" Lisa toasted and sipped.

"And to your new partner!" JoJo exclaimed.

"To Bob Elliott!" They both sipped again.

"To me, the best part of this case was that we were able to get the money returned to the people who were swindled out of it," JoJo said, "and we can thank Megan Harris and your husband Rick for that."

"And the McNeelys, too!" Lisa replied. "It's a good thing they were super rich and had the money to give back. Somehow I feel like they actually wanted to pay it back, Jo."

"To the McNeelys, Megan, and Rick!" JoJo said, as they sipped again.

"Then finally, we had to find out who paid Janet Bannister to kill Jimmy Foster," Lisa said. "That was a real roller coaster ride with a lot of possible suspects."

"My favorite suspect was Mr. Black!" JoJo laughed.

"He was a piece of work, Jo, that Murray Rosenberg!"

"Ninety years old and still full of spunk!"

"To Mr. Black!"

They toasted again. "To Murray Rosenberg!"

"You know," JoJo said, "I was pretty sure it was Cary Garnet who paid Banister to kill Jimmy. He was Jimmy's wingman, but Jimmy got all the glory."

"You had Cary pegged all along, Jo, and he certainly had strong reasons to want to see Jimmy dead."

"He ended up with the wife and the kid," JoJo added, "and then, after Sidney went to the nursing home, Cary even got to share in the old man's money, too."

"Not bad for a wingman!" Lisa joked, "And one handsome wingman, that's for sure!"

"To Cary," JoJo said, as the wine glasses clinked again, "the handsome wingman!"

"But Cary didn't do it," JoJo said, "it turned out to be Roy Prentice."

"A guy that was never even on our radar screen!" Lisa said, with a sip and a smile.

"We got lucky that his ex-wife came forward to accuse him," JoJo added.

"To ex-wives!" Lisa said, as they sipped and laughed, "May we never be one!"

"You know, it's kind of funny," JoJo continued, "after all the shenanigans Jimmy Foster pulled, with gambling, borrowing money from gangsters, cheating the Dreamland buyers, and embezzling millions from his company, in the end the thing that got him killed was fooling around with the wife of a jealous husband!"

"Occam's Razor!" Lisa mused.

"Huh?"

"My dad told me about this guy named Occam. He said when there are a lot of possible solutions to a problem the simplest one is usually the correct one."

"Looks like Occam was right this time," JoJo said.

"And my dad too, as usual!" Lisa added.

"To Occam!" JoJo proclaimed, as she raised her glass and sipped again, "wherever he is!"

"And to my dad, Ernie Goodman, too!" Lisa added.

"Well, we did it, partner," JoJo said with a smile, "it took some hard work, some smart work, and a little bit of luck, but we did it."

"It's been an honor to work with you, Joanne Worthington, and I hope we keep in touch. If there's ever anything you need, you know I'm only a phone call and a short drive away."

"To the newest FBI agent!" JoJo said proudly.

Another glass clink, and another sip, were quickly followed by a hug between friends.

"You know, Lisa," JoJo said thoughtfully, "this was very ironic."

"How so, Jo?"

"Jimmy Foster died while he was developing his Dreamland project," JoJo replied, "and we solved his murder because of John Bannister developing a bunch of photographs.

"I think this should go down in the history books as the developing murder case, Jo!"

"To the developing murder case!" JoJo said, as the partners toasted and sipped once again.

"And through this case the two of us developed into a great team, JoJo!"

"To March and Worthington," JoJo sipped and laughed, "we did it together!"

"To Worthington and March," Lisa added, "the dream team!"

"You know what I think, Lisa?"

"What do you think, JoJo?"

"I think we'd both better take an Uber home!" JoJo said with a grin.

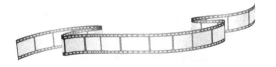

CHAPTER 65

FEBRUARY 16, 2019, 7:00 PM
CARRINO'S ITALIAN BISTRO
PORT ST. LUCIE, FLORIDA

Lisa, Rick, and Lexie walked into the restaurant to be met by a large gathering of friends and co-workers. Lisa was excited to see everyone who had come to wish her goodbye and good luck. A large banner hung above their table.

GOOD LUCK FBI AGENT LISA MARCH

The waiter immediately came over to Lisa and handled her a glass of Kendall Jackson Chardonnay. She sipped the wine, and then took the time to greet, hug, and thank everyone who came.

THE BREAKERS
PALM BEACH, FLORIDA

"I can't believe it's been twenty years we've been together," Louise Schwartz said to her husband, Cary Garnet. The maitre'd escorted them to their table where they were met by a bottle of champagne. After the bubbly was poured they each took a sip.

"Darling," Cary said, "marrying you was the best thing I've ever done!"

CARRINO'S ITALIAN BISTRO
PORT ST. LUCIE, FLORIDA

The assembled group of twenty-two people dined on antipasto, calamari, caesar salad, and chicken parmesan with penne pasta. Each course was accompanied by wine and more wine. It was not often that this group got together for an occasion like this, and they were making the most of it.

THE BREAKERS
PALM BEACH, FLORIDA

"I took the liberty of ordering creme brûlée for dessert, honey," Cary said, as he sipped his champagne.

"My favorite!" Louise smiled, "You are the most thoughtful man I know, Mr. Cary Garnet!"

CARRINO'S ITALIAN BISTRO
PORT ST. LUCIE, FLORIDA

After everyone had finished their main course, and before dessert was served, Captain Bob Davis stood up to speak. He clinked his knife against his water glass several times, hoping to get everyone's attention. When that failed he used his best Captain Davis voice to yell "Everybody shut up!"

That worked.

"We are gathered here this evening," Captain Davis began, "to say our final goodbye to Lisa March."

"What, is she dead?" someone yelled, and the entire group laughed.

"No," Captain Davis laughed, "maybe I should have put that another way. But the bottom line is we're really gonna miss this little dynamo and our loss is truly the FBI's gain."

Captain Davis lifted his glass. "To Lisa, may the best of your todays be the worst of your tomorrows!"

The assembled group stood, lifted their glasses, and said in unison, "to Lisa."

After the toast everyone took their seats as Lisa rose to speak.

THE BREAKERS
PALM BEACH, FLORIDA

"I don't know if you remember, honey," Cary said, "but the very first time I met you was right here in this restaurant!"

Louise reached across the table and touched her husband's hand. "Of course I remember," she said, "you and Jimmy took me to dinner here with my parents to celebrate the closing on our new house."

"That's right!"

"But you know, " Louise said softly, "you never showed any interest in me back then, Cary, only Jimmy did."

"I thought you were amazing," Cary replied, "but I never competed with Jimmy. Once he showed an interest in you I just backed off."

Louise rubbed her husband's arm. "I was really hoping back then that you would be the one to pursue me," she said. "Just imagine how much different our lives would have been if you had."

CARRINO'S ITALIAN BISTRO
PORT ST. LUCIE, FLORIDA

Lisa was standing behind her chair at the table, about to start speaking, when someone yelled "stand up, Lisa!" to another round of laughter.

"Okay you guys," Lisa said with a grin, "now that I'm leaving, you're gonna have to hire another short person to pick on!"

She paused for a moment to collect her thoughts.

"I promised myself I wouldn't cry," she said, waving her hand in front of her face as she felt the tears well up in her eyes, "but I think I broke that promise already!"

"I want to thank you all for being here to wish me well. It's been a great twenty years for me and I've enjoyed every day of my working life with all of you."

THE BREAKERS
PALM BEACH, FLORIDA

"We've gone through a lot to get to where we are today, Louise, and, if I had it to do all over again, I wouldn't change a thing."

"I guess the only thing I regret is that we didn't tell Jeffrey sooner that you were his real dad."

"I thought about that too, honey, but the truth is, I'm not sure if he was ready to handle that information when he was younger."

"I'm so proud that the two of you have built such a great relationship and such a successful real estate business, too."

CARRINO'S ITALIAN BISTRO
PORT ST. LUCIE, FLORIDA

"There are so many people I want to thank tonight," Lisa continued, "but first and foremost, I want to thank my parents, Gloria and Ernie Goodman. My dad was a cop, so I grew up in that environment, and even today he is my best person to bounce cases off of."

"I also want to thank my sweet husband, Rick, who greets me at the door with a glass of KJ Chardonnay and often a pizza to eat. You may not know this, but Rick was willing to sell our home and move, just so I could be closer to my new FBI office."

"And, of course, I want to thank my beautiful daughter, Lexie. I'm so proud of you, Lex, and I'm really looking forward to watching you build a career and a family of your own."

THE BREAKERS
PALM BEACH, FLORIDA

"It looks like Roy Prentice is gonna go on trial for murdering his second wife," Cary said, as he perused the menu.

The waiter came over to their table as soon as he saw Cary looking at the menu. "We have a few specials this evening," he said, "would you like to hear them?"

"Oh, that's okay," Cary replied, I always have prime rib when I come here on Saturday nights."

"And I'll have the Chilean sea bass, please," Louise added.

CARRINO'S ITALIAN BISTRO
PORT ST. LUCIE, FLORIDA

"I want to thank Captain Davis for helping me to grow from a uniformed officer to a detective. You taught me so much, and I promise you, Captain, that I'll work hard to make you proud of me in my new job."

"I already am proud of you, March!" the captain said.

"And I want to thank Danny Torres, my partner for four years. We worked a lot of cases together, Danny, and I couldn't have closed one of them without you."

THE BREAKERS
PALM BEACH, FLORIDA

After the waiter delivered the salads, and walked sufficiently far away from their table, the conversation picked up where it left off. Both Louise and Cary spoke in very soft voices.

"Kathy Jameson told me she went to the cops about the Jimmy Foster murder too," Louise said, as she took a small bite from her salad bowl.

"I heard about that, hon," Cary replied.

"She truly believes her ex-husband paid for Jimmy to be killed by the Bannisters."

"After he threatened Jimmy, and the way he treated Kathy, it's no wonder she thought that," Cary said, as he began to eat.

"She says he told her that he had Jimmy killed, and he threatened to have her killed too, when she was asking for a lot of money in their divorce."

"Roy was always a blow hard," Cary said, "but I guess Kathy believed him. And I'm sure glad she did!"

"If I were her," Louise said, "I would have believed him, too!"

"I guess the cops believed it," Cary said, as he sipped his wine, "and that's what really matters to us."

CARRINO'S ITALIAN BISTRO
PORT ST. LUCIE, FLORIDA

"I want to thank Megan Harris," Lisa continued, "Megan, not only are you the best and toughest prosecutor I have ever worked with, you're also a dear friend, and that's even more important to me."

"And to my new partner, Bob Elliott, who drove all the way from Melbourne just to be here, I want to say I am so impressed with how you handle cases, and I am looking forward to diving into the deep end with you. Together I know we're gonna make a great team."

"Don't drink too much tonight, Bob, you've got a long drive home!" someone yelled.

THE BREAKERS
PALM BEACH, FLORIDA

"So, I guess we can sell that warehouse in Port St. Lucie now," Cary said, "it's in Jimmy's name, but you were the sole beneficiary in his will so that means it's yours now. I'll get the lawyers working on it."

"How much do you think it's worth?"

"I figure we can probably get half a million for it," Cary said, "and now that it's been swept clean by the cops, we don't have to worry about selling it."

"So, now I can close our Swiss bank account and stop paying that damn annual tax bill!" Louise added with a grin.

CARRINO'S ITALIAN BISTRO
PORT ST. LUCIE, FLORIDA

"And last, but certainly not least," Lisa said with a smile, "I want to thank my most recent partner, Joanne Worthington."

"Jo, I pride myself on having great instincts about people, but I want you and everyone else to know that I have never been so wrong about anyone as I was about you."

"I looked at all the fancy dresses and hats, and I thought there was nothing underneath those hats but air."

"I was wrong!"

"JoJo, you are truly a woman of substance, a tough hard nosed cop, and a great detective. Together we closed a twenty-four year old homicide case in less than three months.

"JoJo, I'm proud to call you partner!"

Lisa lifted her glass. "To JoJo," she said.

"To JoJo," the assembled group replied.

JoJo stood and acknowledged her partner's kind words.

"And to all of you," Lisa concluded, "I say thank you, thank you, thank you, from the bottom of my heart!"

The entire room rose to their feet to clap and to honor Lisa March.

"Darling," Louise said, as she held her husband's hand, "maybe we did a bad thing, but it was for a good reason."

"He was not a good person, Louise," Cary replied, "and nobody knew that more than you and me. If I had it to do all over again, I would."

"You would?"

"Eventually, somebody was gonna kill Jimmy, you know that!" Cary said.

"Do you think Dad would have approved of what we did?" Louise asked.

"Maybe yes, maybe no," Cary replied, "but, I think it was for the best that we never told him. I don't think your father would have appreciated the fact that we made it sound like he was the one who paid Bannister for the hit."

"Cary," Louise said, "do you think it's possible that Roy Prentice also paid Bannister to kill Jimmy?"

"So, you think they collected from us and from Prentice for the same job?"

"I'm just thinking, maybe our quarter of a million wasn't enough for them," Louise said, "they were following the cheating husband and the cheating wife, so maybe when they killed Jimmy they got paid off twice."

"Honey, anything's possible," Cary replied, "but, right now, the cops believe that the only person who paid for Jimmy's murder was Roy Prentice."

"For that we owe a big thank you to Kathy Jameson," Louise said softly, "because of her, our worries are over for good."

"To Kathy," Louise said, as she raised her glass.

"To Kathy," Cary replied with a smile.